Nightshade Court

By

Ellen Dugan

Nightshade Court

ACKNOWLEDGMENTS

As always, thanks to my family, friends, beta readers, and editors.

To Charlynn my friend of many years, who helped me figure out how to juggle flaming chainsaws while writing this book. Love ya, Sis!

Thank you to Ken, Mitchell and Eric for the tactical information. To Tara, a talented horsewoman (who likes a horse with a chip on its shoulder.) Thanks for the great information on riding and horses. A special thanks goes to Sarah who discussed with me the truth of a warrior and a bit of police procedure. Thank you all for helping me to make the world of Hemlock Hollow even more realistic. Any mistakes on equine or gun jargon, or with police procedure are mine alone.

This book came out a tad later than was originally planned on as I tried to recover from mono at the age of 57. It was a tough road, and I was hospitalized twice. But a special thank you goes to my editors Mitch and Heather who told me *not* to worry, and that they were ready whenever I would be.

Finally, to LKH for reminding me to allow myself plenty of time to recover from being ill. As she wisely pointed out: "We're supposed to enjoy our art, not punish ourselves with it."
Wise words to live by.

Other titles by Ellen Dugan

THE LEGACY OF MAGICK SERIES

Legacy Of Magick, Book 1

Secret Of The Rose, Book 2

Message Of The Crow, Book 3

Beneath An Ivy Moon, Book 4

Under The Holly Moon, Book 5

The Hidden Legacy, Book 6

Spells Of The Heart, Book 7

Sugarplums, Spells & Silver Bells, Book 8

Magick & Magnolias, Book 9

Mistletoe & Ivy, Book 10

Cakepops, Charms & Do No Harm, Book 11
(Coming 2021)

THE GYPSY CHRONICLES

Gypsy At Heart, Book 1

Gypsy Spirit, Book 2

DAUGHTERS OF MIDNIGHT SERIES

Midnight Gardens, Book 1

Midnight Masquerade, Book 2

Midnight Prophecy, Book 3

Midnight Star, Book 4

Midnight Secrets, Book 5

Midnight Destiny, Book 6 (Coming 2022)

HEMLOCK HOLLOW TRILOGY

Hemlock Lane, Book 1

Wolfsbane Ridge, Book 2

Nightshade Court, Book 3

HEMLOCK HOLLOW ANTHOLOGY

Bewitched in Hemlock Hollow (Coming Fall 2021)

The Queen o Fairies she caught me,

In yon green hill to dwell.

And pleasant is the fairy land,

But an eerie tale to tell.

-The ballad of Tam Lin

CHAPTER ONE

I didn't want to sleep. Because when I closed my eyes nightmares engulfed me.

My dreams were filled with the luminescent green of witch fire, the staccato sound of gunfire, and the horror of the Lycan pack's blood upon my hands. Experiencing the battle of Wolfsbane Ridge every night was horrible, but my subconscious wasn't content with me simply reliving the past. Oh no. It had altered and shifted into something much more horrifying. Now the nightmares were playing upon my worst fears.

Children screamed while trapped inside of a home engulfed in the brilliant green flames of a Witch's fire, and I couldn't save them no matter how I tried. I could only listen to their cries as they died in the flames.

Next, a beautiful male Witch with brilliant green eyes shapeshifted before me. He shouted that he loved me, and yet still he raked me with long talons low across my belly. Suddenly an older man would appear, but the monster always sliced him down for trying to protect me.

In my night terror, the man with the eerie green eyes would transform completely into a monster. Dark, horrifying, and demonic. He stood laughing over the older man's fallen body while gore dripped from his razor-like claws. I shouted in denial and fired my gun until the magazine was empty, but my bullets were useless against him.

The perspective of the dream would change, and all a round me the entire Lycan pack lay dead. I had come to them for sanctuary and had instead brought a battle to their homelands. I heard a whimper and looked down to find a family of Lycans laying on the ground arranged around my feet. The youngest tried to crawl to me, but there was nothing I could do. He always died in my arms.

There was blood and there was smoke and ash falling from the sky like dirty snow. Everywhere was complete devastation. But no matter how hard I tried, how fast I ran, or how many bullets I shot, the outcome was the same. No matter how many times I killed the monster in my nightmares, it was pointless. I simply couldn't protect the people who mattered the most: the children, that brave old man, and the Lycans. They died in the most horrible of ways, and I wasn't able to save any of them.

My own screams woke me.

"Daphne?" The voice was low and familiar.

"Finnlagh?" My voice was raspy.

I opened my eyes and discovered that it was day. The contrast between the horrible dream images and the bright golden sunlight filtering in through the tall window in the room was intense.

"Son of a bitch," I grumbled while trying to shift to a more upright position in the large bed.

Finn sat up from the foot of the bed where he'd been resting. "You are the only female I have ever known to wake up screaming and then start swearing."

I grunted at the comment and did my best to calm down. I wondered what time it was but didn't bother asking. For the past several days I'd watched that light pouring in through the window in the room where I'd been recovering, and I'd given up trying to measure time by the angle of the sun. As far as I could tell it never changed. Instead, I tried to count the nights. How I hated those. The darkness only made the night terrors more vivid.

He pressed a hand to my forehead. "Your fever hasn't returned. Good."

I'd never been so badly injured before and was humbled by how tired and weak I was. While my memories of the first few days were hazy at best due to fever, the only constant in it all was the male next to me. Every single time I had opened my eyes, Finnlagh O'Brien had either been tending to me or watching over me. Often he'd been sitting in an armchair next to my bed, but other times I'd found him sleeping, stretched out at the foot of my bed.

Bottom line? He'd been taking care of me the entire time. Finnlagh had wiped my brow and spoon-fed me broth when I'd been too weak to manage it myself. He'd helped me stand and made sure I didn't fall when I needed to shuffle off to the bathroom. With my left arm in a sling, it had been tricky managing even the most basic of tasks for myself. But he'd been so practical about it all that it left no room for embarrassment.

"Nightmares again?" he asked, getting up to pour me a cup of water.

"Yes," I said, taking the cup.

"Tell me."

"It always starts with a replay of the battle. It turns into something else and I don't know what's real anymore and what's not."

"The dreams will pass," he said, gently resting his hand against my uninjured arm. "Your mind is simply working through the trauma that you have endured."

I nodded. With a sigh I lifted the cup to my lips, drained the contents, and passed it back to Finnlagh. "Sounds as if you've experienced something similar yourself."

"I have," he said, setting the cup aside.

"You've known war, here in the Fae Realm?"

"Yes we have."

I frowned. The fact that he said nothing else only made me curious. I scratched at my head with my good hand and wished desperately for a shower. At my reckoning I'd been convalescing for over a week. My long hair felt heavy and dirty, and the simple night gown I wore was sticky with sweat from my most recent nightmare. I lifted it from my neck and took an experimental sniff.

"Ugh." I made a face over the combination of herbal medicines, sweat, and bandages. "Finnlagh," I began, "I've seen that big metal tub in the bathroom and I want in it. ASAP."

He cocked his head to one side. "ASAP?"

"It stands for: As soon as possible," I explained.

His eyebrows went up. "Perhaps."

"Listen, my hair is going to stand up and walk right off the top of my head if I don't wash it soon," I complained.

"Daphne, you aren't strong enough to manage it by yourself," he said. "We almost lost you. Don't push yourself too hard."

"Well, is there a nurse or someone who can help me?"

"I could help you." His face was straight and his tone sincere.

I considered his suggestion. There had been no double entendre or playful leer from Finnlagh over his offer. In fact, he'd been nothing but kind, caring and compassionate since I'd arrived in the Fae Realm. Besides, I wasn't worried about him seeing me naked. I was pretty sure he already had. He'd been tending to me over the past week– it was far too late for blushes now.

"We would need to remove the sling and keep the bandages on your shoulder dry," he said, thinking it over. "But I think I can help you wash your hair."

"Okay." I nodded. Where once, not so long ago, I would have questioned him or his intentions, now I did not. He'd been nothing but a complete gentleman and more than proven himself to me by his capable and practical care.

I shoved the covers back. "Okay, let's get the show on the road pal."

His lips twitched. "As my lady commands."

I shot him a look. "And here I was just thinking to myself how polite and kind you'd been to me."

He helped me to ease over so I was sitting on the edge of the bed. "Do you promise to stay where you are while I get your bath arranged?"

I swung one of my feet. "Sure."

With a nod he bustled off and soon I heard the water running. Part of me wondered how the Fae worked their plumbing in the realm. The rest of me only cared that at last I could take a proper bath. While he was out of the room, I pulled the night gown up to check to see if there were actual scars across my belly. The skin was irritated, and I got a hell of a surprise to discover that there were faint pink marks, almost as if I had been clawed. *Was that part of the dream real?* I wondered. The bathroom door opened, and I let the gown drop.

There was nothing risqué about Finnlagh helping me

in the bath. Once I had the sling off, I carefully worked my arms out of the sleeves. He gently eased the gown over my head, keeping his eyes strictly on my face. Finnlagh held my uninjured arm and I slowly stepped into the warm water with his help.

I sat down slowly and as the warm water surrounded me, I shut my eyes in appreciation. Silently, he handed me a cloth and a bar of soap and stepped back to one side, allowing me to have a little privacy. I gave the bar a testing sniff, discovered it smelled of lavender and honey, and got straight to the business of scrubbing up. My left side was covered in bruises which I gingerly washed over. Once that was finished, I rinsed myself off.

Finnlagh offered to wash my back and without a word I handed him the cloth and soap. Once he'd finished it was time to wash my hair. After a quick discussion we settled upon me sitting with my head bent forward and my right arm bracing against one side of the tub.

It was the most practical position, as the last thing I wanted to do was to throw my head back and have my healing burns pull tight. He set a few dry cloths over my shoulder to protect the bandages from splashes and slowly poured a pitcher of water over my bent head.

I couldn't help but make a happy sound when he began to rub his fingers through my hair. When he scrubbed his fingers over my scalp I groaned.

"Sorry," I said.

"For what?" he asked as his fingers worked circles across my scalp.

I gripped the side of the tub harder. "For groaning. You've been nothing but a gentleman and I wasn't trying to be provocative."

"Provocative?"

"Well, yeah," I said, peeking at him from under my hair. "Making sex sounds isn't cool when you're being so sweet and helping me wash my hair."

"Groan all you like." He chuckled. "I can take it."

I did my best to bite back any other groans and allowed myself a few happy sighs while he rinsed my hair. However, by the time he had wrapped my long hair up in a dry towel I wasn't thinking happy thoughts anymore. I was gritting my teeth in pain. I had automatically lifted my left arm trying to secure the towel on my head and the movement had hurt like hell.

He held a bath sheet out for me, and I rose slowly to my feet. After he competently wrapped the sheet around me, I stepped out with his help. Without jostling my injuries, he patted my body dry and slipped a clean night gown over my head.

I automatically began to slide my left arm through the armhole and swore out loud at the pain. "Fuck!"

He shook his head. "You moved too quickly."

"No shit!" I tired to blink the black and white spots from my vision.

"If you will allow me?"

Finnlagh eased my arms through the gown, and I

discovered that even getting dressed was currently beyond my capacity. He adeptly tugged the gown down over the bath sheet, and then I managed to unhook it. The bath sheet fell to the floor and before I could say anything else, he scooped me right up.

"Back to bed you go."

"You don't have to carry me," I said, trying to breathe through the pain radiating from my shoulder.

"You are a rather interesting shade of green at the moment," he said lightly.

"It really hurts," I admitted.

He carried me out of the bath and back across the room, where I noticed the bed had been made up with clean sheets. The maid—I guessed it was the maid—was gathering the old sheets in her arms as we moved across the room.

He placed me gently on the side of the bed and asked her to fetch a comb. She bobbed a curtsy and was off like a shot.

I heard a rustling sound and discovered the maid had reentered. She paused only long enough to hand Finnlagh a comb. Afterward, she moved to the fireplace and added more logs to the fire. As I watched, she took the fireplace poker and gave the logs a good jab. The flames flared up and with a satisfied nod she brushed off her hands and left, shutting the door behind her.

To my surprise Finnlagh climbed on the bed behind me and knelt. He slid the towel from my hair and began working his way through the tangles.

"Sorry for shouting at you before," I said, clutching my arm in the sling.

"There is nothing to apologize for. You are in pain." He gently began to comb out my hair.

"Still, I'm sorry."

"Besides your shoulder, how else are you feeling?"

"Weak and shaky," I said. "How many days did I have a fever?"

"Three days," he said.

I frowned trying to remember. "Did I have a fever when I came here?"

"No." He moved to a different section of hair. "The fever began the next day. You had been awake and aware—"

"Were my memories intact?" I asked.

Finnlagh nodded. "They were, and then the fever struck."

"It was bad wasn't it?" I asked. "I figured it must have been, because of how weak I am now."

"The healers and I believe it was caused from the claw marks across your belly."

"Oh shit." My stomach lurched hard. There was something important there. I tried to remember and could not. The effort left me shaking.

"Daphne." Finnlagh's voice was gentle. "You were not infected."

I turned my head to check Finnlagh's face. "Infected?"

"You were attacked by a shape shifter."

"How?"

"During the battle."

"I...I can't remember," I said. "I know there was a battle, but it's all jumbled in my head."

"You are not to worry Daphne," Finnlagh said firmly. "You were *not* infected. The healer and I worked diligently to ensure that the curse was not passed to you."

"You're absolutely sure?"

"Yes. We are sure. Did you know the Witch was capable of shape-shifting?" Finnlagh asked and kept working on combing out the tangles from my hair.

"I didn't know. Not until the night of the battle." I blinked. "Whoa," I said, surprised. "I have no idea where that came from."

"What else do you recall?" he asked.

I began to shiver. "Nothing tangible. Impressions only, except for the horrible images during my dreams."

"Regardless, I can assure you that our alchemist worked with the healers and they created a course of treatment."

"You worked magick on me too. Healing magick. Didn't you?"

He nodded, and I listened intently to Finnlagh while he explained everything he and the healer had done. I realized that I'd been incredibly lucky. No poison had entered into my system. I wondered if the treatments Ashton had been giving himself had helped me escape that.

Ashton.

That had been the Witch's name.

He had green eyes and...My thoughts abruptly shifted. *I had shot him in self defense, hadn't I?* I thought it over and somehow knew that I had killed him. *I'd shot him in the chest seconds before his witch fire had slammed into me*...

In the end, my bullet had been faster than his spell.

Finnlagh's voice broke into my thoughts. "You will unfortunately have burn scars around your collar bone and shoulder," he said.

"From Ashton's witch fire," I said slowly.

"Yes." Finnlagh eased forward to look me in the eye. For a moment he studied my face. "Do you remember anything else?"

I licked my lips against a mouth that had suddenly gone bone dry. "I know that Ashton had green eyes. I also know that I shot and killed him."

Finnlagh nodded. "That is correct."

"In my dreams he turns into a monster, and he kills an older man...Someone who is dear to me."

"I can assure you he did *not* kill that older man." Finnlagh's voice was calm and reassuring.

"But I did kill him—Ashton, I mean." I blew out a shaky breath. "It's odd, but I don't feel any remorse over that. Good gods, what sort of person feels nothing over taking another's life?"

Finnlagh shifted so we were sitting face to face. "A warrior does what needs to be done to protect their allies and their loved ones."

"And my allies are the Lycans?"

"Yes," he said. "You were fighting with the Lycans to protect their pack and others."

I thought about the dream images. "In my nightmares all the Lycans are dead." I couldn't make myself say out loud the rest of the nightmare: The house that burned and the cries of trapped children. Ashamed, I looked away from him and down at my lap instead.

"What is it?" he asked.

"Perhaps the reason I am unable to remember is because I'm simply too big of a coward to do so."

Finnlagh took my chin and lifted it so our eyes met. "You are the bravest woman I have ever known."

"I don't feel brave," I admitted.

"Wounds suffered in battle often leave scars. Emotional as well as physical. You will heal and the scars will fade."

"I'm not particularly concerned about having scars on my body, Finnlagh." I shrugged and the movement caused me considerable pain. It literally stole my breath.

"That's enough for today Daphne," Finnlagh said firmly. "You need to rest."

I nodded, not even offering a token protest to his orders. Instead I let him help me ease back in a semi-reclining position against the pillows.

I told myself to stay awake, but the fact of the matter

was the bath and hair wash had worn my ass out. I blew out a long breath and shut my eyes. I would try tomorrow to remember more, and although I knew it was juvenile I struggled not to give in to self-pitying tears.

I felt the bed dip as he sat beside me. "Can I do anything else for you?"

"No," I said. "But I miss my...family." I sighed. "I can't seem to recall them. Not their names or their faces. Why can't I remember?"

"You will when you are stronger." He rested his hand on my uninjured shoulder. "Be assured that you are well loved Daphne."

"I should go home—" I said. "I shouldn't hide out here while all hell is breaking loose in the mortal realm."

He shook his head. "You're not strong enough to return. How would you defend your loved ones considering the state in which you find yourself?"

"I couldn't," I said. "I'm too weak to do anyone much good at the moment. It's humiliating."

"This is temporary. Allow yourself some time to heal. Besides," Finnlagh said, "the Hunter made me promise that I would keep you out of danger."

"The Hunter?" I asked, frowning at Finnlagh. I knew that title was important, and yet I didn't know why.

"Once you have regained your strength, I will escort you back to the mortal realm myself," Finnlagh said.

"For now, try and rest."

"If I fall asleep, I'll only have more nightmares."

Finnlagh passed his hand over the crown of my head. "And now, you won't."

My eyes drooped immediately. "What did you do?" I managed to ask.

"I charmed you into sleeping. No bad dreams today, only rest."

"That's manipulation," I said as my eyes drifted closed.

"It's a kindness. Rest Daphne. And heal. I will be here when you awaken."

"Tricky, tricky." I rolled over to my good side and was asleep in moments.

***

I woke to whispers.

Although my heart beat quickly, I kept my eyes closed and listened. Whoever they were they were close. I concentrated and after a moment I realized that it was a child's voice. Curious, I lifted my lashes and discovered a pair of huge, tip-tilted eyes peeking over the edge of the bed at me. The eyes were a brilliant green and did belong to a young child.

"Well hello," I said softly.

The child smiled, and it lit up her whole face. I estimated her to be four or five years old. Beside her, a toddler stood clutching her hand.

"Aren't you two cute," I said. "Do you live here?" For a moment I wondered if they were the children of the household staff, but I doubted it. Gingerly I sat up. As I did, I studied the children. Their clothing was exquisite. I'd never seen children decked out in jewels and medieval style clothing made from velvets and satin before.

The girl's dress was a spring green that complimented her bright green eyes and ebony hair. "Finnlagh said you were sleeping," she said, "but you're not."

"Not anymore." I shoved my hair out of my face.

The boy flashed me a shy smile. The toddler waggled his fingers at me but stayed silent.

"Hi cutie," I said to the boy, and it was certainly true. He had a cherubic face, and his clothing was all in shades of amber and brown. It complimented his brown curls and light brown eyes.

"I am called Ravena," the girl announced. "This is my little brother Liam."

"Hi, Ravena." I nodded. "Hey, Liam."

"What's your name, m'lady?" Ravena asked me.

"Daphne."

"Daphne?" The girl giggled. "That's a plant name."

"It sure is," I agreed and found myself smiling.

"Are you hurt?" The child pointed to my sling.

"I was, but I'm starting to feel better."

"I want to see," she said.

"Sure." I patted the bed next to me. She climbed

right up. Her brother followed suit by using the bedside chair. He scrambled up, crawled over the bed, and dropped himself right into my lap. That friendly bounce had me gritting my teeth against the pain.

"I've never met a mortal before." Ravena leaned over to study my face.

"We're not so different." I smiled.

Ravena reached out and picked up a piece of my long hair. "Your ears are different, but your hair feels like mine."

Liam decided he wanted to see my ears as well. He reached for my face to turn my head and I obliged him.

"Ears," he said shyly.

"Nose." I pressed my finger to the tip of his button nose and made a *honk* sound.

The toddler started to giggle. "Honk," he repeated back, trying to mimic the sound.

Ravena began to laugh. "Daphne, you are silly!"

Liam trailed a finger over my sling. "Hurt?" he asked.

I couldn't resist that sweet face. I passed my hand over his curls. "It's an ouchie."

"Ouchie?" He smiled over the word.

"I see you've found your uncle's guest." The voice came from the left, and Finnlagh's mother, Queen Aine, was standing in the doorway. The queen herself had been tending to my injuries since I'd arrived. It still blew my mind that she was a healer.

"Hello ma'am," I said cautiously.

"Lady Grandmother!" Ravena waved at the queen, giving her a sunny smile.

"Grandmother?" I studied the two children. That meant that these two had to be the children of the heir. I tried to remember what I'd been told about the royal family. The oldest brother was married, and he had children—thus securing the line of succession—but I couldn't recall neither his nor his wife's names. And I didn't have a clue who had once told me that information.

"The lady Fallon is searching for the two of you." The queen's voice was serene, and she had a smile on her face as she approached.

"Hide and seek!" Liam cheered and bounced on my lap again.

I managed to stifle a groan.

"We came in here to hide," Ravena said.

There was new movement in the doorway and now a woman appeared. "There you are!"

Liam chortled in delight. "No find!" he said.

I couldn't help but smile. "Gave your babysitter the slip, did you?"

"You imps!" She pointed at the children.

I could hear Finnlagh's voice calling for the children from beyond my room, which only caused the children to giggle more.

"They're here, Finnlagh!" the woman called out. She marched into the room, frowning at the children.

In the light from the windows the woman's hair was

a shining gold. She had milk-pale skin and her straight brows were also the same shade of her hair. She was dressed in luxurious fabrics and a band of jewels sparkled across her brow. Which made me wonder, since the queen had called her *Lady* Fallon, if it was a title or rank.

"The escapees have been located?" Finnlagh entered the room and seemed taken aback to find the children sitting on the bed with me.

"Uncle Finn!" Liam gave another happy bounce and I grunted.

"Forgive them," he said to me, moving quickly to scoop up the boy. "They've never seen a mortal before, and they were curious."

"That's all right," I said. "We're getting to know each other, right Ravena?"

"Yes." She nodded solemnly. "Daphne likes me."

"Come away, Princess Ravena." The Fae female waved the child over and I saw that her eyes were the same unusual cognac shade of Finnlagh's. With those straight brows and eye color, they simply had to be related.

The queen approached and set her basket of bandages on the bedside table. "You two should go with your Aunt Fallon now."

Bingo, I thought. *An aunt.*

Ravena climbed down with the help of Fallon and I smiled at the Fae. "Nice to meet you, Lady Fallon."

The woman seemed startled at being addressed

directly. "I apologize for the intrusion," she said. "The children were curious having heard that Finnlagh had a mortal guest in his house."

"Not a lot of mortal folks up in here, I take it?" I tried for a joke but it fell flat.

"Up where?" Fallon frowned, clearly confused.

Finnlagh passed the toddler to Fallon. Liam bounced once on her hip and waved at me.

"Bye-bye." He waggled his fingers.

"Bye, Liam." I smiled at the girl. "Goodbye, Ravena. It was nice to meet you."

Ravena dropped a flawless curtsy. "If it please you, m'lady, I will return."

I smothered a smile at the formal words. It was adorably cute coming out of the mouth of so young a child. "Sure, come back and visit. I'd like that."

"I will bring you flowers." She flashed me a bashful smile.

"Goodbye, sister." Lady Fallon curtsied to the queen, then to Finnlagh, and ushered the children out.

"Fallon is your aunt?" I asked Finnlagh.

"Fallon is my younger sister," the queen said, reaching for my bandages. "She came into my care after I married the king."

Finnlagh crossed his arms. "Fallon, myself, my brother Diamant, and our sister, Glynis, all grew up together. I think of Fallon more as a cousin rather than my aunt."

The queen unwrapped my sling, eased the shoulder

of the nightgown down, and checked the bandages. "Finnlagh tells me that you managed a bath earlier today."

"Yes ma'am," I said. *Ma'am* seemed the safest way to address her.

"All by yourself?"

"No, ma'am." I met her eyes, so like her son's, and told her the truth. "Finnlagh helped me."

The queen gave her son a considering look. "I see."

I glanced between the two of them. There was some unspoken communication going on there, but I didn't have a clue what information was being exchanged. "He was the perfect gentleman," I was quick to add, thinking his mother was about to give him a lecture.

"My son? A perfect gentleman?" She grinned. "Clearly you have bewitched him."

"Afraid that's not possible," I said as she removed the old dressings. "I didn't inherit any magick from my mother." I flinched. "Hey! I remembered something!"

The queen's shimmering brown eyes searched mine. "Do you recall anything else about your mother?"

I searched through my mind but found nothing tangible. "I only know that she's a Witch, and that I am *not*." I shut my eyes in frustration. "This is going to make me crazy."

The queen patted my hand. "You must give it some time Daphne. Physically you are recovering very well," she said, reaching for a fresh bandage.

I risked a look at my injury and saw that it wasn't as

horrible as I'd feared. Although the wound was puckered and bright pink, the skin was healing remarkably fast. "Wow," I said. "The wound is smaller and looks a lot better than I thought it would."

"You still have a great deal of bruising and a few injured ribs," the queen said.

"Are my ribs cracked?" I asked.

"Not cracked, bruised." She shook her head. "But they will be tender for a time. The bruises on your skin will fade in another week or so. However, I do strongly recommend taking it slowly for the next few days." She slipped the sling back over my head and adjusted my left arm inside of it. "Here you are."

"Thank you," I said automatically and then I blanched. "I am so sorry. I know better than to say that to a Fae. If I have offended you, Your Majesty, I sincerely apologize."

She patted my hand. "Dearest, calm yourself. I am not offended. I understand that it is a custom to say those words in the mortal realm."

"Still, I'm sorry. You're the queen and—"

"Daphne," she cut me off gently. "Try saying, *Go raibh maith agat*, instead."

"Is that Gaelic?" I asked

Finnlagh spoke up. "*Go raibh maith agat,* means 'may you have goodness.' It is applicable in most situations where you would find yourself trying to avoid…"

"I got it." I nodded to Finnlagh. "How do you say it

again? Say it slowly."

Finnlagh smiled. "It is pronounced, guh ruh mah a-gut."

"Guh ruh mah a-gat," I repeated back.

"Yes." The queen smiled. "Now say it all together.

"*Go raibh maith agat,*" I said.

Finnlagh smiled. "Excellent."

I looked directly at the queen. "*Go raibh maith agat,* Your Majesty."

She flipped a lock of her silvered hair over one shoulder. "Are you still having nightmares?"

I shot a glance at Finnlagh. "He told you, did he?"

"It is not uncommon after a battle for the survivors to have temporary memory loss, and to experience disturbing dreams."

"They call that post-traumatic stress in the mortal realm."

"Yes I know," she said.

Before I could ask her any more questions, the queen gathered up her supplies and moved away. "A light supper tonight, I think," she said. "Tomorrow, if you are up to it, a short walk in the gardens and sitting in the sunshine would do you a world of good."

"That sounds wonderful," I agreed.

"*Go raibh maith agat, máthair,*" Finnlagh called as the queen left the room.

"Maw-her?" I tried to sound that final word out. "Does that mean mother in Gaelic?"

"It does," he said.

"May I ask you a question?"

Finnlagh sat in the chair beside the bed. "Of course."

"I figured with your mother being the queen, that she'd have a posse of folks..."I hesitated, trying to come up with the correct term. "Ladies in waiting or courtiers I guess you'd call them, surrounding her wherever she went."

"Here in my home she is free to move about on her own," Finnlagh explained.

"Oh." I nodded. "So in private she's simply your mom, but out there she's the queen."

His eyes slid to mine. "Be aware that she is the queen wherever she goes, be that a private home or a public arena." While his tone had been polite, there was no mistaking the warning in it.

I cleared my throat before speaking. "With your mother taking care of me, it has sort of skewed my perception of her into one that's less formal." I checked his face to see how he reacted to my words.

"That is understandable but going forward you must be cautious Daphne. I have kept you sheltered here and away from prying eyes for the past week, but that time is quickly ending. The moment you step outside tomorrow, all the eyes in Fae will be upon you."

His face was handsome, composed, and pleasant while he spoke, yet his body language read tense. I was surprised to discover yet another side of him. It was cautious, calculating and cool. My stomach gave a quick flip at the realization.

I smiled despite his warning. "You make it sound like I need to have my gun on me."

"I understand that you are an outspoken woman," he began, "but in the Fae realm that sort of blunt honesty will cause nothing but complications."

"Are we talking about politics and protocol?"

He nodded. "Yes, exactly."

I blew out a long breath. "Well you're going to have to help a sister out."

"By Danu, you are *not* my sister." He sounded horrified.

"Jeez Finnlagh, relax. That was slang. You know, an expression?" I rolled my eyes. "I *meant* that you'll have to show me the ropes..." I trailed off when one of his eyebrows quirked.

"The ropes?"

"For fuck's sake." I scrubbed a hand over my face and was torn between screaming in frustration and laughing at the ridiculousness of it all.

"Oh, you are using mortal colloquialisms." One of his eyebrows rose. "Those are aggravating and confusing."

"Yes, they are." I sighed. "Personally, I find it annoying as shit to have to keep explaining them to you."

"It's good to see you acting like yourself again." He chuckled, reached out, and tugged on a lock of my hair. "And for some strange reason I find that I like it when you swear at me."

I shook my head at him. "You are a strange male, Finnlagh."

CHAPTER TWO

I don't know what I'd been expecting when I stepped outside and got my first glimpse of the Fae kingdom. But discovering that it was all like a dreamy photo shoot for a fancy gardening magazine was *not* it.

I paused in the doorway, leaned on Finnlagh's arm, and took everything in. There were blooming trees and shrubs everywhere. Birds sang in the trees, and tall decorative hedges were a brilliant green. I saw an ornate fountain in the center of the courtyard with water that made a sort of tune as it splashed. The water droplets turned to tiny rainbows and glistened in the sunshine.

I tipped my head back to discover wisteria blooming overhead. The flowering vine dripped down in uniform panicles of purple from an ornate wooden arbor. Here the light was dappled overhead, and the stones of the courtyard were sparkling gray and immaculate. *It's like a perfect day in May when everything is in bloom,* I thought.

Two guards followed us and took positions on either side of the door. The males wore leather pants tucked in tall boots and thin chainmail shirts with a metal breastplate. Both of them carried spears tipped with obsidian.

One of the guards offered to accompany us, but Finnlagh waved the suggestion away. As we stepped out from under the arbor, I saw the sky was a tender blue with pearly clouds dancing across it. I paused to admire the topiary next to me. It had been clipped into a flawless form. Despite the perfection, I smelled lilacs which told me it was quite real. The perfume of its flowers was heady and ripe.

I trailed a fingertip over the blooms and marveled. "The lilacs are in bloom here."

"Do you favor them?"

"Yes. I always have," I said, inhaling the fragrance.

We traveled farther out from the courtyard to the garden itself. Even though it was all stunningly beautiful, it didn't seem real. Blooming cherry trees, apple trees, and dogwoods were all flowering in perfect sync. It wasn't so much that the gardens were in the formal style, it was that everything was too symmetrical. In the mortal world those species of trees did not bloom all at the same time. Our trees didn't grow like lollipops on a stick either. Dogwoods especially were more open with an irregular growth pattern.

Blinking the bright sunshine from my eyes, I turned

my head to take in the sheer expanse of the formal gardens that surrounded Finnlagh's home. A meadow of flowers was to our left, and it was all flawlessly pastel, gorgeous, and picture-perfect.

Yet, despite the beauty, the back of my neck prickled, and I felt dread.

I didn't quite manage to control the shiver of unease that ran down my back.

"Are you all right?" Finnlagh asked quietly.

"Yes." I nodded and tried to take in as much of my surroundings as possible without rubbernecking like a tourist.

Although technically I was.

In the mortal realm it was autumn. I knew that and clung desperately to the information. At home the scent of decaying leaves, wood smoke, and the spice of chrysanthemums was heavy on the air. The leaves were yellow and orange, and nature was in its final hurrah before winter set in. "But it's October in the mortal realm," I finally said to him. "How can everything be in bloom here?"

"In the realm of the Light Fae we are blessed with a perpetual spring." Finnlagh's voice was formal and very pleasant.

In fact, his tone was *so* pleasant that I slanted my eyes over to his face. "I see," I said, not quite managing to repress a shiver.

"Are you cold?" Finnlagh asked, starting to shrug out of his jacket.

"No. I'm not cold." Nervously, I smoothed down the fabric of the long dress I wore. It was an olive green, made in a princess cut, and the bodice was fitted with a simple scoop neckline. "Leave your jacket on Finnlagh. I'm fine."

"This garment is called a doublet," he explained, hitching it back on his shoulders.

"It's still a nice-looking jacket, from where I'm standing."

"Is that a compliment?" He sounded so hopeful that it made my lips twitch.

"For the jacket. Not you pal."

"Do you like your gown?"

"Sure. It's certainly better than wearing a nightgown." The dress was surprisingly comfortable, in fact. Its sleeves were three quarter length, and there was a bit of brown detailing around the neckline and at the bottom of the sleeves. It coordinated with Finnlagh's brown pants, linen shirt, and olive-green jacket—no, doublet.

"I am pleased that you like it." Finnlagh gave my good arm a pat. "I chose the fabric myself."

"Oh, you did, did you?" I considered that for a moment. "I wondered why we were all matchy-matchy today."

"Matchy-matchy." He grinned over the words. "Yes, we do match, because it pleases me."

A breeze ruffled the hair away from my face and I shut my eyes for a moment in appreciation of being outside. "This is nice." I sighed happily and tipped my face fully to the sun. "I feel almost human today."

Finnlagh stopped. "Were you not feeling human before?"

My eyes popped open. I couldn't help but chuckle over how serious he sounded. "I'm fine, Finnlagh. I simply meant that I felt better. Saying that you 'feel almost human' is a silly expression. It's a way of making a joke."

"Ah." Finnlagh nodded. "This is another mortal colloquialism."

"Maybe I should start writing a list of mortal slang words and phrases down for you," I said dryly.

Finnlagh smiled at my sass. "I believe I can figure them out as we go along."

The grass was emerald green and lush, but I could detect no loose grass clippings or marks from a mower. The lawn could best be described as absolute perfection. I could smell it and even feel the texture beneath my feet as I walked on it, but a part of my mind was documenting everything, realizing how foreign it all was.

I was admittedly impressed by the elaborate formal knot gardens he took me to. I smiled over the tidy gravel pathways and the scent of rosemary and thyme. But when Finnlagh suggested we take a seat on a pretty stone bench, I sat down slowly. I'd walked maybe a hundred yards so far, and my ribs were aching. I was tiring.

I blew out a long breath and took in the grounds. That small niggling sensation that I wasn't seeing everything that was there grew stronger. While I admired the precisely clipped boxwood hedges, they were after all an integral part of a formal knot garden, I also saw that the herbs and flowers were maintained to within an inch of their lives. I sat looking over the knot gardens and instead of relaxing I felt tense.

It was a surprise to realize that I longed for the cheerful riot of colors, textures, and plants of a cottage garden. These knot gardens were so orderly that it took some of the fun out of it. Almost as if an herb wouldn't dare branch off in a different direction. Gods forbid a flower should bloom without permission. I cast my gaze on a nearby row of peonies. While they were lovely, they too had been shaped—pruned so that the flowers bloomed in a visible pattern.

Where is the wildness? I wondered, and then it hit me. That's what was wrong with the gardens. While they were lovely, they were too perfect, unnaturally pristine, and far too regimented.

"What do you think of our gardens?" Finnlagh asked.

"Well, they're certainly tidy," I said before thinking better of it.

He smiled. "Are they not to your taste, my lady?"

"I didn't say that," I argued.

Finnlagh stood, walked a few feet over to the left, and plucked a peach colored peony from a bush. "An offering." He sketched an elaborate bow and offered it.

"It's pretty. Tha—" I cut myself off. *"Go raibh maith agat,"* I finished instead and took the flower.

"I think we've walked far enough today." Finnlagh offered his arm. "Let's start back."

"Okay." I tucked the peony behind my ear and accepted his help to stand. My ribs protested the movement and I gasped. "I'm going to need a moment," I whispered, waiting for the pain to ease.

"I will have a chair brought out to the courtyard after we return," Finnlagh said. "You can do as my mother suggested and sit in the sunshine."

"I won't argue with that," I said, moving forward slowly.

I'd started to get used to the view on the return trip. His home was a grand manor house. The gray stone was warm, and the mullioned windows glistened in the sunlight. I kept telling myself to just take in the overall picture and not to focus on the details—otherwise I'd get twitchy.

Up ahead of us two Fae females in gorgeous pastel gowns walked along the garden path. They were talking and laughing with each other, but when they spotted Finnlagh and me they stopped, stared, and began whispering to each other.

When we were only a few feet away they both sank into a deep curtsy. "Your Highness," they said in unison.

With their foreheads parallel to the ground I took in

the elaborate hairstyles. Their coiffures had a medieval style, yet there was something modern about it as well. A blonde with braids wrapped around the back of her head in a sort of halo dipped down the lowest. Ribbons were worked lattice style in the round center of the golden braids, making me think of a pie top. At each intersection of ribbon there was a pearl.

"Prince Finnlagh." The pie top straightened back up and dimpled prettily. "We've missed you this past week."

The second female raised her head and smiled at Finnlagh too. She had dark sandy blonde hair done in two thick braids that went well past her knees. They were crisscrossed in embroidered ribbons and she wore jewels at her ears and gemstones at her throat.

Both of the Fae females were gorgeous. I felt the tension in Finnlagh's arm as he continued to hold mine and wondered why. Was he embarrassed or perhaps annoyed?

Finnlagh exchanged pleasantries with the pair and in return they flirted outrageously. The first blonde even trailed her fingers down Finnlagh's arm as she spoke to him. I felt him react to the touch but didn't hazard a guess if that was a good or bad reaction.

This is like high school all over again, I thought as they yammered on. *Mean girls, the handsome popular guy, and a new female who might be competition for his attention.* I was hard pressed not to laugh at the ridiculousness of the situation as both of the Fae females avoided direct eye contact with me.

It was like I wasn't even present.

"Hello." Sliding my arm from Finnlagh's, I stuck out my right hand. "I'm Daphne. It's nice to meet you."

They recoiled violently from my offer of a handshake.

"It spoke to us!" the pie lattice said to her braided pal.

"*It* sure the hell did." I stepped a tad closer.

The Fae with the pie lattice hairstyle stumbled back and dragged the braided female with her. "Keep it away from us! Please, Your Highness!" she cried.

"*It?*" I scowled at the pair. "Not too big on manners in the Fae realms, are you?"

With a horrified squeak, the two picked up their pretty skirts and fled.

"What was that all about?" I asked Finnlagh as the pair ran away and disappeared around a bend in the shrubbery.

Finnlagh ran his hand over my good shoulder. "Daphne."

I turned back to him. "What?"

He sighed. "In the future, do not attempt to introduce yourself. That's a breach of protocol. Allow *me* to introduce you, instead."

I rolled my eyes. "Well, you could have told me that ahead of time, pal."

"Yes, I should have." Finnlagh nodded his head in agreement. "However, I did not anticipate that Sorcha and Laoise would be laying in wait."

"And *I* did not anticipate being treated like I was invisible, or lesser than, because I'm a mortal," I complained.

"They are ladies of the court and from noble families. They have had no contact with the mortal world."

"Well, let me make a mental note of what to expect the next time I see them." I pressed my first finger to the center of my forehead. "Currently adding ignorance, snobbery and *rudeness* to the list of personality traits of the ladies of the court."

"Daphne." Shaking his head, Finnlagh chuckled. "Not only were they jealous of the time we have spent together, they were also frightened of you."

"Frightened?" I asked. "Seriously?"

"I am very serious."

"Golly." I batted my eyes. "And I wasn't even *trying* to scare them. I'll do a better job next time. I promise."

Finnlagh took my arm again. "I hope that you were using sarcasm."

"Hope springs eternal," I said, as we continued on our walk.

I told myself that I shouldn't feel guilty for messing up Finnlagh's social life, but honestly those jealous ladies of the court *had* managed to offend me. I made up my mind to let it go. After all, I didn't want the encounter to ruin our outing. "Look on the bright side," I said, patting his arm consolingly. "When I return home, you can take back up with all your lady friends."

"Lady friends?" he asked.

"Your lovers," I said patiently.

Finnlagh shrugged. "They will get over their disappointment, soon enough."

"Oh yeah?" I raised my brows. "Are you planning on ducking out tonight to go and make it up to them?"

Finnlagh paused and tilted his face down to mine. "Expecting me to abandon you so soon m'lady?"

I held my breath as his eyes searched mine. "Finnlagh," I said after a moment, "I don't believe it has ever been my luck to be with a male who was faithful." Even as the words left my mouth, I knew them to be true.

One of his eyebrows quirked. "And because of your past experiences, you do not expect me to be."

"Are you claiming that you would be faithful?" I countered.

He shifted, and now we were standing face to face. "I believe I made my feelings on that subject perfectly clear that night at Wolfsbane Ridge. Are you able to recollect what I said that evening?"

We stood in the garden under that bright Fae sunlight, a few inches away from kissing. I stared up into his face and a series of images flashed into my mind. A kiss with him under the stars. A dream-like interlude by an autumn pond where Finnlagh and I had made love. It had been incredibly mind blowing and the stuff of fantasy.

"Oh my gods." I felt the blood rush to my cheeks. "Was any of that *real*?"

He smiled. "Would you like it to be?"

"Wait. You've asked me that before." I shivered.

He slid his arms around my waist and pulled me closer. "You have remembered our time together."

"Yes, I have," I said in a voice that shook.

He lowered his forehead to mine. "Our time together haunts me."

His words had my belly flipping. "Finnlagh," I said, "my memories are still hit and miss so I'm not quite sure…Were we actually physically together, or was it all some sexy illusion?"

Gently, he kissed my temple. "It was not an illusion."

His words caused my belly to tighten and my thighs to clench. "Well, holy shit."

He grinned. "You say the sweetest things, my lady."

Shaken at the realization I rested my cheek against his shoulder. "Where does that leave the two of us, Finnlagh? Are we friends, or are we more?"

"We are more." His voice was husky, and when he ran his hand down my hair, I trembled.

I lifted my head intending to kiss him, but his attention was snapped away from me. His body tensed, and he went on guard. "What is it?" I whispered.

"We are not alone here," he said after a moment.

"Are we talking about a threat, or is it folks simply being nosey and spying?"

"Let's continue our walk," he said in a completely different tone.

"All right." I nodded and played along. I could feel the tension in his hand where it rested at the small of my back.

I kept watch on our trip back to the house but saw nothing other than flowers and trees. There was now, however, a group of Fae in the courtyard of his home. As we drew nearer, I noted their plain clothing and figured they were all probably a part of the household staff. They were all casually speaking to each other as they worked, and it was a happy and productive sound.

Besides the guards at the door, someone was now strumming a lap harp, and the tune she played was gorgeous. Another Fae female was carrying a basket of flowers inside, and an older male was sweeping the already clean stones. He had an air of authority around him and seemed to be supervising two younger males who were cleaning the windows.

We'd barely hit the courtyard stones when three children came rushing from around the side of the house. They spotted Finnlagh, cheered, and ran toward him. I recognized Ravena and Liam right away, but there was a second boy and he appeared to be around six or seven. He had brown hair and was grinning from ear to ear, trying to beat his sister in a race to get to their uncle.

I moved back as the older children grabbed ahold of Finnlagh. He gave them both hugs and the kids were laughing and talking a mile a minute.

Liam had tried to keep up with the older children. In his rush to get to his uncle, he tripped and started to fall. I was the closest so I rushed forward, managing to get my good hand between Liam's face and the pavement. Still, he landed with a hard splat.

He started to wail and despite the pain from moving too quickly, I knelt down to his level. "Let's see, sweetie," I said, helping him to stand and brushing him off. He had a couple of minor scrapes across the palms of his hands. Otherwise he seemed all right.

"Hurts!" he cried.

I wiped away his tears with my thumb. "I know," I said to the two-year-old. "But you'll be okay."

He held up the palms of his hands for me to see. "Ouchie?" he asked.

I dutifully dropped a kiss on each palm. "There you go. All better."

He flung his arms around my neck. "Ooof!" I said, and promptly lost my balance. With no way to catch myself, I wasn't able to stay standing. I landed on my butt, and the jarring from hitting the ground caused me to see stars.

"Be careful, Liam!" Finnlagh scolded the toddler.

"I'm okay," I wheezed, even as the boy climbed in my lap for a cuddle.

"Well, well," a new male voice said. "Isn't this a charming scene?"

I raised my eyes and discovered an elegant couple

moving toward us.

Instantly the courtyard fell to silence, and everyone present, including the two older children, bowed deeply to the couple. Confused, I checked my surroundings and discovered that I was the only one not bowing or curtsying.

The good news was that I was *probably* exempt from bowing as I was on the ground with a lap full of royal toddler. The bad news was that the male and female were continuing to walk forward, and they had an entire retinue of folks following behind them. Guards and courtiers, I supposed. And none of them looked very happy.

The Fae male in front was striking. He wore a shining silver headpiece which sat across his brow, accenting dark blonde hair that fell straight past his shoulders. His complexion was fair, and the male's eyes were steel blue. His mouth was unsmiling and surrounded by a neat, short beard.

His robes—let's go with robes, because I simply couldn't think of a better name to call his outfit— were deep blue with elaborate silver thread shot throughout. He wore some sort of flowing pant, but as his robes fluttered back I saw that his chest was left bare. A lean, nicely toned chest and six-pack abs were on full display. It was a *lot* to take in, and immediately I lowered my eyes away from all the pale skin.

"Brother." The man had paused in front of Finnlagh and me. "Is this the lady in your care?"

Finn rose from the bow. "Hello, Diamant."

The heir, I thought. *Terrific.*

Finnlagh tried to help me to me feet. It was awkward as Liam continued to cling to me for dear life. The boy tightened his grip around my neck and inadvertently jostled my healing burns. I grit my teeth over the pain *and* the strain on my ribs but held on to the child. Dropping him would be beyond bad. I slid Liam to my right hip and secured him in place with my good arm.

"Brother," Finnlagh began, "may I introduce to you Daphne Hart?"

"Dab-nee." Liam tried to pronounce my name and bounced happily on my hip.

I couldn't help but flinch in pain at his bounce.

"I see you have made yet another conquest, my lady," Finnlagh's brother said.

I smiled and made brief eye contact. "He's a sweet boy, Your Majesty."

"Majesty?" He chuckled at that. "I am the heir. Not the king. You will address me as, Your Highness."

"I beg your pardon." I checked his expression and tried to get a read on whether he was angry or not. "I thought you must be the king," I said. "Maybe it's the way you carry yourself."

Apparently, that was the right thing to say as his lips turned up in the smallest of smiles.

"I am Prince Diamont, the eldest son of King Donal, and first in line to the throne of the Fae." He gestured to the lady on his arm. "This is the mother to my heir. My wife, the Princess Oona."

I shifted my gaze to her. The princess had an olive skin tone and deep brown eyes that were set off by straight bangs and elaborate dark eye makeup. Her raven-black hair was intricately braided up into a coronet, and the rest flowed loose over her shoulders "Ma'am," I nodded politely to her.

The princess' gown was indigo with silver threads running throughout. The garment was cut in the sheath style. A jeweled chain crisscrossed beneath her breasts, and in contrast to the other ladies I had seen, her dress was cut much slimmer, with sheer tight sleeves. Around her neck was an elaborate jeweled collar. It gave her a sort of Nefertiti look. *Wow. She is gorgeous,* I thought.

"You should curtsy to us, mortal," she said, and the look the princess gave me was filled with such suspicion that I went from admiration to caution.

Smoothly, Finnlagh stepped in. "Perhaps, this once you will allow an exception, sister-in-law? She is injured after all, and yet holding on to Prince Liam."

"And would you care to explain why you dare to touch *my son*?" The princess' voice went up on her last few words and everyone present stiffened.

Even though I was uneasy, I made sure my tone of voice was matter of fact. "He tripped and fell down. I knelt to help him—"

"And Liam clung to her," Finnlagh finished for me.

"Dab-nee kissed my ouchies," Liam said soberly.

"She *what*?" Princess Oona scowled.

Prince Diamant appeared confused by the word. "Ouchies?"

"Ouchies," Liam said again, showing his scraped hands to his father. "Dab-nee kissed it."

"It's a mortal custom, sir," I said, hurrying to explain the expression to a prince of the Fae. "A kiss to make it all better."

"All better!" Liam grinned and pressed a sloppy kiss to my cheek.

Prince Diamont smiled at his son. "I see. Well it appears to have worked. Prince Liam tends to howl over the slightest bump or bruise."

"A little soap and water and he'll be good as new," I agreed. Liam gave another happy bounce, and I caught my breath against the pain in my ribs.

"Daphne?" Finnlagh rested his hand on my back.

"Okay, Liam," I said as my stomach lurched from the pain, "time to go to your father." I leaned forward to transfer the child over, and Liam went to his father's arms.

I tried not to make any noise at the discomfort that the movement had caused, but I failed. "I beg your pardon, sir," I said, wiping at the sweat that had popped out on my lip. "I'm obviously more tired than I realized."

Silently, I pressed my hand to my ribs and ordered myself not to throw up, or to pass out on the heir or his wife. Because I felt like it could go either way.

"Lady, are you unwell?" Prince Diamant asked and

set the toddler down.

"Seamus?" Finnlagh gestured to one of the men standing guard in the courtyard.

"Sir?" Instantly, a big and stocky man stepped forward.

"Will you please escort my guest inside?" Finnlagh said.

"Yes, Your Highness." The guard nodded and took me firmly by the elbow. Unfortunately, he grasped my injured arm and tugged.

I flinched away from his grip and saw stars. "Damn it!" I swore as black and white spots danced in front of my eyes.

"Seamus!" Finnlagh reprimanded the guard sharply.

"I apologize, sir," Seamus grumbled.

I staggered, trying to catch myself. "I don't feel so good," I managed to say. A roaring sound filled my ears, and everything went black.

***

I opened my eyes to discover that I was propped up in bed again, and the queen herself was checking my bandages. "Hello, Your Majesty," I said carefully.

She frowned. "When I told you to take a walk in the gardens, my dear, that suggestion did *not* include picking up and holding toddlers."

I opened my mouth to speak, but the queen raised her brows, and I hesitated. Between the look of disapproval on her face and her current state of dress—which was far more formal than any I'd seen her in previously—I was suddenly very nervous. "Liam took a nasty tumble," I tried to explain.

"So I hear." The queen shook her head. "But in your attempt to help, you have reopened your wound in the process."

"At least I managed to keep him from bashing his face on the stones of the courtyard," I muttered.

"You also picked him up." She frowned. "You have bruised ribs, dearest. I didn't think I had to explain to you that there was to be *no* lifting."

"It wasn't planned," I said, glancing down at my shoulder.

The left half of my dress had been pulled down to my waist and I sat in a white linen undergarment. It sort of reminded me of a long one-piece slip. Gently, the queen and a maid helped me remove the olive-green dress I'd been wearing. The maid silently took the dress and the blood-stained bandages away.

The queen applied a clean dressing to my injury, and while she worked, she gave me a firm lecture on overdoing it on my first day up.

"Liam fell, and was crying, so I tried to comfort him," I said in my defense.

"Yes, I know." The queen refastened the sling. "The entire house is a buzz over it."

"Have I broken some protocol?" I asked as she helped me get resettled.

"I would be more concerned about fainting and landing in the arms of the heir." Her voice was dry as toast.

I did a double take. "I face planted on Prince Diamant?"

"That's one way of saying it," the queen agreed.

"And the hits just keep on coming!" I said, shutting my eyes in mortification.

"Now, now." She stood and patted me on top of the head. "I think my step-son and his courtiers found it all very exciting."

I groaned and covered my face with my good hand.

"Prince Diamant is quite proud of himself for catching you," the queen said. "In fact, the courtiers are raving at his quick and *heroic* actions."

"Christ Jesus," I mumbled from behind my hand.

"I hear the Bards have already begun to compose ballads," she said.

I had to look to see if she was kidding, but the queen stood by the edge of my bed and appeared to be completely serious.

"Ballads?" I asked.

"Yes." She nodded soberly. "This all may go to his head for a few days. But not to worry. Although Diamant is a bit vain, he is, at his core, kindhearted."

The queen's lips quivered as I continued to stare. She started to snicker. That rolled into a full out laugh, and before I knew it, I was holding my ribs and chuckling too.

"There. Your color is much improved." She smiled and began to gather her things.

"I very much appreciate you taking care of me, ma'am," I said.

"Of course. You are my son's honored guest. Besides, my youngest grandchildren seem very fond of you."

"Oh." I brushed that aside. "That's the 'mom' vibe. All kids can spot a mom. They instinctually know to go to a mother for help..." I trailed off. That had popped right out of my mouth almost as if I was a mother myself. *Was I?* I struggled again to remember.

The queen cocked her head. "Daphne, have you remembered something?"

The thought that I might have children and that I couldn't remember them made my heart slam into my throat. *What sort of woman forgets her own children?* I silently chastised myself. *And what about my own mother?* I knew she was a Witch, but I could not recall her face or even her name.

"It's not a memory," I tried to explain. "It's more like an inner knowing..." My head started to pound, and I lifted a hand to rub at my forehead. "I think between you tending me as my healer, and the way you speak to me—that sort of gently lecturing tone. It has made me wonder about my own mother."

She smiled. "That is lovely of you to say."

Finnlagh walked into the room with another servant trailing behind him. "Mother," he said to the queen, "how is she?"

"The wound has only slightly re-opened," the queen said, passing her basket to the new servant. "I have changed the bandages, but she must take more care in the future."

"I will personally see to it that she stays in bed for the remainder of the day," Finnlagh announced, taking a seat on the side of my bed.

"I'll stay put," I said, shifting against the pillows. "Trust me."

Finnlagh narrowed his eyes. "I couldn't help but overhear your conversation in the hall."

I raised my brows. "Oh?"

"The children's fondness for you is because you are kind, sweet, and generous, Daphne," he said. "That is why the children are drawn to you."

"*Pfft.*" I rolled my eyes. "I have never been called *sweet* in my life," I countered, and then wondered how I was so certain of that fact.

He smiled and picked up my hand. "And you find being called sweet offensive?"

"Damn straight," I said. "I'd prefer to be thought of as strong and capable."

"Now, children." The queen shook her head. "No quarreling."

"Yes, ma'am," I said immediately.

"I must go," she said. "The king expects an update on the wellbeing of our guest."

There was a commotion out in the hall, and I turned

my head in time to see Prince Diamant, his wife, children, and a half dozen courtiers all come trooping into the bedroom.

What fresh hell is this? I wondered, tugging the blankets a bit higher over my chest.

"Queen Aine, how is the patient?" Prince Diamant asked, stopping near my bed.

"She will be well with rest and care," the queen said.

"Excellent," Prince Diamant said, bowing to the queen as she made her exit. She acknowledged his bow with a smile and a pat to Liam's head. Everyone else in the room bowed very low to show their respect to her.

I spoke to Prince Diamant after the queen left. "I apologize for passing out and landing on you, Your Highness."

Prince Diamant's gaze went straight to Finnlagh's hand holding mine. "You came to the aid of my son, at the expense of your own health, m'lady. I was happy to assist you in your time of need."

"You are very gracious to say so." I nodded and noticed that Ravena was standing quite close beside her mother. "Hi sweetie," I said.

The child cast a quick glance over toward her mother and thrust out a handful of lilacs. "I brought these for you, Daphne," she said, stepping forward. "Uncle Finnlagh said they were your favorite."

I slid my hand out from under Finnlagh's to accept the posy. "That was very kind of you, Ravena."

The child smiled, nodded, and ducked back to her

mother's side. Prince Diamant, I noted, completely ignored her. He did, however, literally have his hands full. He kept one hand on his eldest son's shoulder and Liam's hand firmly grasped in his other.

Prince Diamant slid his fingers over his youngest son's hair. "Soon brother, we would like to see both you and your guest at court," he announced.

"Oh, that's a kind offer but I—" Finnlagh shut me up by clamping his hand warningly over my leg. Instead of arguing in front of his family, I lifted the lilacs to my nose and inhaled their fragrance.

"We would be delighted," Finnlagh said smoothly. "I am sure Daphne would find a visit to court very enlightening."

Princess Oona curled her lip. "Finnlagh, you can't possibly be thinking of keeping this mortal female as a pet, are you?"

"Now, now, *mo chroí.*" Prince Diamant chuckled as he continued to stroke Liam's hair. "Finnlagh has always had his own interests."

"As you say, my lord." Princess Oona dipped her dark head demurely, but the tone was insolent.

Prince Diamant ignored his wife's behavior. "I look forward to seeing you again, Daphne."

I wasn't sure how to best respond, so I smiled slightly and nodded in acknowledgement of his words.

"At the very least, husband," Princess Oona said, "see that the mortal is cleaned up and presentable before she is in our presence again."

What a bitch, I thought.

"I am sure Finnlagh will see to that," Prince Diamant said.

"Of course." Finnlagh inclined his head. "I will personally oversee Daphne's care."

His brother smiled slowly. "I have no doubt."

I glanced between Finnlagh and his brother. There was some subtext here, and it made me uneasy. Trying to lighten the mood I smiled at Prince Diamant. "I promise that I will do my best not to faint the next time we meet, sir."

"It is not your fault," Prince Diamant said. "I sometimes have an overwhelming effect on mortal females." He gave a mock sigh. "It is a trial to me, yet I have learned to live with it."

"Wow, you are *so* brave," I said, before I thought better of it.

The heir threw back his head and laughed. "Oh, I like this one."

At the heir's amusement the Fae courtiers immediately laughed as well. The group's reaction struck me as a very high school sort of insincere, nervous laughter.

He left with his sons, and Princess Oona sent me a long, considering look and then followed. The rest of the flock of courtiers were quick to bring up the rear.

The maids scurried out behind the group and Finnlagh went to close the door behind them all. He shrugged out of his coat and hung it by the door. As I watched, his shoulders dropped in obvious relief.

"Finnlagh?" I asked.

Finnlagh held up one finger, in a silent request for time. He stood waiting at the door and listening. After a moment he nodded and bolted it. He strode straight to the bed, leaned over me, and got up in my face. "You took an unnecessary risk today."

"Your mother said that I would be fine," I pointed out.

"No." He took my chin in his hand. "That was not the sort of risk I meant."

I pulled my head away. "What's gotten into you?"

"You have unknowingly put yourself in real danger, Daphne."

"Danger from what?" I asked.

"From my brother."

CHAPTER THREE

I blinked at the intensity of Finnlagh's tone. "You think I'm in danger—from your brother?"

"I don't think," he said. "I know."

I opened my mouth to argue and checked myself. "Are we secure in this room?"

"I will be staying with you, your physical well-being is not in jeopardy."

"No." I shook my head. "I *meant* is this room private. I was asking whether or not we might be overheard."

He sat beside me on the bed so that he was facing me. "This is my room. We will not be overheard."

"Good." I nodded. "First off, I don't see how I could be in danger from your brother. He seemed like a self-important pretty boy to me."

Finnlagh's eyes grew wide. "I will suggest that you *never* speak that way about him outside of this room, nor to anyone else. Not ever again."

"So he has a big ego, eh?"

"Daphne." Finnlagh rested a hand on my leg. "For your own personal safety do not underestimate my brother, or his pride."

I tipped my head to one side as I thought about what Finnlagh had said. "That's interesting," I said. "Because your mother told me that while Diamant was vain, he did have a kind heart."

Finnlagh's eyes grew wider. "The queen said that to you?"

"She did," I confirmed.

Finnlagh sat back. "I find I am *very* surprised that she shared that with you."

"She also told me that the Bards were busy composing ballads about your brother catching me when I passed out. She seemed to think that was hilarious."

Finnlagh shook his head over the news.

"Which makes me curious," I said, drumming my fingers on my thigh. "Does your half-brother get along with your mother, Queen Aine?"

"Yes, he does. She's the only mother he has ever known," Finnlagh said. "The king's first wife was slain while my brother was young."

"Slain?" I asked. "As in murdered?"

"Assassinated," Finn said. "During the war with the Dark Court."

"A war with the Dark Court?" I narrowed my eyes. "Are we talking like Seelie and Unseelie courts?"

"In a way…" Finnlagh paused. "It's complicated and

rather difficult to explain."

I frowned. "So you do have wars?"

"Yes, unfortunately we do. The Fae realms are not so different from the mortal world."

"Realms?" I asked. "As in plural—more than one?"

"Yes."

"To be clear, I am in one realm right now, but there are other Fae realms?"

"There are many." Finnlagh nodded.

I filed that bit of information away. "What's the story with your sister-in-law?" I asked next. "Is she prejudiced against mortals like those other ladies of the court I met today?"

"That is not my story to tell," Finnlagh said.

"Well, from her reaction to me I figure it's one of a few scenarios," I said. "Either she's bigoted toward other species, she's never seen or been around a mortal before, *or* she's got a superiority complex."

"Oona is not like the other females of this realm," Finnlagh said.

I frowned. "Are you saying that she's from another realm or something?"

"Yes." Finnlagh nodded. "She was a princess of the Dark Fae."

"Oh…" Suddenly, I remembered something I'd once been told about marriages in the Fae realm. "Was her marriage to your brother *arranged*?"

"Yes." Finnlagh reached over and tucked a stray lock of hair behind my ear. "Their union brokered a peace treaty."

"Peace treaty? So you're saying their marriage stopped a war?"

"Yes," Finnlagh said. "The birth of Prince Riordan bound the treaty."

I did my best to smother an exhausted yawn. "How so?"

"Because now a child of both the Dark and Light Fae is heir to our throne. The Dark Fae are loathe to make war against one of their own."

"No kidding?" I asked. Despite my fatigue, my curiosity was piqued. "So your brother and sister-in-law actually didn't know each other before they were married?"

"No they did not," he said, easing closer. "They met at the signing of the treaty and were handfast immediately afterward."

"They were strangers when they married..." I trailed off thinking that over. "Are they happy now?" I asked. "I mean obviously they're *together*, they have kids but —"

Finnlagh flashed a lop-sided grin. "I'm afraid you are confusing duty and the necessity to provide an heir for the realms with romantic love, Daphne."

"But he's your brother," I argued, even as he took my hand. "Surely you have some sense of whether or not he's happy or—"

Finnlagh leaned forward and pressed his mouth to mine. His kiss was firm, and he lingered over it for a moment.

Was it a slick, fancy move? No.

Did it affect me? Yes.

He eventually lifted his mouth, but his eyes stayed locked on my face as he spoke. "The only happiness I care about at the moment is yours, Daphne. When you fainted today, it frightened me."

"I'm sorry that you were worried," I said automatically. "I feel like I screwed up my first day being up and about."

"You did nothing of the kind. Seamus on the other hand has been reprimanded for being so careless with you."

"Who's Seamus?"

"The guard that caused you so much pain."

"To be fair, Seamus wasn't the only reason I passed out," I said. "I overdid it today by picking up your nephew. I was trying not to throw up when I handed Liam off to your brother. Seamus sort of pushed me over the edge when he grabbed ahold of my arm."

Finnlagh trailed a fingertip along my jaw. "He hurt you and still you defend him?"

"I doubt his hurting me was deliberate," I said. "You simply gave an order and he tried to follow it as quickly as possible."

"Perhaps I shall rethink his punishment."

"Jeez!" My eyes went wide. "You didn't throw him in the dungeons, did you?"

"Oh, it's much worse than that..." his voice trialed

off menacingly.

Horrified, I pressed a hand to my throat. "What did you do?"

"I put him on the guard rotation to watch over my brother's children," he said, deadpan. "Liam is a hellion. He will run Seamus ragged."

I patted my heart back in place. "Ha-ha, Finnlagh. Very funny."

"Seamus won't think that it is. None of the royal guards enjoy watching over the children. They are quite the handful."

"Ravena and Liam seemed okay to me."

Finnlagh smiled and took my hand again as he spoke. "Riordan, the eldest, he's the ringleader and often talks the other two into mischief. He seems to take a delight in watching the other two get in trouble."

I leaned back against the pillows. "So Riordan is a shit disturber, is he?"

"Shit disturber?" Finnlagh began to laugh. "That would be an accurate description of my brother's eldest son."

"I enjoyed seeing the gardens today," I said around a yawn. "Maybe we can go out again tomorrow."

"Perhaps," he said. "Only if you promise to rest."

"Honestly, I could go for a nap," I agreed.

"Then I will allow you to rest." He started to stand.

"Hang on a second." I reached for his closest hand with my good one. "You said before this was *your* room. Am I to take it that I've been sleeping in your bed this whole time?"

He nodded. "Yes. It was the safest place for you to be."

"I see." I thought that over. "So, all this time you've either been sleeping in that chair or across the foot of the bed?"

"I trusted no one else to guard you." He pressed a kiss to the back of my hand.

His quiet words and actions touched me. "That was very gallant of you, Finnlagh."

His lips twitched. "Thank you, my lady."

I studied him as he released my hand and sat in the chair. For the first time, I noticed that he looked worn out.

"Can I get you anything?" he asked as I continued to stare at him.

I had put him out of his own bed, and still he hadn't complained. In fact, he seemed fine with sleeping in a chair. I wouldn't have thought to use the word *sweet* when it came to describing Finnlagh O'Brien. But yet, that's exactly what he was.

"Why don't you stretch out here, instead of sitting in that armchair?" I patted the spot beside me on the bed. "Seems only polite, since I've booted you out of your own bed."

His jaw dropped, and I found Finnlagh's reaction to be endearing. He genuinely was nervous to lay next to me. And the fact that he was confirmed my theory about the sweetness of his character.

"Are you sure?" he asked.

"You look pretty wiped out," I said, managing to keep my voice casual. "You might as well lie down and be comfortable for a change."

He pulled off his boots and let them drop to the floor. "All right."

"When was the last time you slept?" I asked.

"I don't remember," he said, standing.

"Well, come on." I patted the empty space beside me again. "You aren't going to do me much good as a bodyguard if you are dead on your feet."

He eased down on the bed, on top of the blankets with exaggerated slowness. "I don't want to jostle you," he said by way of explanation when he very slowly stretched out on his back.

"I'm okay," I said, trying not to grin.

He folded his arms behind his head, shut his eyes, and sighed.

As I was propped up, I could still see his face. Slowly, he began to relax. "Better?" I asked him after a moment.

His eyes popped back open. "Yes. Are you sure you are comfortable with me sleeping in the bed beside you?"

"Well..." I tucked my tongue into my cheek. "These bandages and sling are crazy sexy. I can only hope that you will manage to restrain yourself."

"I would *never* force myself upon—"

I snorted out a laugh. "Finnlagh, I know that. I was

only making a joke."

"Ah." He narrowed one eye at me. "Well, that's good then."

I waited a beat. "You don't snore or anything, do you?"

"Not any louder than you do."

"I do *not* snore," I said, offended.

"You do, and it is adorable." He grinned. "It is probably because you sleep with your mouth open."

"Well, that's not my fault if I've been sleeping with my mouth open. I've been drugged with whatever the healers gave me," I argued. "You can't hold that against me."

"Yes, you are correct, my lady." He yawned and shut his eyes. "It was churlish of me to have said otherwise."

"Churlish?"

"Boorish," he said. "Perhaps ill-mannered might be a better word…"

I rolled my eyes. "Smart ass."

"Get some rest, Daphne," he suggested.

"You too," I said, closing my own eyes.

I woke up some time later from another round of nightmares and discovered that it was fully dark outside. I burrowed my face into the firm pillow searching for comfort but discovered that it wasn't a pillow at all. My cheek was pressed against Finnlagh's chest.

At some point I had kicked off the covers, rolled onto my good side, and had snuggled up against him.

Finnlagh was still lying on his back, with his hands tucked behind his head. Apparently, he hadn't moved a muscle since he'd first laid down.

I, on the other hand, not only had my head resting on his chest; one of my legs was thrown across his and I was pressed up tightly against his side. I was pretty sure that I had never been much of a nighttime cuddler and was surprised to find myself in this position. Carefully, I began to ease back. When he stirred, I froze.

My gaze traveled up to his face. He was still sleeping. The soft light from the candles on the mantle and the fire burning across the room created enough illumination for me to make out his features. Since I was laying so close to him, I took the opportunity that had presented itself and studied him.

Damn, I thought. *He really is beautiful.* His dark blonde hair tumbled over his forehead and his lashes were ridiculously long. Those thick brows stood out, and if my left arm hadn't been in a sling or my good arm pinned beneath me, I would have never been able to resist running a fingertip across his cheekbones or that sculpted mouth of his.

However, it was more than his looks that captivated me. Over the past days I'd discovered for myself that Finnlagh O'Brien, Prince of the Fae, was a caring and kind male. His courtly elegance and sardonic sense of humor had intrigued me at first. But the unexpected sweetness and his sense of chivalry? That was a lethal combination. Chivalry wasn't exactly a common attribute in this day and age, and Finnlagh wore it very well indeed.

As I continued to study his features, I again recalled our dream-like time together by the pond. Admittedly, it had been incredible, and I was barely able to repress a shiver of longing. I also discovered that, injured or not, I wanted to make love with him again.

Down, girl, I thought. *Let him sleep.*

He rolled toward me, and I held my breath waiting to see if he was going to wake up. We were nose to nose now and my leg was still hooked over his. Cautiously, I started to ease my leg off.

His hand suddenly moved. He caught my ankle, and I jumped in reaction.

"Finnlagh?" I asked quietly.

"Daphne?" He said with his eyes still closed.

"Er, sorry," I murmured, trying to do the right thing and to ease further away. I stopped the moment his fingers tightened on my ankle. I flashed my eyes up to his and discovered he was fully awake and watching me.

"What are you sorry for?" His voice was low.

"Sorry to have invaded your space..." I trailed off when his fingers slid from my ankle to the back of my knee. I swallowed hard. Hard enough that I was sure that he heard.

"I am not sorry," he said with his eyes still on mine. "I am very happy to find that you have turned to me in the night."

"It wasn't deliberate," I tried to explain.

"No." He hitched my leg higher over his hips. "It was instinctual."

"I...um..." I stammered. "It's not fair." I tried to remove my leg. "To you. Let me just—"

He pressed closer, brushing against me, and I lost my entire train of thought. "I'm content to simply hold you," he said. He moved his other arm from behind his head, and now I was encircled in his arms.

We stayed like that for a while, and finally I broke the silence. "What you said to me earlier today, about how our time at the pond haunted you?" Nervously, I licked my lips. "Well, if I'm being honest, Finnlagh, while I may not remember much about my past...That event is crystal clear and it's haunting me too."

In answer, he kissed my forehead and my heart begin to pound. "Every night," he said, brushing kisses all over my face. "Every night I dream of you. Only you."

"Finnlagh," I whispered as he gave my knee a squeeze. "I want you, but I'm not sure if I'm up for this. Maybe we shouldn't."

In answer, his hand slipped under the gown and slowly moved up the inside of my thigh. "We absolutely should," he said, as his fingers slid even higher.

I wasn't wearing anything under the gown. I bit my lip trying to hold back a moan as he found that out for himself. Softly, he began to test my readiness.

"Daphne." His voice was low. "Do you trust me?"

"I do," I said honestly. "But I'm afraid I'm not going to be able to live up to either of our expectations after our previous time together."

"Hush now." He silenced me with a kiss.

Slowly the kiss became deeper and hotter. Eventually when he lifted his mouth from mine, I was lucky to remember my own name. He rolled to his back and quickly shoved his pants down past his hips. Before I could blink, he was reaching for me and lifting me easily. I slid my leg over his waist and straddled him.

I braced my weight with my good arm against his chest and leaned forward to kiss him again. The kiss was explosive. Finnlagh took my hips in his hands, positioned me, and began to push his way up inside.

I gasped and shut my eyes at the slow penetration. Once he was sheathed to the hilt, he anchored my hips with his hands. It was everything I had to hold still and let him set the pace. Our mouths met again, and the kiss continued even as I kept my good arm resting on his chest for balance.

The care which he took because of my injures only turned me on more. He was amazingly tender, and his lovemaking was slow, deep, and intense. When I told him I wanted to sit more upright, he bent his knees and raised his legs which allowed me to lean back a little and use his legs for support.

The gown puddled around us as we slowly rocked together. He reached for my breasts, but between the gown and the sling on my left arm, he couldn't get to them. I was about to try and pull the gown over my head with my good hand when he stopped me.

Finnlagh grabbed the hem of the gown with both his hands, and with a wicked lifting of one eyebrow, he tore it in half.

The contrast of his slow, careful strokes and the quick violent tearing of the gown had me shuddering. Now that the gown was split up the middle, he was able to have access to my breasts and he gently filled his hands with them. Clamping my thighs down on his hips, I enjoyed the ride.

I felt the orgasm build. It went from a shimmer to a burn, until eventually when I went over the edge, Finnlagh was right there with me.

Afterwards he tucked me along his side, and feeling safe in his arms, I slept deeply. With no bad dreams chasing me.

***

The next several days were spent trying to regain my strength. Every morning after breakfast, Finnlagh and I would take a stroll. We started out with short trips, but as my strength returned we would go for even longer walks. He took me on tours of both his home and the surrounding property, which was a massive estate.

We typically had lunch in the courtyard under the pergola, while the sunlight shone through the wisteria vines and blossoms. In the afternoon—with the queen's permission—I began to rework my left arm. Some days I read in the library after lunch, or I took a nap while Finnlagh attended to his duties—always within the house though. We ate our supper together in a big formal dining room, which was surprisingly intimate. Our nights were spent alone in Finnlagh's bedroom, making love in his ornate bed.

After a few days of being up and around, I started to learn the names of the Fae that worked in the household. There was an older gentleman whose name was Bagley, who was fairly intimidating. I was pretty sure he was the butler, as he was definitely in charge of the entire staff.

The cook was a kind, grandmotherly type of female named Moira. She wore an apron to protect her clothes, and her hair was always neatly tamed into a bun on top of her head. The head gardener's name was Darren. He was the one responsible for the grounds and for the flowers that were arranged all over the house.

I spent one afternoon following him around while he redid or freshened up the interior flower arrangements. I learned he was married, and he and his wife were expecting their third child. The maid who had helped the queen tend to me and also tidied up Finnlagh's room was a shy young Fae named Imogen.

Imogen had a crush on one of the footmen, a freckle-faced young male named Hamish. He was tall and slightly awkward, but Hamish was always smiling.

After a week, I was able to remove the sling. The

queen declared that my ribs were healing too and so Finnlagh and I celebrated by walking arm-in-arm to the stables. It was further than we'd ever walked before, and I was looking forward to the exercise as well as seeing more of the estate. However, I was less than excited when I discovered that a few guards were to accompany us.

Seamus was back from his rotation guarding the children and did seem relieved to be re-assigned to Finnlagh. He had given me a stiff, obviously forced apology upon his return, and I tried to put him at ease. His response had been to scowl.

I guessed he held a grudge. Either that or he didn't like mortals.

The walk was wonderful and the stable set up was huge to my inexperienced eye. Finnlagh and the manager of the stables ended up spending quite a long time talking about the horses, but I didn't mind. I could tell as I watched him walk up and down the stalls that he genuinely loved the horses. Delighted to be out of the house, I stayed back and took everything in.

While Finnlagh finished up his conversation with the manager, I strolled outside the stable to look around. I had spotted a nearby paddock and so I headed in that direction. Seamus trailed behind me, shaking his head and grumbling under his breath the entire way. Flipping my braided ponytail behind my back, I decided to ignore him.

There was a rider in a bright red jacket working with

a white horse and I leaned on a fence to watch. Birds were singing from a branch of a nearby tree, and the breeze was light and as frisky as the horse being exercised. I lifted my face to the sunshine and breathed in the fresh air. I was wearing the olive-green dress again today and was pleased to discover that after the long walk my wounds only mildly ached.

I was finally starting to feel like my old self. I was clearer headed, definitely stronger, and the nightmares had all but disappeared. Maybe that was due to the care I'd been given, or maybe that was from the nights I'd spent with Finnlagh.

We had made love every night since that day I'd invited him to share the bed with me. I had to give him props for coming up with ways we could be together that didn't jostle my healing wound or aggravate my ribs.

I heard the horse approach and snapped my head around. The female rider walked the horse over to the fence where I stood. "How are you this fine day, my lady?" she asked.

"Fine, than—" I cut myself off from saying 'thank you' in the nick of time. "I am well," I finished, looking up to meet the rider's eyes.

She's such a tiny thing, I realized. The female was one of the shortest adult Fae that I'd ever met; even sitting on the horse it was obvious how petite she was. She did look sharp in her riding outfit. I admired the bright gold buttons on the crimson velvet jacket. Her leggings were white, and her riding boots and cap were black. When she smiled down at me I saw that under her cap her hair was a sunny blonde. My attention was pulled from the rider when the horse shook its head. Cautiously, I moved farther back from the fence.

"You're not frightened of horses, are you now?" the rider asked.

"Ah, no," I said. "Not especially. It's only that I haven't been around them much." On cue the horse tossed its head again and I jumped.

"Colleen is spirited," she said, "but there's no reason to be nervous around her."

"Okay," I said uneasily. "The horse is pretty that's for sure."

"That she is." The rider nodded at the compliment and I noticed her eyes were a friendly green. "Would you like to touch her?"

"Oh, that's all right," I said quickly. "I'll pass."

"Have you never touched a horse before?"

"Nope," I said. "I'll stay clear. Wouldn't want to get bitten."

The rider laughed. "Colleen here won't bite you. But I will warn you to stay clear of the ass end."

"Duly noted," I said as the horse and rider moved closer still.

"Pat her on the neck," the rider invited. "It's less stressful for the horse and for you."

Cautiously I reached out and patted the horse's neck. When she swung her head toward me, I froze. I patted her neck again. The horse allowed my touch, and I ran my fingertips over her creamy white mane. Since the horse seemed fine with me, I ran my hand over her neck again.

"Hello, Tara!" Finnlagh's voice came from behind me.

I eased back and checked over my shoulder to see Finnlagh smiling at the woman.

"Good morning, Your Highness," she answered.

"Daphne, this is Tara," Finnlagh said, slipping his arm around my waist. "She's one of the finest horse trainers in the realm."

"I appreciate the compliment, sir." Tara said it sweetly, but her grin was mischievous.

"I just met Colleen the horse," I said to Finnlagh. "I got to pet her. Er, at least I assume Colleen is a female horse."

Tara chuckled. "Colleen is a mare, aye."

"Oh, okay." I nodded. "Female horses are called mares and males are stallions?"

"Most male horses are in fact geldings," Finnlagh explained.

"Oh." I nodded. "Snip, snip."

"Geldings are more affable," Tara explained. "While a mare is a bit more—"

"Sassy?" I guessed.

"Correct." Finnlagh gave my waist a squeeze. "Which means that a talented rider, such as our Tara, would prefer a more spirited mare than a gelding."

"Now Colleen here, she has a bit of attitude," Tara said, giving the mare a pat. "She does what I tell her, but only because she thinks it's what *she* wants to do."

Tara's explanation made me smile. "Oh, I get it. You're more like partners?" I guessed.

In answer, Colleen whinnied.

"Yes, you're smart and beautiful," I said to the horse. The horse side stepped closer to the fence and feeling braver, I patted her neck again.

"Do you have time for a ride today, sir?" Tara asked Finnlagh.

"No," he said, sounding resigned. "Not today.

"You should go, Finnlagh," I said, taking my hand away from the horse. "Go and do something fun, you've been watching over me for days. Seamus can walk me back to the house."

"I can have one of the grooms saddle your horse for you, sir." Tara made the offer, and I could see that Finnlagh was debating it.

"Get out of here." I reached up, took ahold of both sides of his face, and planted a firm kiss on his mouth. "You go do your thing, and I'll walk right back to the house and take a nap."

"If you're sure?" Finnlagh asked.

"Absolutely." I nodded. "You know exactly where to find me when you get home."

"And where might that be?" he asked.

I went up on my toes to whisper in his ear. "I'll be in bed, waiting for you."

"Maybe we should go back straight away," he said, completely serious.

"Scram." I nudged him, making him chuckle. "Seamus?" I said next.

The stocky guard stepped forward. "My lady?"

I gestured in the direction of the house. "Let's get this show on the road."

Seamus frowned in confusion. "What show?"

"It's an expression," I said, rolling my eyes. "It means, 'let's get going.'"

"My lady." Seamus held out an arm.

With everything settled, I took the guard's arm in my right. I lifted a hand at Tara and Finnlagh. "Have a nice ride you two. See if you can keep the prince in line, will you Tara?"

Tara touched the brim of her hat. "I will take excellent care of His Highness, my lady."

"Seamus?" Finnlagh called. "Protect the lady with your life. Or yours will be forfeit."

"Yes, Your Highness," Seamus said without blinking an eye.

I considered what Finnlagh had said as Seamus and I began our walk. Seamus was an older Fae, and his blonde, curly hair was starting to turn white at the temples. While I wasn't pleased being stuck with the sour old guard, I *was* happy knowing Finnlagh was getting a break and doing something he loved.

We walked in silence for the first ten minutes until I finally spoke. "Seamus?"

"My lady?"

"You don't like me very much, do you?"

"May I be frank?"

"I'd rather you be Seamus," I quipped.

"Pardon?" He looked at me as if I'd completely lost my mind.

Okay, I thought, releasing his arm, *this guy has zero sense of humor.* "I meant," I said, "that I'd rather have you be honest with me than put on an act. I'd prefer it if you were truthful."

"While it is not my place to comment on such things, m'lady…" Seamus said.

"I hear a *but* coming."

"But, another bride from the cursed Dark Fae race would be preferable to *you*."

"Jeez!" I laughed. "Don't hold back there, Seamus."

He nodded. "Very well, as a mortal you are unsuitable and completely improper as a companion for the prince."

"So you have a big hate on for Dark Fae, and you're prejudiced against mortals too, is that it?" I said, giving him side-eye.

"The Dark Fae assassinated our Queen!"

"So I was told," I said calmly. "It was also my understanding that the marriage of Diamant and Oona brokered a peace between the realms."

"*Prince* Diamant and *Princess* Oona!" Seamus sputtered, sounding scandalized. "Do not dare to presume to speak their names so informally!"

"Relax, Seamus," I said, since the guard was beginning to turn a rather alarming shade of red. "You're gonna give yourself an aneurysm."

"Hear me, mortal. It would be safer for you, and certainly far better for the prince if you were back with your own kind!"

"Safer for me?" Now I stopped walking. "Do you care to explain what you meant by that?"

"No." Seamus sneered. "I do not care to explain myself to an inferior being."

"Wow." *What a bigoted asshole,* I thought.

My neck prickled. Feeling suddenly uneasy, I took a moment to consider him as a possible opponent. My eyes traveled up and down the older man. While Seamus' hair was starting to go gray at his temples, he had the type of bulk that often hid a lot of muscle. It would be best not to underestimate him physically. Not to mention he'd already hurt me once. I certainly wasn't going to give him an opportunity to do so again.

The more distance I can put between us the better, I decided and started to power walk back to the house.

I no longer felt safe being alone with him. I didn't think he would attack me, but I had a hunch that he wouldn't bother defending me from an attack either. As I made it to the top of a big hill, the house came into view. Giving myself a chance to catch my breath, I paused. Out of the corner of my eye I saw movement and spun to face it.

There was a face peering out at me from the leaves

of a nearby tree. "Who's there?" I asked quietly.

I stared hard at that face and slowly it changed color. It melded into the leaves as if it had never been. From the bottom of the hill I could hear Seamus muttering about the injustice of having to guard a mere mortal.

"You can take off Seamus," I called from over my shoulder. "I am more than capable of finding my own way back now."

"The prince would be furious if you walked without an escort!"

"Is that right?" Tossing my head, I picked up my skirts and took off at a run.

"Stop!" His voice came from behind.

I could hear the jangle of his chainmail shirt against the breastplate he wore as he started to jog up the hill after me. It crossed my mind that all that metal was probably horribly uncomfortable to run in—and that thought goaded me on like nothing else could have.

Soon I was back at the edge of the formal knot gardens and a good fifty yards ahead of the guard. I was tiring but decided to push myself and run the rest of the way back to Finnlagh's house anyway. I pressed my arm against my bruised ribs and jogged past Darren and a few assistant gardeners, who all stopped what they were doing to gape at me.

"Hey, guys," I called to them as I ran past. By the time I made it to the courtyard, I had dropped my pace down to a walk and Bagley had come out to greet me.

"My lady?" Bagley's raised beetle brows said it all.

"Whooee!" I bent over at my waist and tried to catch my breath.

"Is something amiss?" Bagley wanted to know.

"Well the flat shoes aren't bad for running," I said, panting a bit. "Thank god they buckled, but it sucks jogging in a dress, let me tell you."

"I see," Bagley said soberly. "May I get you anything?"

I straightened up and smiled at the man. "I could probably use some water to drink right about now."

"Of course." Bagley inclined his head. "If you would care to follow me inside, I can have some refreshments set out for you."

I heard the jingle of Seamus' chainmail as he approached. "What were you thinking?" He was more out of breath than I was. "Do not *ever* run away from me like that again!"

I ignored the guard. "Lead the way, Bagley," I said, nodding to the butler.

"Now, see here!" Seamus dropped his hand on my shoulder.

"Hands off!" I warned, shrugging free of him.

"You little…" Seamus growled, grabbing ahold of my long braided ponytail.

"Hey!" I yelled, and when he roughly pulled me backwards by my hair, I reacted defensively.

Glancing over my shoulder to judge his location, I gave a swift back kick to his kneecap. His leg buckled instantly. He released his grip on my braid, and I followed through by turning and bringing my right elbow back. Hard. The elbow strike connected with the bridge of his nose and made a loud crunch.

His nose exploded with a spray of blood, and Seamus went down to his knees. Immediately, I grabbed the spear he dropped and turned the weapon on him, holding the blade to his throat.

"Now," I said, very calmly. "You might want to rethink that whole, 'she's inferior because she's a mortal,' mindset."

"*Bhitseach bheagl*," Seamus swore at me. Then he spat blood out on the stones of the courtyard.

The gasp from the assembled staff had me guessing that Seamus had just called me something very unflattering.

"Ah, good." I nodded. "I see that we understand each other." I took the blade away from his throat, flipped it pointy end up, and tapped the end of the spear on the ground. "Bagley?" I addressed the butler. "I could use a snack."

"My lady." Bagley made an *after you* gesture.

Now that the adrenalin was fading, I was starting to ache. However, I'd be damned if I let anyone know that. Holding my head up, I sailed into the house, taking Seamus' spear with me.

CHAPTER FOUR

I ended up going to the kitchen, while Moira the cook, Imogen, and Hamish stared at me with very large eyes. Bagley had escorted me to a chair and brought me a glass of water right away. I pulled out a neighboring chair and rested the spear against it, keeping the Fae weapon close at hand.

Moira shook off her surprise and plied me with chamomile tea and cookies in short order. I sat at the table in the kitchen and chatted her up, eventually joined by Darren, who had come in with a huge basket of flowers from the gardens.

I tried to play it cool while Darren arranged the blooms in big containers, but the truth was between the impromptu jog and performing an elbow strike to Seamus' nose, I was hurting.

A lot.

I tried to discreetly keep my left arm pressed against my side to support my bruised ribs, but I was fairly miserable. I excused myself after my cup of tea and a few cookies—they weren't sitting well—and when I scooted the chair back from the table, everyone in the room jumped.

"The tea was lovely," I said evenly to Moira as if they hadn't all over reacted.

She nodded, and as I watched I saw that Darren tried not to smile. I braced my hand on the table, took a deep breath, and attempted to stand.

"My lady," Darren said, gently taking my right arm. Once the gardener had assisted me to my feet, he stepped back immediately.

I inclined my head. "I appreciate your kindness, Darren."

"I am your servant, my lady," he said, gallantly handing me a pink peony blossom.

With a nod to him, I tucked the flower behind my ear and went up to the room I'd been sharing with Finnlagh, taking the guard's spear with me.

Shutting the bedroom door, I limped over to the bathroom gritting my teeth the entire way. I locked the bathroom door in an abundance of caution and rested the spear against the wall beside the tub, keeping it within easy reach. I got the water going, made sure it was hot, and stripped down and climbed in. I didn't bother trying to pull my ponytail up and out of the way; it would hurt badly if I tried to raise my hands over my head. Instead I carefully sat and slid down until I was up to my chin in the hot water.

Hoping to soak the aches and pains away, I shut my

eyes and rested the back of my head against the rim of the tub.

Good news? I was able to jog, *and* I had defended myself from an angry Fae who outweighed me by at least seventy pounds. Of course, I'd caught him off guard—I could admit that. He hadn't expected a female to know self-defense moves, let alone to be able to effectively employ them. But worst of all I'd taken his weapon *and* threatened him with it in front of the household staff.

That would burn Seamus' ass more than anything.

"At least it worked." I laughed at myself and shifted in the tub trying to get more comfortable. The truth was that I hadn't used self-defense tactics in years. I typically relied on a weapon. *I wonder what ever happened to my handgun after the battle on the ridge, anyway?* I frowned over that thought for a moment, but the memories of the ridge seemed so out of focus.

For a moment I wondered why that was…But then those thoughts drifted away too. I was exhausted.

When the bathwater cooled, I let half the water drain out. I refilled the tub with the hottest water I could handle and kept right on soaking. The heat was helping my ribs although my right elbow hurt like a son of a bitch. I sincerely hoped Seamus' nose hurt worse. After hearing the crunch and seeing all the blood spray from his nose, it was a good bet that I'd broken it.

Finnlagh would probably be upset about what had happened, and I hoped he wouldn't be too angry with me. At least Bagley, and most likely Darren, had witnessed the incident, so it wasn't merely my word against Seamus'.

Shutting my eyes again, I tried to relax.

A brisk knock on the bathroom door had me jolting awake.

"Daphne?" Finnlagh called through the door.

I sat up with a splash and discovered that the water had cooled considerably. "Yes?" I said, checking to see that the spear was still within reach.

"Are you all right?"

"Yes."

The knob rattled. "Why is the door locked?"

"For extra security," I said. "I'd unlock it for you, Finnlagh, but I'm still—" I broke off as he let himself right in the bathroom. "—in the tub," I finished.

"How long have you been in here?"

"I don't know." I pulled the plug and psyched myself up to climb to my feet. "The water is cold. I must have dozed off."

Finnlagh spotted the spear and stopped in his tracks. "It's true then. You disarmed Seamus."

"Sure the hell did," I said. "Seamus shouldn't have grabbed ahold of my hair and yanked me back by it. It pissed me off."

"He did *what*?"

I held up a hand. "I'll explain it to you in a minute. For now, can we postpone the lecture until after I figure out how to climb out of the tub in the least painful way possible?"

Finnlagh leaned in, put his hands under my arms, and lifted me easily to my feet. "Have you reinjured yourself?"

"Not seriously," I said. "I am pretty sore though." *And bone tired too,* I realized.

"Let's get you dried off. I will deal with Seamus later." Finnlagh helped me step out of the tub. A few minutes later I was in a clean nightgown with my wet hair wrapped in a towel. He escorted me to a chair and when I asked for a comb, he fetched it himself and brought it to me.

I tried to explain to Finnlagh what had happened. But with no fire in the room, I felt chilled. Determinedly, I pulled the leather tie from the end of the braid and attempted to work through the tangles in my hair. But after a few minutes I had to let my hands drop. It hurt too much to comb out my own hair.

My teeth started to chatter a moment later, and before I could blink Finnlagh had me back in the bed, covered with a blanket. He started shouting for Bagley, Hamish, and Imogen.

"Finnlagh, I'm only sore and cold," I tried to protest, but he ignored me.

Bagley came and went. Shortly thereafter, Imogen bustled into the room with a warm blanket. She spread the blanket over my lap and started to work on towel drying and then combing out my hair.

I was amazed at how calm Imogen stayed while

Finnlagh barked orders at the folks who came at his summons and rushed around the room. Hamish popped in and rebuilt the fire. As soon as Hamish's task was completed, Finnlagh called the footman over to him. He spoke quietly, but whatever he'd said had Hamish leaving the room at a dead run.

"Finnlagh, calm down," I began. "I'm all right."

"You will be quiet!" Finnlagh pointed at me.

"Hey!" I snapped. "If you think I'm going to sit here while you shout at me, you're in for one hell of a rude awakening, pal."

In the blink of an eye, he went royal. "By Danu, you will stay put in that bed until I return. Is that understood?" His tone was grim, and I blinked at the change in his demeanor.

"I'll stay in the bed because I'm tired and cold," I shot back. "*Not* because you told me to."

"Imogen?" Finnlagh shifted his attention to the maid who stood beside me. "You will remain with the lady until I bid you leave."

Imogen silently inclined her head in acknowledgement of the command.

Finnlagh glared at me one final time and was out, slamming the bedroom door behind himself. I heard the distinct click of a lock being turned and realized that Finnlagh had locked me in with Imogen.

"Well," I said, turning to look at the maid, "it's just you and me, kid,"

"I am not afraid to be alone with you, my lady." Her

light green eyes were solemn. "You would never hurt me."

"Please," I said, "call me, Daphne."

"As you say, Lady Daphne." She nodded and gently rubbed the towel over the ends of my long hair.

"No. Not *Lady* Daphne..." I sighed. "Never mind."

"I saw you defend yourself from Seamus," Imogen said as she worked the comb through my hair. "I watched it all from the kitchen window."

"Oh, yeah?"

"Bagley said to Moira that Seamus was a brute, and that he deserved his comeuppance."

My eyebrows raised. "Bagley said that, did he?"

Imogen nodded. "He did."

I smirked. "Well, I guess I gave everyone plenty to talk about."

"Oh, yes, Lady Daphne," Imogen said, starting on a new section of my hair. "You have."

I started to smile at the absolute sincerity in her tone. Sarcasm didn't seem to be a concept grasped by the Fae as far as I could tell.

"Now, Darren the gardener," Imogen continued, "he thinks you must be a warrior, perhaps even the warrior bride of legend."

"Nope. Not a warrior or a bride. Sorry to disappoint." I chuckled, and immediately regretted it. I pressed my hands to my sore ribs and groaned.

"Hamish swears that you must be," Imogen said next. "He says Prince Finnlagh would never be betrothed to any female unless she was a warrior *or* a member of the nobility."

"Imogen," I said patiently, "Finnlagh and I are *not* betrothed."

"As you say, Lady Daphne."

"I don't have a title and seriously, we aren't getting married."

Imogen didn't argue, she simply nodded and kept working on my hair.

"I don't know why you'd automatically assume we were betrothed," I said. "I'm sure that Finnlagh has had other relationships. And besides, his other lovers couldn't have all been aristocrats."

"I wouldn't know, Lady Daphne."

"How long have you worked here, Imogen?"

"For the past three years," she said, setting aside the comb.

"Have you ever seen or met any of Finnlagh's other romantic partners?"

"You are the only one I have ever had a conversation with." Imogen took the damp towel from my shoulders and set it aside.

"The *only* one?"

"Well, His Highness has never had anyone live in the house here with him before."

"Yes, but he had to have had dates, or guests, to the house before me."

Imogen shrugged. "Would you like me to read to you, Lady Daphne?"

"Read to me?" I did a double take. "Ah no. I'm good. It was kind of you to offer all the same."

Imogen nodded and walked across the room. She stood beside the door, folded her hands, and simply stood there.

"What in the world are you doing?" I asked.

Imogen slanted her eyes over at me. "I am waiting for His Highness to return."

"All the way over there?"

"Yes, Lady Daphne."

"You can drop the *lady*, I asked you to call me Daphne."

Imogen's eyes went huge in her face. "Oh no, my lady, I could never do that!"

"Well would you at least sit down? You're making me nervous standing over there."

"I must defend the door," Imogen announced, and she was completely sincere.

"Oh, for the love of god." I tossed the covers back and climbed out of bed. My feet had barely hit the floor before Imogen came running at me waving her hands.

"My lady get back in the bed at once!"

"I'm only going to the bathroom," I said.

"You should not be on your feet." Imogen bit her lip and looked so upset that I spun away from her, stalked over to the bath, and slammed the bathroom door shut.

Taking a deep breath, I went over to lean on the sink. I counted to ten trying to calm down. Then, I counted to ten again.

I scowled at my reflection in the mirror. "Locked in my goddamn room in some fancy palatial home by a prince of the Fae no less..." I blew out a long, annoyed breath. "This is one jacked up faerie tale."

"My lady?" Imogen's voice came through the door.

"What?" I asked crossly.

"Do you require my assistance?"

"No!" I snapped. "I can pee all by myself, been doing it for years." So saying, I took care of business, washed my hands, and exited the bathroom, grabbing Seamus' spear along the way.

Imogen was hovering beside the bed as if unsure of what to do next. "My lady?"

I rolled my eyes as I stalked back toward the bed. "I'm getting back in the bed. Calm down, Imogen."

She nodded and silently began to wring her hands.

Seeing her do that infuriated me. "Oh for gods sake! Would you *please* sit in the chair and relax?"

Her eyes flashed wide and she dove into the padded chair beside the bed. It took me a second to realize that she had only complied because I sounded angry, and most importantly, because I was holding the spear.

My eyes traveled from the weapon and back to the maid's pale face. I walked around to the far side of the bed, laid the spear across the foot, and climbed in. Imogen watched my every move as if expecting to be struck. Ashamed of myself, I sat back against the pillows, pulled up the covers again, and finally faced her.

"Imogen," I began, "I am sorry that I frightened you. I only wanted you to sit down and relax. There's no telling how long it'll be until Finnlagh returns. I am sore, tired, and annoyed—mostly at myself. I should not have taken it out on you. Please forgive me."

Imogen flinched in surprise. "You apologized to me?"

"Uh, well, yeah." I flipped a section of drying hair over one shoulder. "That's typically what decent people do when they need to own up for behaving badly."

Imogen seemed to think that over. "Is that a common practice among mortals?"

"Apologizing?" I frowned at the unexpected question. "It is. Usually."

"No one has ever apologized to me before."

"I'm sorry to hear that," I said, and then waited a beat. "There, now you have two apologies under your belt."

A smile quivered on Imogen's lips. "You are very amusing, Daphne."

"Hey!" I grinned. "You used my first name. I thought I was going to have to threaten you with the spear to get that to happen."

"Well, we are locked in here together." Imogen demurely folded her hands in her lap. "You are distraught, *and* you have a weapon…I thought it would be in my best interest to humor you."

I grinned. "And there's a bit of snark!"

Imogen tilted her head. "I am not sure what *snark*

means."

"It means your comment was snide but made with humor."

"I shall endeavor to make more snark for you in the future, in that case," she said, completely serious.

I couldn't help but chuckle. "I like you, Imogen."

"I like you as well, Daphne."

We ended up being locked in the room for the rest of the afternoon. At some point I woke up to discover that Imogen had propped her feet up on the edge of the mattress and was snoozing away. It made me smile. I stayed still, hoping the maid would be able to continue to rest. As far as I could tell she worked her ass off. She deserved a break.

I shut my eyes, snuggled back under the covers, and was asleep again in moments.

***

When Finnlagh came to bed that night he held me close, but we did not make love. I woke in the morning surprised that I'd slept for so long. When I got back from the bathroom, I found him getting dressed for the day. He was in much more formal looking attire than I had seen previously.

"What's up?" I asked around a yawn.

"I have matters I must attend to." He sat in a chair and pulled on his boots. "I have been called to see the queen."

"Oh, yeah?" I said. "What's that all about?"

"That would be all about you."

"I take it this would be in regard to the incident with Seamus?" I sighed. "How much trouble did that cause for you?"

"It has become a diplomatic issue, and now an inquiry has been made."

"Tell whoever is *inquiring* to talk to Bagley, Imogen, and Darren. They saw the whole thing."

"Darren and Bagley were questioned yesterday." Finnlagh finished with his last boot, stopped, and looked at me. "I never imagined Seamus would act out against you in that way."

"Finnlagh, I know that." I said, going over to him. "I also hope that *you* know that I wouldn't do an elbow strike on someone without provocation."

He pulled me into his lap. "He should have never laid his hands upon you."

I smiled. "It's a safe bet Seamus will think twice about it before he tries it again."

"As will everyone else," Finnlagh said wryly. "The tale is spreading across the realm like wildfire."

I shrugged. "You're looking pretty spiffy this morning."

One of his eyebrows rose. "Spiffy? What does that word mean?"

"It means that you look very fine." I ran my fingers through his hair.

He took my hand, dropped a quick kiss on it, and

stood with me still in his arms. For a moment I thought he was taking me to bed, but instead he gently put me back in the chair.

Finnlagh went straight to a wardrobe and selected a sapphire colored jacket. Without a word, he shrugged it on. He went to the mirror and straightened the hair I'd recently mussed. He was obviously preparing to leave.

"I guess you have to leave right this moment?" I said.

"I do, yes," he said, starting for the door.

"You could at least give me a proper kiss goodbye." My words had him stopping in his tracks.

He spun on his heel, came back, pulled me up to my toes, and kissed the hell out of me.

"Well that's more like it," I said and pressed another smacking kiss on his mouth. "Tell your mother that I said hello."

"I will." He smiled. "For me, please rest today."

"Sure thing," I said.

He ran his hand down my hair. "Stay in the house. *Indoors* and out of trouble."

"Sheesh." I rolled my eyes. "It's not like I'm going to go arm wrestle the household staff."

Finnlagh shook his head. "Your word, Daphne."

"Fine. I will stay in the house and be bored out of my mind."

"I will return in the afternoon." He pressed a kiss to the top of my head and headed for the door. He opened it to reveal Imogen. She bobbed a curtsy to Finnlagh as he left.

"Good morning, my lady." She smiled and was holding an armload of material.

"Hey, Imogen. What do you have there?"

"New gowns for you, my lady."

"Gowns?" I asked. "What in the hell am I supposed to do with those?"

Imogen laughed. "Wear them."

Imogen may have been soft spoken, but she brooked no nonsense, and I was dressed in a dark blue gown a short time later. This one was also cut in the princess style lines and featured a scooped neckline. The sleeves were shorter, ending at the elbow and the dress was surprisingly comfortable. There was a touch of embellishment around the neckline and hem but other than that it was plain.

"Perhaps, my lady," Imogen began, "you would care to wear the jewel that I found in your clothing when you arrived—"

"I'm starving!" I said, cutting her off. The last thing I needed was a jewel.

She nodded. "I will tell Bagley to set up your meal in the dining room."

"Can I eat in the kitchen, instead?"

Imogen did a double take at my request, but I insisted. A few minutes later I was following Imogen down to the kitchen, and it scared the hell out of Moira when I waltzed in.

"Sweet Danu!" Moira jumped and patted a hand to

her ample bosom.

"Good morning, Moira." I nodded, trying not to laugh.

Hamish sat at the table polishing the silver and nodded. "Good morning, my lady."

"Hamish." I smiled. "I've been told to stay out of trouble today, so I figured I'd come hang out with you guys in the kitchen."

Moira began to sputter at the announcement.

"You don't have to fuss over me," I told the cook. "I can make my own breakfast."

Moira was clearly offended at the suggestion. "I would prefer that if you are going to be in *my* kitchen, that you stay out of the way."

"I was only trying to help," I began.

Moira pointed to the table. "Sit. I do not care to have people underfoot while I am working."

I sat. "Yes ma'am."

"*Humph.*" Moira flounced over to the stove.

There was a twinkle in Hamish's eye while he sat at the table. He was trying to hold back his laughter, but his shoulders were shaking slightly.

It was Bagley who ended up smoothing things over. The butler only hesitated a moment when he found me at the table.

"I've been ordered to stay out of trouble," I said to Bagley.

"Let us see what we can do about that." He nodded, spun neatly on his heel, and brought me a cup of tea in short order. Smoothly, it was slid in front of me, and Imogen added a plate of buttered toast.

I found that I was starving and started on the toast immediately. "So," I said to everyone assembled. "I hear that Bagley and Darren were questioned about what happened with Seamus?"

At the stove, Moira bobbled the skillet and Hamish dropped the candlestick he'd been polishing.

Interesting reaction, I thought.

Bagley cleared his throat. "I did speak to the prince about the incident yesterday, my lady. It was unfortunate that it transpired at all." He moved to the far side of the kitchen and began to talk to Moira.

"I wish I would have seen you break his nose." Hamish said, so only I could hear. "How did you manage it?"

"Elbow strike," I explained.

"The prince was so enraged that he went straight to the king's council yesterday," Hamish said.

"Oh, is *that* where he went?" I said.

Imogen handed me a dish of fruit preserves. "It is rumored that Seamus has been threatened with banishment."

"Imogen!" Bagley scowled at the maid. "We do not discuss matters that are beyond us."

I considered that and noticed that while Bagley look seriously displeased, Imogen appeared unfazed by the reprimand.

I sampled the preserves, found them to be excellent,

and considered my next move. Imogen clearly had more information. I was about to ask her but was distracted by the plate of eggs Moira set in front of me.

"This looks fabulous, Moira," I said, tucking right in. I couldn't remember the last time I'd been so hungry.

A few moments later Bagley left the kitchen, doing whatever it was that he did. When Moira stepped out as well, I turned my attention to the freckled-face young man across from me. "Tell me, Hamish," I said, "what sort of mission did Finnlagh send you on yesterday afternoon?"

"Oh, 'twas just an errand..." Hamish kept on polishing and did not meet my eyes.

I ran my tongue over my teeth. "Don't bullshit me Hamish."

"My lady?"

Imogen cleared my empty plates. "You should tell her, Hamish," she said.

Hamish cleared his throat. "The prince bid me go to the queen and give her an urgent message."

"What was the message?" I asked.

Hamish's face went red. "I could not say, my lady."

I narrowed my eyes. "You can not say, or you don't know?"

"Yes." Hamish gulped audibly.

I glanced over at Imogen to see how she was reacting to all of this. When she realized I was watching her, she spoke. "His Highness is most concerned with your health and wellbeing, my lady."

"I get that," I said to the couple. "I also know that you two are acting very guilty."

Imogen folded her hands at her waist. "Hamish and I only wish for you to be happy while you stay here."

I wasn't going to get any more information out of them. Bagley appeared in the doorway and cleared his throat. "May I escort you to the library, my lady?"

"Why?" I asked, confused by the out of the blue request.

"Prince Finnlagh made arrangements for you to have visitors while he was out for the day."

"Visitors?" I asked, rising to my feet.

"If you will follow me please?" Bagley requested.

Too curious not to see who my visitors were, I followed along up the stairs and down a long hallway.

"The Princess Glynis and her fiancé, Mr. Beau Stone," Bagley announced and then bowed out.

I stared at the pretty blonde for a long moment and then, suddenly, I knew her. "Glynis!" I rushed forward to give Finnlagh's sister a hug.

"Daphne!" She held me close. "You look well."

"It's good to see you!" I laughed and accepted a hug from her mortal fiancé, Beau, next.

"We wanted to surprise you," Glynis said, linking her arm with Beau's. As they stood side-by-side, Glynis was a few inches taller than her fiancé. Glynis wore a long pale blue-colored tunic and close-fitting gray pants that were tucked into dark boots.

Her tunic was encrusted with beads and sequins... *No,* I comprehended, *those aren't sequins.* They were, in fact, jewels. There was a thin silver and sparkly band in her hair as well. Worn low across the forehead, it kept her hair back from her face.

Beau was wearing dark pants, a loose linen type of shirt, and a blue-gray jacket that was made from a heavy jacquard fabric.

"Wow, you two look great, but you didn't have to get all dressed up for me," I teased the couple.

"Geoffrey asked us to come and see you," Glynis said, as we all took a seat. "He was worried you might need to see a familiar face."

"Geoffrey?" I smiled but didn't recognize the name.

"Your grandfather," Beau said patiently.

"My..." I trailed off, trying to remember.

"I knew it," Glynis said to Beau. "She's been here for too long. The memories of her mortal life are fading."

I frowned. "What are you talking about Glynis?"

"Daphne," Beau reached in his pocket and drew out a sachet. "Take this."

"What is it?" I asked him.

"St. John's Wort." Beau pressed the fabric pouch into my palm. "Keep this with you. It should remain on your person at all times."

Confused, I glanced from the little bag back to the couple. "Why?"

Glynis pressed her hand over mine, folding my

fingers around the sachet. "That herb can help keep you from completely losing your memories while you are a guest here in the Fae realm."

Automatically I squeezed the pouch, and as soon as I did my daughters' faces popped into my mind. *How could I have forgotten my children?* "Kayla and Kenzie, how are they?" I asked Glynis immediately.

"They are safe and happy." She nodded. "The girls, your parents, and their young ward are guests of the Shaw family on Wolfsbane Ridge."

"My parents..." I clutched the bag of herbs tighter and instantly recalled why I'd been taken to the Fae realm. It had been for my safety, so I could recover from my wounds from the battle. "If you are here, who is guarding my family?" I asked her, suddenly panicking.

"Your grandfather and the Lycan pack are protecting them." Glynis rested her hand on my arm. "Daphne, you are missed. Your friends and family need you back in Hemlock Hollow."

"Hemlock Hollow..." It sounded so familiar, and the longer I held that sachet in my hand the more my memories began to swirl. The raw emotions that accompanied them hit me like a sucker punch to the gut. Horrible images flashed through my mind and my memories returned with a vengeance all at once...

Defending my home against a reanimated corpse... I'd shot it in the chest with a short barrel and it hadn't vanquished it. I relived stopping a teenage Witch from throwing a dangerous spell while in my ice cream parlor and felt the pain of burns across my hand all over again. In my mind's eye, I watched my brick house being engulfed by witch fire with my daughters trapped inside.

"No," I whispered as tears began to roll down my face.

Now I was able to remember that it had been Glynis who had gotten my girls to safety. On the heels of that was the recollection of the day when Ashton Lowell had invited me and my daughters to come live with him. I was horrified at my utter foolishness in believing that my children and I were both loved and safe with him.

"Breathe," Glynis said. "Try and breathe."

"I trusted Ashton...Thought that we loved each other. Otherwise I'd have never moved in...But it was your brother that I called when my girls had fallen victim to a curse." I lifted my eyes to Glynis' and shuddered at the memory of how hard it had been to keep them from hurting each other.

"That was wise." Glynis nodded. "Go on."

"Finnlagh was there for me when I'd been desperate for help," I heard myself say. "He worked his magick and healed the girls. Afterwards we sat on the porch and I told your brother, *thank you*, even though I shouldn't have."

"I'm sure he didn't mind," Glynis said softly.

"He teased me about owing him a debt, and—" My

voice broke. It took me a moment to continue. "And I offered Finnlagh ice cream for life." Now, I began to cry in earnest.

"Daphne?" Glynis rested her hand on my arm. "Let the memories flow over you. Don't fight them, it will only make the process more painful."

I nodded in acknowledgement of her words and felt the pain of Ashton's lies again, as I re-experienced finding out how my lover had betrayed me with Jessamine Albright, my best friend. In my mind, I once again lived through the shock of finding his ritual room and all the dark magick accessories it had contained.

"Oh god." My words were a broken whisper. "I was sleeping with the god-damn necromancer. I'm so ashamed."

"It is not your fault." Glynis patted my back.

"It is!" I insisted. "Don't you understand? I put my children and parents' lives in jeopardy by trusting that manipulative, lying bastard! Ashton Lowell is responsible for the deaths of at least three people, and probably the curse laid against my own children. He's been the source of the unrest, intolerance and hatred of the other Supernatural species growing within the Witch community."

Beau stepped closer. "Daphne, no one blames you —"

"*I blame me!*" I shouted. "My children have been traumatized, my parents were forced to flee their home, and the Lycans died trying to defend their territory. All because of me!"

"My lady?" Imogen stepped in the room. "What is wrong?"

Furious, I squeezed the herbal sachet tightly in my hand and suddenly flashed back to the ridge once again…Surrounded by smoke, fire, and blood, I relived the moment that I'd fired my gun on Ashton Lowell. My bullet had hit him in the chest, I saw the impact, and his retaliatory spell had struck me an instant later. Blasted to the ground, I'd been left lying alone and in helpless agony until my grandfather and Finnlagh had found me. Being forced to re-experience it again made me ill.

Sweat popped out on my upper lip, and my stomach began to roil. "Excuse me," I said, dropping the sachet to the floor. "I'm going to be sick."

Bolting from the library, I ran up the stairs for Finnlagh's bedroom and past a few servants. I heard them ask if I was all right, but I couldn't answer. I hit the bedroom door at a dead run and rushed across to the bathroom. I barely made it in time before I threw up everything I'd eaten for breakfast. I heaved over and over until nothing was left.

Weak and shaken, I climbed to my feet and wobbled over to the sink. I rinsed out my mouth, splashed some water on my face and carefully staggered back to the bed I'd been sharing with Finnlagh. I managed to climb in the bed and lay on my side. Curling into a ball, I waited for the shaking and the sickness to pass.

The shame, however, wasn't going anywhere. That and the guilt all but smothered me.

Imogen came in and stood beside the bed. After a moment, she rested her hand on my shoulder. "Can I fetch anything for you, my lady?"

In answer I reached up and grabbed for her hand. I didn't trust myself to speak, yet I did not want to be left alone. If I opened my mouth, I knew that I would scream and bawl like a baby, so I shook my head, *no*, willing myself not to make a sound.

I felt the bed dip as Imogen sat next to me. "It is all right." She gave my hand a squeeze. "I will stay with you until the prince arrives."

I nodded, lay there crying silently, and held Imogen's hand.

"You are safe here," Imogen whispered, running her hand gently over my hair.

I almost laughed over the idea of the young Fae sitting guard over me. I might have taken down a Fae warrior, but I'd fallen apart at being forced to recall the traumatic events of the past few months. I squeezed my eyes shut and wished that the awful memories would simply go away and leave me in peace.

Imogen began to sing. The melody was like a lullaby, and the sweetness of it had more tears falling. Exhausted from the emotional trauma and from being violently ill, I drifted off listening to the maid's quiet, comforting song.

***

"Daphne."

Finnlagh's voice woke me, and I shifted toward it seeking comfort. He was there, sitting at my side and holding out his arms.

"Hold me," I said, wrapping my arms around his neck.

"I am here."

"Don't let go," I whispered in the crook of his neck and then pulled him down to lie on the bed with me.

"I won't let go," he said, settling half on top of me.

I heard Imogen leave, quietly shutting the door behind her.

"Take me away from here, Finnlagh," I whispered. "Take me somewhere quiet where we can be completely alone."

"I would take you anywhere you ask, *mo ghrá*."

"Take me back to our special place. My one beautiful memory where the light was golden, and it was quiet and still by that pond."

"Of course," Finnlagh said, pressing a kiss to my throat.

"I need you Finnlagh," I whispered. Then I felt his body's reaction to my words. He was hard as a rock and I groaned at the discovery of it.

"Hold tight to me," Finnlagh warned.

I squeezed my arms around him as tightly as I could and felt a falling sensation. It was like the drop of a roller coaster. When it stopped, I opened my eyes and discovered that I was sitting in his lap. Once again we were in the tall emerald grass beside that magickal pond. All around us trees were brushed with red and orange and the air smelled like autumn.

The light was still that same incredible tawny color, and I let out a shuddering sigh. "It *is* a real place."

Finnlagh pressed a kiss to my forehead. "It is."

"Where are we, truly?" I asked.

"We are in a realm outside of time. It is another realm of the Fae."

I kissed him. "Make love to me, Finnlagh, like you did the first time."

One of his eyebrows quirked. "Are you sure? You are still recovering from your injuries. I would not want to cause you pain."

I pulled his head down to mine and kissed him again. "Take me here, Finnlagh. I'm tired of thinking. I only want to *feel*."

He responded by kissing me softly, and although it was wonderful and romantic, it left me wanting so much more. I pulled my mouth away from his.

"You don't need to hold back anymore, Finnlagh," I said, meeting his eyes. "And you don't have be so gentle with me."

The cognac color of his eyes shifted. There was the slightest flickering of russet in them and as I watched, his facial expression changed. "I will ask you this only once," he said. "Are you certain?"

I met his eyes without flinching. "Yes. I am sure."

CHAPTER FIVE

Finnlagh swooped in for a hard kiss, and I found myself flat on my back in the grass. There were no pretty words, and there would be no careful lovemaking this time. Instead it was all fire and fury.

While our mouths dueled, I yanked his trousers open and pulled him free. I chewed on his bottom lip, and he shoved the skirt of my dress up and out of his way. I wrapped my legs around his hips and guided him to my entrance. With one hard thrust he was deep inside me.

Throwing back my head, I screamed in pleasure. Finnlagh grasped the neckline of my gown and yanked, tearing it and freeing my breasts. He latched on to one and began to suckle. I reached around to his hips and dug my nails in, pulling him closer.

The pace he set was fast and intense and I held on for dear life. With a small bite to my breast, he moved back and pulled my legs up higher. He slammed forward, and it was exactly what I wanted.

"Like this?" he gritted out as he surged inside me

again and again.

I was right on the edge when I met his eyes. "More," I dared him.

To my surprise he completely withdrew, and I protested the loss of his body from mine. Before I realized what he was about, Finnlagh rolled me over and tugged me up to all fours. He yanked what remained of my dress away from me. Once I was completely naked, he moved in close behind. I held my breath and waited for him to continue, but he did not.

Turning my head, I looked at him from over my shoulder. "Finnlagh," I said. "Don't tease me."

"I would never tease you," he said.

"Finnlagh!" I demanded, as he kept me waiting.

He grabbed ahold of my hair with his free hand and pulled my head back. "Yes?" he asked very pleasantly.

I squirmed.

"Did you need something?" he asked.

"Stop teasing me!"

"Then hold still," he suggested politely.

I growled in frustration even as I felt him nudge at my entrance. My feminine muscles contracted, and he hissed out a breath. Slowly, he pushed his way inside, and from this angle he stretched my core so tight that now *I* was the one hissing in reaction to the fullness of it.

He went deeper and deeper until he bumped against my cervix. For several heartbeats he remained still, allowing my body time to adjust. Finally, he began to move slowly. His pace was deliberate, and it was agonizing, wonderful and maddening all at the same time.

Impatient for completion, I pushed back against him. "Finnlagh." I tried to turn my head again, but he held me firmly in place with one hand clamped on my hip and the other tangled in my hair. It didn't hurt, in fact my body was reacting happily to being held so tightly. Very happily.

"You will not move unless I allow it," he said, and to my surprise he gave my backside a light swat.

"You should know," I said, "that if you start this game, I *will* retaliate in kind."

His voice was a low rumble. "Do you promise?"

"Absolutely," I shuddered.

With a low laugh, Finnlagh leaned forward, pressing his chest tight against my back. Releasing his grip on my hair, he wrapped both his arms around me. Sitting back on his haunches, he drew me with him until I was sitting upright. Held tightly against his chest, I was now in his lap and he was still deep inside of me.

I gasped as he reached down and ran his fingertips across my most sensitive area, while his other hand began to fondle my breasts. His fingers danced over me, and I began to tremble as my orgasm built.

He whispered in my ear of all the things he wanted to do to me, with me, and it sent me right over the edge. The orgasm crashed through me, and I shouted myself hoarse. While I was still shaking, Finnlagh guided me forward to my hands and knees again, and now he began to surge inside of me. It was wild and rough and exactly what I needed. I threw my head back and came again. I was still shouting from the pleasure when he found his own orgasm a few moments later.

Together we collapsed in the soft grass at the edge of that magickal pond, and I had a moment to think to myself that Finnlagh O'Brien had probably ruined me for any other male, for the rest of my life. No one would ever be able to make me feel the things that he did.

I lay in his arms shuddering, exhausted, and trying to catch my breath. "That was great," I managed to say. "You do good work."

He popped open one eye to look at me. "I am your most devoted servant, my lady."

I couldn't help the snort of laughter that escaped.

I dozed in his arms for a time, and eventually he woke me with gentle kisses and lingering caresses. Now night had fallen, and the stars were in the sky. I rolled on my back, pulling him to settle over me. Above us, in the heavens, shooting stars blazed across the sky. As he thrust home, I held him close and blinked unexpected tears from my eyes at the beauty of it all.

***

I woke slowly, snuggled close to Finnlagh. With a satisfied hum, I opened my eyes but was shocked by my surroundings. "What the fuck?" I said, sitting up quickly.

Finnlagh stretched beside me. "You always say the sweetest things when you wake."

I scowled at the discovery that we were back in Finnlagh's bed and no longer on the banks of our pond. "How did we…When did we get back?"

Finnlagh sat up, and the sheet pooled at his waist. "I brought us back while you slept."

"Why did you…" I paused, distracted by his naked chest and all the lean muscle on display.

One of his eyebrows rose. "Yes?"

I shook my head and tried to focus. "*Why* did you bring us back?"

Finnlagh ran his hand over my long hair. "It was for the best. Time runs differently in the other realms."

"Right." I nodded. "I knew that."

"No. I mean that our perception of time is distorted while we are in the other Fae realms."

"So, what seems like an hour is actually…Several hours?"

"No." Finnlagh dropped a kiss on my shoulder. "More like weeks."

I did a double take. "Explain that to me again."

"To clarify," Finnlagh said with a smile, "what would seem like hours to a mortal, would be weeks in *that* realm. To those of my kingdom, several days would have passed."

"So how long were we physically away from *here*?"

"A little over a week."

"No way," I said.

"Check the wound on your left shoulder," Finnlagh suggested.

I glanced down and saw for myself that the wound appeared very different indeed. "Holy crap. It's healed."

Finnlagh rose from the bed and brought me a robe. "How do your ribs feel?"

I climbed out of bed and shrugged the robe on. Experimentally, I lifted my arms over my head. "I feel better," I said.

In fact, there was no pain at all. I twisted from side to side and had no twinges, and zero soreness. I went directly to the mirror, held the robe open, and saw for myself that the bruises that had decorated my ribs were gone as well.

"Daphne." Finnlagh's voice was low and husky.

I turned away from the mirror to face him. "Yes?"

"I want you again, *mo ghrá*."

I looked him up and down as he stood there naked before me. "I can see that."

He held his hand out. "Come back to the bed. It has been forever since I loved you."

I rolled my eyes. "It's probably only been a couple of hours."

"In which realm?" he said. "For me, it feels like forever."

I shrugged the robe off and it fell to the floor. I walked towards him, and he swept me off my feet. He kissed me then, and it was romantic as hell.

"That's a pretty slick move, pal," I said when he came up for air.

"I have a few more to show you," he replied, laying me on the bed.

"Well, now that I'm healed up…" I trailed off, waiting until he joined me. Once he did, I gave his shoulder a quick shove. He fell back to the mattress with a chuckle, and I rolled on top of him. "I may have a few moves to show you, too."

Finnlagh tucked his hands behind his head and smiled. "Feel free to do with me as you wish."

"Damn right I will. You might want to hold on to something," I warned, beginning to work my way down his chest with small love bites.

Later, I left Finnlagh sleeping, put on my olive-green dress, and silently let myself out of the bedroom. I went downstairs, heading for the kitchens determined to hunt up a snack. I was starving. Whether from the travel between realms or the sexual marathon with Finnlagh, I wasn't sure. All I knew was that I needed something to eat.

Following the aroma of fresh baked bread, I walked into the kitchen, waved at Imogen, and watched her jump a foot straight up in the air.

"My Lady Daphne!"

"Hey, Imogen." I headed for the bread on the counter. There were two loaves, and they were still warm and smelled fantastic. "I'm starving. Figured I'd make a sandwich or something."

Imogen rushed to my side. "You're back!"

"Uh, yeah." I tore a chunk of bread off the nearest loaf and popped it in my mouth.

"Allow me, my lady." Imogen shooed me toward the table.

I spotted a bowl of plums on the counter and snagged one before I sat. "You don't have to fuss. Some cheese, fruit and bit of that bread would be great."

I wolfed down the plum while Imogen bustled around. In moments I had a plate of cheese, another plum, some berries, and a slice of the rustic bread. Imogen brought me a cup of cider and a dish of butter, too. I slathered some butter on the bread. "This tastes great."

"I am very happy you are back and looking so well," Imogen said.

I reached out for her hand and gave it a squeeze. "I feel much better," I said.

"I am so glad."

"Take a load off, girlfriend." I patted the bench beside me.

"Oh! I couldn't!"

"Sure you can." I gave her a firm tug and she gave in and sat. "See how easy that was?"

Imogen grinned. "I've missed you, Daphne."

I released her hand and patted her shoulder. "It was very kind of you to have sat with me the other day when I wasn't feeling well."

"Of course." Imogen smiled shyly.

"Can't seem to quite recall what it was that made me so upset…" I picked up the cup of cider. "Feels like that was weeks ago." I shrugged it off and took a sip of the cider.

Hamish walked in, spotted me, and smiled. "Lady Daphne, I am happy to see you have returned."

"*Go raibh maith agat,*" I said, and smiled at the footman. "How've you been, Hamish?"

"Busy," he said with an aggrieved sigh. "Bagley has been running us ragged since you and the prince departed."

"Sorry," I said automatically. "Anything else been going on around here?"

"Well, that horrible guard was punished." Imogen proceeded to fill me in on the goings on at the house while I ate. "Darren the gardener told me that *he* heard from a guard at the royal palace that the prince had in fact been in very important summits the day that you left."

"Summits?" I asked.

Imogen nodded. "Yes. There were meetings with his mother *and* her advisors, historians, and the royal astrologer."

"Astrologer, eh?" I chuckled. "I'm an Aries. With the moon in Leo. Double fire signs. I've been told that means I'm passionate, independent, a born leader, and I prefer to be in charge."

"Who told you that?" Hamish asked.

"Huh." I sat back and thought about it. "I can't seem to recall." *And I should know that,* my inner voice said. *Hadn't she drilled me on the elements associated with each sun sign when I'd been a child?*

"My lady?" Imogen's voice cut through my thoughts.

I came back to the here and now. *Perhaps my memories are finally starting to return,* I thought. I held my breath waiting to see if I could recall anything else, but there was nothing. *Damn,* I groused silently, *it sure would be helpful if I had some sort of context to these random recollections.*

"Daphne?"

Imogen was staring at me, a look of concern on her face. I took a sip of cider and tried to pick the conversation back up where I'd left it. "Anyway," I said, "Finnlagh had mentioned that he was meeting with his mother about my skirmish with Seamus."

Imogen shook her head. "You do not understand the gravity of the entire state of affairs, my lady. This situation is far beyond the incident with the guard."

I took another drink. "So I'm guessing when the royal astrologer gets involved, it's a big deal?"

Hamish's eyes went wide. "My lady, the prince had been protecting you as his betrothed!"

I choked on the cider. "The prince and I are *not* engaged, Hamish."

Hamish waved that away. "His Highness would never stand by and allow an attack upon your person to go—"

"An attack that I handled all by myself," I interjected.

"He could not allow that to go unanswered!" Hamish declared. "His Highness made sure that the court knew of the importance of your safety, *and* of your position within his life."

I narrowed my eyes at the pair. "And you two got all of this from Darren?"

"Yes," Imogen and Hamish said in unison.

"And Darren got the information from gossiping with a guard at the palace?"

"You are more important to the Fae than you realize, my lady," Hamish said.

I frowned. "Meaning what?"

"There is a legend regarding a prince of Fae, Lady Daphne." Imogen's green eyes were huge. "According to the legend a prince of the Fae will wed a warrior bride. Their union will unite all the realms of the Fae and the Supernatural races on earth."

"Seriously?" I asked.

Hamish leaned forward. "It is rumored that you are, in fact, that very legend made flesh, Lady Daphne."

"Made flesh?" I shook my head at the phrasing. "Hamish, that all sounds like a romantic faerie tale to me."

"And are you not in the realm of the Fae having a romance?" Imogen asked.

"Well," I said, taking another bite of cheese. "I

suppose you have me there."

I heard footsteps and glanced over to discover Finnlagh standing in the doorway. Hamish bowed and immediately left the room, and Imogen popped up to her feet.

"I woke and you were gone," Finnlagh said to me.

"Seemed to me that you deserved a bit of a nap." I gave him a sassy smile. "Besides, I was starving. Imogen here, she filled me in on gossip and fixed me a plate. She's my hero."

"Your Highness." Imogen curtsied to Finnlagh. "I was keeping Lady Daphne company."

"That was most appreciated, Imogen." Finnlagh inclined his head.

Imogen offered to fix him a plate as well, and Finnlagh sat down, taking the spot that she had vacated. The two of us sat in the kitchen sharing a cozy snack, but when Bagley walked in, he bobbled the tray he'd been carrying.

"Your Highness." He bowed to Finnlagh and next to me. "Lady Daphne." It was obvious he did not know what to do with himself, since Finnlagh and I were seated at the kitchen table. The spot was reserved for staff, not the lord of the house.

"Hi Bagley. Did you miss me?" I grinned at his discomfiture.

"It was certainly quiet while you were away," he said. Clearing his throat, he addressed Finnlagh. "Your Highness, I am very pleased that you have come back in time for your scheduled return to court."

"Return to court?" I asked.

Finnlagh nodded. "Bagley? Will you see to it that suitable garments for Lady Daphne and myself are ready for this evening?"

"Of course, Sir." Bagley bowed and left.

"Imogen?" Finnlagh addressed the maid.

She snapped to attention. "Sir?"

"I will leave the lady's formal preparations in your capable hands."

Imogen bobbed a curtsy and took off at a run.

"Formal preparations?" I asked. "What in the world is going on?"

Finnlagh snatched the last piece of cheese from my plate. "As much as I would prefer to keep you here all to myself, we have been summoned to the Royal Court by my father."

"Am I being called on the carpet about breaking Seamus' nose?"

He shook his head. "I do not believe that is the *real* reason for His Majesty's summons."

"But to be clear, the king has summoned us?"

"Yes."

"Yeesh," I said. "That sounds a little ominous."

Finnlagh wasn't smiling. "It is ominous."

"Well shit." I blew out a long breath. "You better spill the tea and bring me up to speed on court politics."

"What did you just say?" His eyebrows rose. "I'm afraid I am unfamiliar with those mortal colloquialisms."

"I *meant* that you need to fill me in on all the royal gossip. As many pertinent details as possible…And give me a quick run down on the court protocol so I'm ready to face both your parents—and their court."

Finnlagh dropped a kiss on my nose. "I will do my best."

"And Finnlagh?" I said, resting my hand on his thigh. "I'm honored to meet your father. I will do *my* best not to embarrass you in front of the court.

Now he smiled and kissed me on the mouth. "*Mo ghrá*, you never could."

***

"I feel absolutely ridiculous," I muttered to Finnlagh as we stood in a hallway later that evening, waiting to be announced. "Why are we dressed in matching outfits? It makes me feel like I am at some weird grown up version of senior prom, or maybe a fancy Ren Faire."

Finnlagh smiled down at me and took my arm in his. "Tonight, we are wearing the colors of the royal household. My house."

"Oh." I thought that over. His mother, brother and sister-in-law, even Glynis had all worn shades of blue and gray whenever they had dressed formally. I simply hadn't put it together before. A banner displayed on the nearby stone wall caught my eye. It was a coat of arms, and I saw a crown, some sort of flower, and a bird in silver set against a lapis blue background. I glanced around the room and realized that while the Fae present at Court were glittery and elegant, no one else was wearing the colors of gray, silver, and blue.

"So you use color coding for quick identification, eh?" I asked.

He frowned in confusion. "Coding…Sorry?"

"The distinct colors must make it more convenient for spotting the members of your family," I said.

"That is one way to think about it."

I shrugged. "My game plan *had* been to be on the lookout for crowns, or someone sitting on a throne."

Finnlagh chuckled and leaned closer to me. "I am very pleased to see you in my colors." His voice was low and warm. "You look beautiful, Daphne."

Normally I would have rolled my eyes at his flattery, but Imogen had pulled my hair back so tightly that I wasn't sure that was even possible. The maid had braided the front of my hair away from my face, into an elaborate weave that left the back section of my hair to hang straight down between my shoulders. I'd never had my hair done so intricately in my life. I'd barely had a chance to compliment her on her skills before she bundled me into a high waisted gown of gray and silver brocade with navy trim.

Before we'd left, Imogen had produced a red-orange jewel tied on a long silver ribbon. "You should wear this, my lady." She said, tying it around my neck. "I hope that it brings you illumination."

"Illumination?" I asked, peering down at the jewel as it rested against my bodice.

Imogen patted my shoulder. "All of the other ladies at court will be decked in jewels. You should wear this tonight, especially."

"It's pretty," I said, and thought to myself that the jewel was oddly familiar...

Now Finnlagh and I stood arm-in-arm outside of the throne room in his parents' castle. The awareness that I was in fact wearing the colors of the royal household made me gulp nervously. I chanced another quick peek at Finnlagh, but he was smiling and nodding at folks. Truthfully, I wanted to ask him *why* I was wearing his colors.

I was not a member of the royal household; I was merely a guest. Perhaps it was for my safety? Centering the dark blue sash tied beneath my breasts, I reminded myself how potentially precarious the situation was. My stomach tightened over that thought, and I did my best to keep a pleasant expression on my face.

But it was incredibly difficult not to be distracted by the gorgeous surroundings. Dazzling though the Light Fae were, we were in the thick of the Royal Court. Everyone was listening and watching every single thing that we did. Scanning the room, I assessed the exits and kept my eyes open for any weapons and possible threats, just as he'd once taught me...

Just as who *had once taught me?* I wondered.

I tried to recall the face of the person who had trained me in self-defense tactics, weapons, and how to secure a perimeter. He was an older male, that much I knew. But even as I struggled to recall his identity, it faded away from me.

These glimpses of my past were exasperating. Concerned by my lack of ability to recall my own past from the mortal realm, I scanned the crowd again.

While I saw no weapons being openly carried, one of the first things that I *had* noticed upon our arrival was that the majority of Fae who were present all had similar expressions of disapproval on their faces. The Fae bowed or curtsied low to Finnlagh, while I had received only the barest of acknowledgments—or outright scorn.

So far, every Fae had looked down their nose at me. The self-deprecating side of me wondered if it was because I was the shortest individual at the castle. By mortal standards, my height was typical for a female— five foot six. However, all the Fae had to be at least six feet tall.

An elegant and—spoiler alert—gorgeous Fae couple dressed in green and gold sashayed their way over to us. They greeted Finnlagh, bowing low to him, but when Finnlagh introduced me to the Lord and Lady Greenfield they actually sneered.

Finnlagh had warned me to expect some hostility, and I was doing my best not to react to the bait. "Lovely to meet you," I managed to calmly say to the

Greenfields. But it wasn't easy to smile at the pair.

Finnlagh spoke to a different couple after the Greenfields had moved along, and I took a deep breath, telling myself to stay cool. I would get through the evening. Finnlagh had asked so little of me, the least I could do was to meet his father.

The royal family had been kind enough to allow me to stay in their realm while I recovered, and that meant I owed them my gratitude. If I had to wade through alligators and assholes to make sure his parents were both happy, then so be it.

I was beyond relieved when I heard Finnlagh's name being loudly announced.

Finnlagh began to step forward, and as my arm was in his, he drew me along with him. "Once, you stated that you owed me a debt." His voice was low as we walked away from the others.

I nodded and gave his arm a squeeze. "Being introduced to your father is my honor, Finnlagh. I'm happy to repay your parents' hospitality."

"That is not what I meant," he whispered.

"Then what do you mean?"

"I am warning you that I am about to collect upon that debt."

"Okay." I was concerned by how serious he sounded. "There's no need to be so grim. I would never go back on my word, Finnlagh."

He dropped a swift kiss on my mouth. "You have made me very happy, *mo ghrá*."

I was amazed that he'd kissed me in public, but his words and reactions were absolutely confusing the hell out of me. "You've called me that before," I said quickly, as the doors were starting to open. "What does *mo ghrá* mean?"

He tilted his face down to mine and smiled. "It means, 'my love.'"

I stumbled a bit hearing that. But there wasn't time to respond because suddenly we found our way blocked by a large group of Fae. At the center of the pack stood Lord and Lady Greenfield.

"So this is the mortal who is causing all of the trouble?" a male from the group asked.

"Stand aside," Finnlagh said, and I felt his muscles tense as I held his arm.

Lord Greenfield stepped forward. "I find it hard to believe that this *mortal* female managed to injure a guard of the Fae."

"Try harder," I said.

"It spoke to me." Slowly, he slid his long, pale hair over one shoulder. "Perhaps Seamus had been so startled to hear himself addressed by a mere mortal, that he was caught off guard."

The crowd laughed, and I shifted my weight in preparation for a fight.

"An inferior mortal might disarm a Fae guard," Lord Greenfield said to the crowd, "but never a member of the nobility."

"Perhaps, you'd care for a personal demonstration,

Lord Greenfield?" I pitched my voice to be heard.

Finnlagh clamped his fingers down on my arm. "Daphne."

"Are you challenging me, mortal?" Lord Greenfield smiled down at me, and it changed his appearance from pampered and pretty, to spoiled and mean.

"Consider this a polite warning," I said, dropping Finnlagh's arm. Swiftly, I summed up my opponent. He was supermodel elegant, and very tall...But he was also soft.

At his back, the Fae lord's pack of friends obviously thought that my warning was amusing. They spoke to him in Gaelic, and I didn't have to understand what they were saying—their tone was crystal clear. They were urging Greenfield on.

"I would strongly suggest that you stand down, Lord Greenfield," Finnlagh said as the Fae lord stepped closer.

Prince Diamant suddenly joined the group, with his wife right behind him. "Brother," he asked mildly, "is there a problem?"

"The mortal has issued a challenge to Lord Greenfield," one member of the group announced.

Princess Oona raised her brow. "Did she really?"

"Well this *is* exciting!" Prince Diamant rubbed his hands together. "Nothing like a bit of court intrigue to liven up the evening."

"Perhaps, the mortal pet simply needs to be beaten into submission." Lord Greenfield brushed his lace cuffs back. "Allow me, Your Highness, to show you how it is done."

"Do you want me to intercede?" Finnlagh asked me.

"Nope. I got this," I said, not taking my eyes off my opponent.

Finnlagh grinned. "Take him down, *mo ghrá.*"

Lord Greenfield reached out for me, but I caught his hand with both of mine. Quickly grabbing his pinky finger and ring finger in my right hand, I also took ahold of his index and middle fingers with my other hand. I yanked his fingers apart in opposite directions, while at the same time bending his wrist down and away from me. I heard—and felt—the bones in his hand pop out of place.

Lord Greenfield screamed in pain and tried to pull his hand away. But I held on.

"Stop! Stop!" Lord Greenfield's voice was girlishly high and shrill.

"Do you yield?" I asked pleasantly, even as the Fae male dropped to his knees.

"Aye!" he screamed.

"Does anybody else need a goddamn demonstration?" I asked, casting my eyes around the group of shocked courtiers.

When no one took me up on that, I let go of Lord Greenfield and stepped clear. He snatched his hand back, held it close to his chest, and stayed on his knees.

"Well," Prince Diamant laughed at the turn of events. "Now that we're all acquainted, I will escort my brother and his guest to the king." Diamant held out his arm to me.

"Your Highness." I inclined my head to the heir and accepted his arm.

Finnlagh held out his free hand to his sister-in-law, and Princess Oona accepted it with a slight nod of her head. Together we all walked into the adjoining chamber. The crowd of Fae that had previously gathered parted before us as we entered the throne room. I saw four decorative chairs fanned out at the far end of the space. Seated upon two of those chairs, on the dais, were obviously the king and queen. They too were all dressed in various shades of gray and blue.

Deliberately, I lowered my gaze and wondered how much trouble I was in now. *No eye contact,* I reminded myself, as the room fell to silence. *Curtsy low, and only speak after I am spoken to.* I'd taken on a cruel lord and I wasn't sure what would happen next, but it would be beyond stupid at this point to offend the king and queen of Fae.

If I hadn't already…

Diamant escorted me to stand directly in front of the thrones. He left, and Finnlagh stepped beside me. When he bowed, I knew that was my cue to curtsy. I had practiced but had no idea if I could pull it off correctly. Finnlagh shot an arm around my waist to steady me, and I did my best, wobbling only slightly.

"Finnlagh, my son. You honor us with your presence at court after so long a time away." The male voice was deep, smooth, and sounded, well…majestic.

Finnlagh tensed. I could feel it where his hand rested against my waist. "*Go raibh maith agat,* Your Majesty," he replied and straightened.

That was my cue to rise and I did, making sure to keep my eyes on the foot of the dais.

"I am delighted to meet you at last Daphne, friend to my daughter, the Princess Glynis."

I lifted my eyes. "Your Majesty." I dipped my head again automatically, because holy shit, I had never in my life seen anyone who looked more kingly than Finnlagh's father.

King Donal's hair was white and silver, and he wore the crown well. He had a neat, short beard that was also brushed with silver. The king's robes were midnight blue and trimmed in shimmering gray fur. He was not smiling as he studied me, and his eyes were a piercing aqua blue color. There was an aura of power around Finnlagh's father. An absolute authority. It made me nervous.

To his right, Prince Diamant had taken his place with Princess Oona at his side. Diamant snapped his fingers for wine, while Oona arranged her lapis blue skirts around her.

Finnlagh gave my arm a tiny squeeze, and I launched into the short speech that we'd prepared. "I am most appreciative sir, for your hospitality. I am very grateful to Her Majesty, Queen Aine, for her healing skills, and to your son, Prince Finnlagh, for his generosity while I have been convalescing."

"You look very well, Daphne." This was from the queen, and I slanted my eyes over to her. She was seated on the king's left and was smiling warmly. Queen Aine was lovely in a deep cut gown of cornflower blue velvet that managed to seem both modern and medieval all at the same time. Today there were jewels in the queen's hair, and they were dazzling.

"Your Majesty." I bowed my head again.

"It's wonderful to see you blooming," she said.

I smiled at her. "You are very kind, Your Majesty. I do feel much stronger."

"Stronger, eh?" Prince Diamant snickered. "I do believe that Seamus was very lucky to only have received a broken nose...As was Lord Greenfield."

The laughter that followed was loud with a mean sort of undertone. While the court had a chuckle at Lord Greenfield's expense, I forced myself to keep a neutral expression on my face and didn't move a muscle.

"I do recall hearing about an incident...Something about our guest having an unfortunate altercation with Seamus?" The king's eyes narrowed as he looked me over. "But what's this about Lord Greenfield?"

"You missed the fun, father!" Prince Diamant said.

"Lord Greenfield threatened to beat the guest of the prince," Princess Oona said, "and the mortal defended herself from his violence."

"What?" the king demanded.

I wanted to say something in my own defense, but I

did not. I couldn't speak unless I was addressed directly. *Fucking royal protocol,* I thought bitterly.

Lord and Lady Greenfield pushed their way forward. The lord was still sobbing, and his wife was trying to hold him up. "The mortal is an evil Witch!" Lady Greenfield pointed her finger at me dramatically. "Look what she has done to my husband!"

"She warned you, you pompous fools!" The comment was from Princess Oona.

That's twice she has defended me, I thought. *What is up with that?* I risked a glance at the princess. She was stoic and unsmiling, yet she had spoken up for me even as the court grew more agitated.

"Your Majesty," Finnlagh spoke over the crowd. "Lord and Lady Greenfield's claims are outrageous. Considering the current unrest between our realm and the Dark Fae, and the supernatural species in the mortal world, inflammatory statements and dramatics will only make the situation more tense."

"Ask her!" Lady Greenfield cried dramatically. "I'll wager there are sorcerers in her family! She's spelled Prince Finnlagh! Why else would a son of the royal house be cavorting with some low mortal whore?"

A collective gasp sounded from the court at this new insult. I felt the tension in Finnlagh's body. He was furious.

"Silence!" The king's voice was firm and had all the members of the court cringing. "Well, girl?" The king now spoke directly to me. "Did you spell my son or assault a guard of the Fae?"

I slid my gaze toward Finnlagh, and he nodded ever so slightly. "I have no magick nor did I assault the guard, Your Majesty," I said as politely as possible. "I *defended* myself from Seamus when he manhandled me." I nodded over at Lord Greenfield. "Today, I stopped Lord Greenfield in his attempt to do the same."

"I see," the king said. His eyes were the color of an iceberg. Cold and merciless, they sent a shiver of fear down my spine. "Have you anything else to say for yourself?"

I reminded myself to breathe. While the older man was stunning to look at, he was every bit as intimidating. I licked my lips nervously and spoke with care. "Like today, there were witnesses to Seamus' behavior."

"Yes, they have been spoken to," King Donal announced. "Did you truly keep the guard's spear?"

I nodded. "Yes sir, I did."

"Dare I ask where you keep it?" Prince Diamant asked me, sipping from his goblet.

I faced the heir. "The spear is next to my bed. I prefer to keep it close at hand. In case I ever have to defend myself again."

"Perhaps," King Donal said, "our guest should have brought the spear with her this evening."

"Well, I would have, Your Majesty," I said tartly, "but it clashed with my dress."

The King burst out laughing, and the rest of the court

joined in. Beside me, I felt Finnlagh exhale. I guessed he'd been holding his breath.

"Lord Greenfield," the king addressed his courtier, "you have insulted our guest and threatened her person. You and your wife are hereby banished from court."

The Greenfields gasped and the crowd parted. As one, the court turned their backs upon the couple as they left the room.

For a few moments, the silence was deafening. I looked from the retreating couple and back to Finnlagh.

The king spoke again. "You are brave, aren't you mortal?"

In deference, I inclined my head. "When I have to be, Your Majesty."

"I have always admired your courage, and I see why my son is so taken with you." King Donal smiled.

"*Always* admired my courage, sir?" I asked, confused.

"My daughter Glynis speaks very highly of you."

That's right, I thought, *Glynis.* She had been to visit me. She and her fiancé. I'd become ill when they visited…

My musings stumbled to a halt as Finnlagh started to speak. "Your Majesties. Father and Mother, we have a request."

"*We?*" I said to Finnlagh.

"Yes, we." He smiled at me and shifted his attention to his parents. "We have come here today to ask Your Majesties' permission and blessing, so that we may be handfast."

CHAPTER SIX

For a split second it was silent in the chamber. Then everyone began to talk at once.

"No," the king said, thumping his fist on the arm of his throne.

"Handfast?" I said to Finnlagh. "What in the hell are you doing?"

"You told me, father." Finnlagh pitched his voice over the noise of the court. "You said that I needed to take a bride by the winter solstice or that you would choose one for me."

"I told you to find a suitable and fertile bride!" King Donal argued. "A prince of the Fae must wed to bring either wealth or security to his house."

The king's words shimmered in my mind. I'd heard them before. I flashed back to a memory of talking with Glynis. She'd been telling me about Finnlagh and saying there had been pressure on her brother to find a suitable bride soon...

"What about the prophecy, husband?" The calm

voice of the queen cut through the uproar of the crowd. "The legend that a prince of Fae would take a warrior bride. She would be neither Witch, Lycan, or Fae…And that this bride would somehow be linked to all supernatural races as well as the mortal clans?"

"Speak, wife," the king said, and the crowd fell to silence.

"Daphne Hart is a mortal and yet she is not," the queen said. "Her mother is a Witch, and her father is a mortal. Yet while Daphne has no magick, she is an ally to the Lycans of Wolfsbane Ridge."

The queen's words about my parents hit me like a ton of bricks. In my heart I knew they were right…And as to the Lycans, that felt every bit as true. But they were all debating about me as a wife for Finnlagh. No one had asked me how I felt about it. I was being discussed as if I were a piece of property—and not a person.

"This is insane," I said, but no one heard me. I began to try and speak again but was drowned out by Finnlagh arguing with his father.

"Only a true warrior could have so easily disarmed a guard of the Fae," Finnlagh spoke over me.

"Finnlagh…" I squeezed his arm. "Let's not get carried away—"

He smiled. "You gave me your *word*, Daphne."

I narrowed my eyes. "The handfasting, is this the debt you were speaking of?"

"It is." Finnlagh nodded. "Be my wife, and mother

to my children."

"Goddamn it," I muttered, shaking my head at him. "You tricky bastard."

"My warrior bride." He patted my arm. "You say the sweetest things."

"You are twisting this whole legend to work to your advantage," I pointed out.

"Making you my wife is the one sure way that I can ensure your safety," Finnlagh said. "I gave your grandfather my word. Will you go back on your oath?"

"Have you spoken a *gesa*, mortal?" the king asked me.

I knew that word. It was old Irish and it was a type of vow, but one that if broken would haunt you through this life and the next...*Be careful what you offer the Fae.* I heard that older male voice again in my mind. I tried to recall why that voice sounded familiar. Oddly, I felt a warmth against my chest from where the jewel lay that Imogen had given me. Reaching for it, I closed my eyes and bore down trying to recall who the owner of that voice was to me.

The memory slammed into me a heartbeat later...

I was picked up, and fresh pain rocketed through me. It hurt so badly that I cried out. I forced myself to open my eyes and saw that my grandfather was standing right there, big as life, and he was shouting.

"Take her. Get my girl out of here!" my grandfather insisted.

My eyes traveled up and attempted to focus on the

person who was holding me. It was Finnlagh O'Brien.

"I swear to you, Geoffrey," Finnlagh said, "she will be safe."

"Go!" My grandfather gave my hand another squeeze. "She has to survive."

"Do not die, Daphne," Finnlagh ordered as he carried me away from the battle. "I forbid it."

"Geoffrey," I said as a piece of my missing past fell into place with a thud. "My grandfather's name is Geoffrey Sullivan. He has been the Hunter for Hemlock Hollow for over fifty years and I was to be his heir." I met Finnlagh's eyes. "He asked you to take me from the battle and you swore to keep me safe."

"And so I will keep you safe." Finnlagh ran his hand over my back. "Do you also recall the day you declared that you were in *my* debt?"

"I do," I said, because suddenly—*I did.* "We were sitting under a full moon. I told you how much I appreciated your help and that I could never repay you."

Finnlagh nodded. "I asked if you admitted to owing me a debt, and you agreed. We clasped hands on it."

"I remember," I said, searching his eyes. The cognac color shimmered and I knew that for all that he tried to act unaffected, his emotions were involved. He was vulnerable in that moment. I had the ability to embarrass him in front of his family and the entire Royal Court.

He is my friend, my lover, and a champion to me and

my...I let the jewel drop back to the bodice of my gown, and my thoughts trailed off. I couldn't say why I felt like I owed him so much more. However I knew, down in my heart, that Finnlagh had once saved someone very, very precious to me.

"You are putting me in one hell of a spot, Finnlagh," I whispered.

Finnlagh smiled. "Are you going to renege on your promise?"

To do so would make me appear to have no honor, but there had to be a way out of this mess...So everyone could save face. All I had to do was to stall and buy myself enough time to try and talk some sense into him. "Finnlagh, may I speak to you privately?" I asked and tugged on his arm.

"*Well?*" the king demanded impatiently.

My time had just run out, I realized. Taking a deep breath, I faced the king. "I will honor the debt I owe your son, Your Majesty."

"It is settled." The king thumped his fist on the arm of his chair. "Let us make it official. Send for the High Priest!"

"Official? Priest?" I balked. "There's no need to rush —"

"Wonderful!" The queen clasped her hands together.

"We will see them bound by handfast, tonight," the king decreed.

"Tonight?" I squeaked.

"Thank you, Your Majesty." Finnlagh bowed to his

father, then turned to me with a huge grin on his face.

"You tricky son of a—" I started to swear, but he cut me off by dipping me dramatically backwards and kissing me in front of his parents and the entire royal court.

"How romantic!" Queen Aine was laughing merrily when he finally let me up for air. "Do you have a ring for your betrothed?" the queen asked her son.

The word *betrothed* had my stomach dropping to my shoes. "Finnlagh, we need to talk. Right now."

"Patience, dearest," Finnlagh said, and his tone was so glib that I seriously considered decking him.

In fact, the only thing that kept me from doing so was the fact that we were standing in front of his parents—the king and queen of the Fae.

"No, Mother, I do not have a ring," Finnlagh said calmly, hooking his arm through mine. "Not yet."

The queen smiled. "I believe I can help with that."

"Oh, that's not—" I shut up when the queen rose to her feet.

Queen Aine tugged a ring from her right hand. She stepped down from the dais and held out a ring. The aquamarine colored jewel was set in a silvery band, and it shimmered in the light. "Your father, the king, gave me this ring many years ago."

"Mother." Finnlagh's voice was filled with wonder.

"It was a symbol of his promise to me," the queen said, loud enough that only Finnlagh and I could hear. "He asked me to wait until we were free to marry and swore that this gem was a promise that he would not turn away from me, no matter what the obstacles before us."

She took Finnlagh's hand and placed the ring inside of it. "For Donal and me, passion came first, and that slowly turned to love. Despite the challenges we faced, we found our way together and I can see that it is the same for the two of you as well."

I stood there silently, holding on to my temper by my fingertips. Finnlagh folded his fingers over the ring. He murmured his gratitude to his mother, pressing a kiss to her cheek.

Queen Aine kissed my right cheek and my left, as the king descended from the dais behind her. "So, the warrior bride of legend is among us?" King Donal smiled. "It will certainly be comforting to know my son's children will be in such capable hands."

My son's children? My heart raced as panic began to set in. *Wait!* My mind screamed. *Don't I already have children?*

While I stood there with my mind running a million miles an hour, Finnlagh clasped King Donal's forearm in his. "I am relieved and grateful to have your blessing, Your Majesty."

The king raised his brows at Finnlagh. "Seems to me you would have wed her with or without my permission."

"Wed *and* bed," Diamant said, leaping from his throne. "And who could blame him for surrendering to his passion?" The heir laughed and slapped his brother on the back. He began to tease Finnlagh about his wedding night duties, and Finnlagh told his brother to shut his mouth.

The queen took my hand, drawing my attention back to her. "The gown you are wearing will be most suitable for a handfasting ceremony. However we will need attendants for you Daphne."

"Well, I…er…" I stammered.

"What about Princess Ravena and Prince Liam?" Finnlagh asked.

Diamant's head swung around. "You wish to include my children in your ceremony?"

My children. My heart slammed in my throat, and I could feel my memories trembling on the edge of returning.

Finnlagh shrugged at his brother's question. "It is a custom in the mortal world to have the young nieces and nephews of the bride and groom to be in the wedding ceremony, isn't that right, Daphne?"

I managed to nod, even as I broke out in a nervous sweat.

"I will have someone send for the children," Queen Aine said, and with a snap of her fingers a servant rushed to do her bidding.

The queen and Princess Oona took over from that point. My request for a moment to speak with Finnlagh was ignored, and I was whisked away while preparations for the impromptu ceremony were put in place.

Shortly thereafter, I found myself standing before a tall mirror while the queen's ladies fussed over me. Large white flowers were being woven into my hair, and although I felt they were too much, I stayed silent, going over everything that I *could* remember…

My grandfather's name was Geoffrey Sullivan. He was the Hunter. I was to be his heir. My mother was a Witch, my father was a mortal…But what were their names? I had a horrible feeling I had children out there somewhere too. Were *they* the voices I'd heard screaming in my nightmares? Were they still alive? Was that why I owed a debt to Finnlagh? Back in the throne room I had felt that he'd once saved someone precious to me…What else would have made me swear an oath to a Fae?

I came back from my musings with a start and frowned at the reflection of the woman staring back at me dressed in an elegant gray gown. *Who am I?* I wondered. *Why was I standing silently and allowing others to plan my life?*

The stranger reflected back had no answers. As it was, I barely recognized myself. My skin was very pale, my cheekbones sharp, and my blue eyes seemed dazed and far too big for my face. "This isn't right," I said out loud.

"What isn't, dear?" one of the queen's ladies asked, touching my shoulder hesitantly.

I can't go through with the ceremony, I decided. Not

when I wasn't even sure exactly who I was.

"My lady?"

"Stop with the flowers," I said, gently pushing her hands away from my face. "Stop. Stop everything." Grabbing a flower at random, I pulled it out of my hair.

"You are a bit pale," one of the ladies said. "Are you not happy?"

"Happy?" I yanked out another flower. "I am about to be bulldozed into marriage and I can't even recall most of my past."

"Now, now," she said, reaching for my hair again. "A bit of nerves are to be expected in a bride."

"Stop it!" I snapped. "Everybody back off and let me breathe."

"She is only overwhelmed at the speed of which she is about to be bound by handfast," another lady in waiting piped in.

"At least you know your groom, my dear." A third lady in waiting smiled. "*Intimately* from what I hear."

That comment had all of the ladies tittering.

"Consider yourself lucky," Princess Oona said over their laughter. "At least you are not being forced to wed a stranger."

My head was pounding, but I glanced over to the princess anyway. "I am sorry that happened to you, Your Highness."

Princess Oona shrugged. "I was raised knowing what my duty would be. Unlike you, I had no choice."

The oldest of the ladies in waiting tried to smooth

things over. "We all know that the king and queen would only tolerate Prince Finnlagh's defiance for so long. It is high time that he settled down and fulfilled his duty to provide an heir for the realm."

"Provide an heir?" I balked at the comment. And that was when Finnlagh's proposal—if that's what you could call it—began to sink in.

Be my wife, and mother to my children.

Those had been his exact words. There'd been no talk of him loving me, and that was a relief at least. Yes, he had called me, 'my love,' in Gaelic—but for all I knew that was as casual of an endearment as a mortal calling someone 'babe'.

Not that it mattered, I assured myself. Because hadn't I sworn to never fall in love again? After the last personal betrayal I'd suffered, I had vowed to simply enjoy any future partners physically—but to never give my heart away. I knew better than anyone that marriages rarely lasted...

I sucked in my breath as another bit of my past fell into place. *Zane, my first husband, had been unfaithful. And Ashton had not only been unfaithful, he'd tried to...* A sharp pain throbbed in my temple, and all my thoughts screeched to a halt.

"Perhaps," Princess Oona said, sounding sly, "there is an heir already on the way. Is that why Finnlagh is in such a rush to wed, and the bride is so pale?"

Was that *why Finnlagh was so passionate?* I asked myself as my heart began to pound in my chest.

Because he needed an heir and was in a hurry to get one?

Confused and overwhelmed, I lifted a hand to rub at my temple. The ladies that were gathered around stopped as one and stared at me. All of them had concerned or pitying expressions on their faces.

"Oh, shit," I whispered as the reality of my situation sank in. *I could very well already be pregnant,* I realized. I'd used no birth control, and I'd been with Finnlagh at least once a day for weeks at my best recollection. Suddenly nauseous, I staggered over to a chair and sat down. "I think I'm having a panic attack."

The ladies began to rush around again, and thankfully Princess Ravena entered the room. I saw that the child was dressed in shades of blue and silver like the rest of the royal family. Ravena smiled a bit as she handed me a posy of lilacs.

I tried to smile at the Fae child. *She's such a delicate thing.* In the throes of anxiety, my mind bounced wildly. *Kenzie was so much sturdier when she was this age...*

"Kenzie?" I whispered, and promptly dropped the flowers. *Why was that name so familiar to me?* I shut my eyes and willed my memories to return as the chatter of the ladies swirled around me. Against the bodice of my dress, the jewel Imogen had given me began to vibrate.

Lifting my hand, I gripped the red-orange stone again and held on. Immediately, it grew warm to the touch. "Wait. Where are *my* girls?" I heard myself say.

"They should be here…"

"Everyone out!" Princess Oona commanded with a clap of her hands.

That's right, my inner voice said. *I am a mother to girls. Two daughters. The youngest of my daughters is named Kenzie, and my oldest girl has hair the same shade of auburn…As my mother's!*

A scene filled my mind: I was standing in a hot summer backyard and practicing with my compound bow. My Grandpa Geoffrey was there giving me grief and rolling his eyes. My girls were laughing with him even as I tried to practice. The oldest of the two grinned at me, and my heart slammed against my ribs.

"Kayla!" I whispered her name joyfully as I suddenly remembered. *Her name is Kayla. She has blue-green eyes and won prizes for her archery. Archery that her great-grandpa Geoffrey taught her.* Relieved tears filled my eyes at finally being able to remember my girls. "Kayla and Kenzie." I spoke their names out loud and felt a missing part of my heart click back into place

I began to tremble yet continued to clutch the jewel. It had heated up so much that it was painful to hold, but it didn't matter. Because the harder I grasped it, the more I could recall.

My parent's names and faces flooded in next. My father's image popped into my mind. His name was Allen Grant. He *was* a mortal, had brown hair, and was a pharmacist. My mother's name was Poppy, and she was a gifted green witch. Her gardens had won the best garden award in Hemlock Hollow for three years straight. My brother Derrek was kind and yoga loving. He had moved away to start his own business. Last but not least, there was young Harper, the blue-haired teenage Witch my parents had taken in.

"My family!" I missed them all so much in that moment that the emotions had me slipping from the chair and dropping to my knees on the floor. "I remember my family."

"Who are you?" I heard someone ask. "Claim your name and your power."

And suddenly I did know who I was, and I knew exactly how to reclaim my power.

"I am Daphne Hart," I said, and began to stand. "I am a descendant of one of the first supernatural beings to settle in the hollow. My ancestor, Brigit O'Reilly, left me this sphalerite necklace, and the gem has the powers to help the wearer discern reality from illusion."

"You have regained your memories at last," Princess Oona said.

"I have." My voice grew stronger, fueled by the memories that had fully returned to me. "My grandfather is the Hunter of Hemlock Hollow and I am his heir. I have two children who need me and allies that require my support. I have a life and a business to run and a goddamn war against corrupt Witches to win. I took out an evil necromancer and managed to survive his attempts to kill me. But there is still work to be done. I have to return to Hemlock Hollow."

"Are you all better, now?" Princess Ravena asked.

I wiped the tears away and glanced around. "Where did everybody go?" Other than myself and the princesses, Oona and Ravena, the room was now empty.

"I sent the ladies in waiting away." Princess Oona rested a hand on my shoulder. "I thought you needed privacy."

I considered the gesture of support. "That was surprisingly kind of you."

Her lips twitched. "I have my moments."

I rubbed a hand over my face. "How could I have possibly forgotten my own children?"

"You've been in the Fae realm for too long," she said, giving my shoulder a brisk squeeze. "Surely you were warned about the perils of Fae for a mortal?"

"I was told I could be lost," I said as I climbed to my feet.

"And so you were. The Fae realm clouds the senses and makes you lose parts of yourself." She nodded toward the gemstone I still held. "That jewel has helped you to regain all of your memories. Keep it close."

I tucked the gem inside the bodice of the gown where it could lay against my skin and keep working. "I've got to get the hell out of here and back to my children," I said, starting for the exit. I tried the door and found it locked.

"I have spelled the door. It is sealed," Princess Oona

said, calmly.

"Open it." I spun to face her. "Or I'll climb out the goddamn window. I can't stay here and play faerie tale wedding. I have to return home to the hollow."

She smiled. "How far do you think you can go in a castle full of courtiers and guards, without my help?"

"And are you offering to help me?"

She lifted her brows as if amused. "If you wish to return home to the mortal world I can help you, Daphne Hart. However you must do something for me in exchange."

"What do you want?"

The princess took her daughter's hand. "I need you to get a friend safely to the mortal realm."

"A friend?" I said.

"I will assist you in getting out of the castle. My allies will see you through the Fae realm and to my friend. Then you can return back to your family."

"Who are your allies?" I asked.

"The Dark Fae. There is a small faction of my people here, working for change."

This was no time for me to get into the intricacies of Fae politics. A feeling of urgency was sweeping over me, and I stuck out my hand to Princess Oona. "Deal. You and your people get me out of the castle and back to my daughters, and I'll take your friend with me."

She clasped my hand. "Excellent."

I nodded. "Let's move."

"Your Highness?" The voice of one of the ladies in

waiting came from out in the hall. "The High Priest has arrived. The queen is on her way to escort the bride to the prince."

"We must hurry," the princess said to me. "We don't have much time."

"Your Highness?" There was a knock on the door. "Is all well?" The doorknob rattled a second later.

"Right." I nodded. "How do we get out of here?"

Princess Oona hitched Ravena on her hip. "Follow me." She walked over to the wall, pressed a stone, and the entire wall shifted.

"Wow," I said, impressed at how well hidden the passage had been.

The alarm had been raised out in the hall. There were several Fae banging on the door, and I could clearly hear their shouts.

"That mortal must have done something to the princesses, Oona and Ravena!"

"Hurry! Open the door!"

"The mortal was clearly disturbed. Call for the guards!"

"For fuck's sake." I shook my head over the Fae's automatic assumption that *I* had done something to the princesses.

"Come!" Princess Oona beckoned me to follow and stepped into the passageway.

I lifted my skirt and ran after her. "How long will your spell hold the outer door?" I whispered.

With a scraping sound the wall behind us slid back

into place, leaving the three of us in darkness. "Long enough for us to get away," Princess Oona whispered. "Stay close."

"You got it." I reached out and rested my hand on her shoulder. Blindly, I followed the princess down the corridor. As far as I could tell we were hugging the right wall. The floor began to gently slope downward as we traveled farther away. In a few moments my eyes adjusted, and I could see a light far ahead.

"Hurry," Princess Oona hissed. We picked up the pace, almost running toward the light.

Illuminated in a pool of light, a Fae male was waiting and holding a torch aloft. As we drew closer, I saw that he stood with a female too, and the couple was dressed differently than any other Fae I'd seen.

They wore tunics and pants all in shades of green and brown. The outfits were rustic looking, hand made perhaps. The male wore large copper hoops in his ears, and a thick cuff of metal on each wrist. His long, curly brown hair was pulled back from his face, and that face was striking. It was made only more so by dark, tribal looking face paint. He wasn't quite as tall as other Fae males I'd seen, and his build was definitely more muscular.

"Torian," Princess Oona greeted him.

"Your Highness." He inclined his head in deference, and I saw a neat moustache and goatee with a short beard riding along his jaw line.

The female accompanying him had long brown hair

with the front secured back by a top knot. She too had dark makeup worked across her upper face. It made me think of a painted-on mask, and the tribal pattern accented her pale green eyes. For a split second she reminded me a bit of…

"Imogen," Oona said, acknowledging the female.

I did such a hard double take that I almost fell over. "*Imogen*?"

"Daphne." She grinned. "You seemed surprised to see me."

I blinked at her. "What the fuck?"

"Has the jewel done its work?" she asked.

"That's right," I said, slowly. "You were the one who gave it to me."

"I found it in your clothes the day you arrived in Fae," Imogen said. "I recognized the gem and was aware of its powers to cut through illusion. I saved it for you, to return when you were ready."

"We haven't much time," Princess Oona said. "The alarm has been raised."

"This way." Torian motioned for us to follow him.

"What is your place in all of this, Imogen?" I asked as we moved deeper into the bowels of the castle together.

Imogen linked her arm in mine. "I am Dark Fae. I came here to this realm to be eyes and ears for the Princess Oona."

"So you're a spy?"

"I was placed in Prince Finnlagh's household, for his

protection," Imogen said firmly.

"Aw, hell. Finnlagh." I hissed out a breath. "What will he think when he discovers the three of us are missing?"

Princess Oona glanced back over her shoulder. "That we were captured by the evil Dark Fae, no doubt."

"I doubt it," I said. "You didn't hear the comments out in the hall. Seems the ladies assumed that 'the mortal' had done something terrible to the princesses."

"His Highness, Prince Finnlagh, would never believe that of you, Daphne," Imogen said as we started down a set of stone steps.

"He's not going to be thinking anything good about me once he finds out I've left him and gone home."

"The prince loves you," Imogen insisted.

Ahead of me, Princess Oona stumbled. Torian paused, took the child in his arms, and passed the torch back to Imogen.

Imogen took the lead and I matched pace with the princess. "Are you all right, Princess Oona?"

"I will be as soon as I know that you and my friend are with off the *Leipreachán*."

"Lep-ra-haun?" I tried to sound it out. "And who is your friend, by the way?"

"An ally," she said. "One of the bravest Fae in all the realms."

"Hurry," Torian said. "We are almost there."

I heard the sound of water before I saw it. The stairs ended at a stone ramp with a small boat tied to it. A mist rose from the underground river. It was gothic, creepy, and foreboding.

I skidded to a halt. "You have *got* to be kidding me," I muttered to myself. "Didn't I see this scene once in *The Three Musketeers* movie?"

"Highness." Torian handed Princess Ravena back to her mother, and then he hopped lightly inside the boat. He headed to the stern and picked up the oars.

"Get in!" Imogen took me by the elbow and helped me step into the boat.

"Come on, Imogen." I held up a hand to Imogen, figuring she was the friend that I was helping to get out of Fae.

"I am not leaving," Imogen said, giving my fingers a squeeze. "I must stay and help Her Highness secure the children. Torian will take you to the Fae who needs to leave the realm."

"Promise me, mortal," Princess Oona said. "You will see to it that my friend is safe while they are in the mortal realm?"

"Of course," I said. "I will do my best."

"I owe you a great debt," Princess Oona said.

"You helped me, I am helping you," I said. "We're even."

"I will see you again." The princess nodded and stepped back.

"Good journey, Daphne," Imogen said, starting to release my hand.

I gripped her fingers harder. "Can you get a message

to Finnlagh for me?"

She nodded. "I can."

"Tell Finnlagh that my memories have all returned and that I have to go home to be with my daughters. We have been under attack in the hollow, Imogen, and I have to protect my family."

"I will tell him," she said. "I promise you."

I let go of her hand, and Imogen untied the boat. She pushed it clear from the dock. Instantly it spun around in the current, and Torian guided us neatly away and out into the river proper.

I lifted a hand in acknowledgment, and a second later the mist surrounded us. I couldn't see Imogen or the princesses any longer.

I shivered in the damp night air. "Where to now, Torian?" I asked the Fae.

"We will travel down the river for several leagues, to meet with the *Leipreachán*."

I looked slowly over my shoulder as to not rock the boat. "Did you say, Leprechaun?" I asked him.

"Aye. The *Leipreacháns* fled the realm of the Dark Fae many years ago. A few have secretly integrated into the society of this realm, as some can pass for Light Fae. Others do not."

"What do you mean, *pass*?"

"Those that do not meet certain requirements remain out of favor."

"Requirements?" I asked.

"Their height," he said succinctly.

"Are you telling me because they aren't as *tall* as the other Fae in this realm they are discriminated against?"

"Correct." In the low light, Torian's eyes flashed a golden-green. "Anything not golden or perfectly tall is considered out of favor in the realm of the Light Fae."

I stayed silent and thought about what he'd said. We passed out from under the castle and the river widened up immediately. The sky was mostly cloudy, but the moon was peeping out sporadically.

Torian worked with the current of the river, and we were moving at a good clip. His comment had me thinking, and I recalled all the nobles I'd seen at court. They'd all been tall, willowy blondes. True, there were plenty with sandy to medium brown hair in addition to all the blonde Fae...But come to think of it, the *only* truly dark hair I'd seen at court had been Oona's and Ravena's. With a sigh, I realized that the Fae weren't so different than mortals after all. There was politics, intrigue, war, and prejudice here too.

Torian was rowing for all he was worth. The moon peeped out again, and I spotted a second set of oars in the bottom of the boat. "Let me give you a hand," I said, hooking them in their holders.

"Are you not recovering from an injury?" he asked.

"I am," I said. "But it seems to me that it would be better to reach our destination as quickly as possible. They're sure to send scouts down the river looking for us."

"That is true. I am not easy out on the water. We are

too exposed," Torian said.

"Agreed." I dipped the oars in the water and pulled.

"Her Highness will do her best to stall, however, the Prince Finnlagh is bound to search high and low for his missing lover."

I grimaced hearing that. Finnlagh would be pissed. I had promised to marry him, thereby fulfilling my debt, and now I'd run off before we could be bound by handfast.

No. Not run off, I corrected myself. *I am returning home to my children.*

Yes, I still owed him a debt. However, it was not going to be fulfilled tonight. Technically I hadn't gone back on my agreement. Instead I was simply getting out of the realm before I could be railroaded into a fast wedding ceremony in front of the entire royal court.

It was, in a way, a very Fae-like maneuver.

Or maybe I was simply justifying my behavior because I *did* feel guilty about causing Finnlagh hurt and embarrassment. I grimaced over my shoulder. "I appreciate that extra slice of guilt you piled on me, Torian."

"That was not my intent." Torian shrugged. "The royal court will most likely say you refused his hand and were emotionally overwrought."

"I'm no hysterical female running from a bridegroom." Offended at the description, I blew a tendril of hair from my eyes. "What I am is a woman who needs to return to her family and her own people.

We are at war. They need me."

"Spoken as a true warrior." Torian grunted as he worked the oars. "If the prince loves you, warrior bride, he will understand in time."

"The warrior bride." I dipped the oars in the water and pulled in synch with Torian. "I'm *never* going to hear the end of that, am I?"

"I doubt it," he said, and I could hear the smile in his voice.

"You're such a comfort to me, Torian," I said.

He pointed over my shoulder. "That is the channel we need to take."

"On it," I said and rowed with him for all I was worth. The faster we got to the Leprechauns the better.

My left shoulder was not happy with the rowing by the time we headed for the shore a few hours later. We banked the boat and Torian leapt out. I carefully climbed out and helped him pull the boat up higher on the steep shore. He tied the ropes onto a tree while I checked the area. There was a heavy wood on both sides of the river. I tried to judge the time by how far the moon had traveled across the sky but gave up. There were far too many clouds now.

I heard the horse before I saw it. I ducked, hunkering down by the boat, and Torian crouched down beside me. Silently, he pulled a blade from his waist and passed it to me.

I took it and waited to see who was approaching.

The woods fell to silence, and I heard the call of a

bird.

Beside me, Torian let out an identical call.

"The *Leipreacháns* have arrived," Torian whispered to me.

"Torian!" The voice was hushed and female.

"We are here," he said, rising to his feet.

I stood with him and a petite figure appeared at the top of the bank. She was blonde and wore a deep red jacket with glistening gold buttons. It was Tara, the horse trainer.

CHAPTER SEVEN

Behind Tara, several males stepped forward. They were small, shorter even than she was, and dressed in shades of deep green and red. My eyes moved over the group and saw that every one of them was wearing a red coat and gold buttons, making me wonder if their jackets were a military uniform.

"My lady." Tara held out a hand. "Welcome to the territory of the *Leipreacháns*."

Now Tara's petite stature made sense. "You're part Leprechaun, aren't you?" I asked.

Tara smiled. "My father is a *Leipreachán,* my mother was a Light Fae."

I tucked the knife I'd been given in the gown's sash at my back and reached for Tara's hand. With her help, I was able to climb up the bank.

"The royal guard is a league away," Tara said to Torian. "We must get to the mortal world without delay."

Around me the Leprechauns fanned out and moved

back into the woods. They were taking a defensive position. They expected a battle.

"Torian," I began as the Fae male climbed up the bank easily, "I didn't push while we'd been in the castle. It was obvious Princess Oona thought it too dangerous to say out loud. Who is the ally I'm taking back to the mortal realm?"

"That would be me." Tara said sketching a bow. "I was an active part of the Dark Fae uprising, but my position has been revealed recently, and now am in need of sanctuary."

"There is a price on her head," Torian explained.

"I see." I nodded. "Well, once we get back to the mortal realm, you are welcome to stay with me and mine," I said. "It's the least I can do."

Tara smiled. "I will take you up on that. Are you ready?" she asked.

"Yes." I nodded. "I need to get back to my family."

Tara jogged over to her horse and leapt. She seemed to defy gravity only to land in the saddle as easily as I might sit in a chair. The horse was massive and solid black. I'd never seen such a big horse, and when Torian nudged me forward, I balked.

"Er…" I said. "You don't expect me to get up on that horse, do you?"

"Yes," he said.

"Tara," I said. "You know that I don't ride."

She held out a hand. "There is no time to go on foot."

"The royal guard has been spotted!" one of the Leprechauns called out.

"God damn it," I swore, knowing I was out of options. "Well somebody help me up on the damn horse. I have no idea how to climb up there by myself."

Torian made a basket with his hands and boosted me up. He was scary strong, and the only reason I didn't fall off the other side was because he kept ahold of my skirt once I was seated behind Tara.

"Grab hold of my waist," Tara instructed.

"Okay." I took a hold of her and was tall enough to see over her head. I shifted my weight and tried to get comfortable, but I'd never sat on a horse before.

Torian stepped back. "Go! Tara," he said, "be well."

"*Go raibh maith agat,*" I said to Torian.

He raised a hand in response. Tara pressed her heels to the horse's sides, and we took off. It was terrifying riding on a horse for the first time in the dark. I did my best to hold on to Tara and to *not* fall off.

As we tore through the woods, I saw dozens of Dark Fae males moving stealthily forward. All of them were carrying weapons.

"Is there about to be a war?" I said in Tara's ear.

"Yes!" Tara cried and she sounded happy about it.

"Oh, shit." I gulped hard. "It's not because of me leaving the realm is it?"

"No!" Tara laughed. "The Dark Fae are rising up. Danu be praised!"

Now Imogen's earlier comment about securing the

princess' children made sense. There was a rebellion happening in the realm. Princess Oona had used my escaping the handfasting ceremony as a way to distract the royal court *and* to get herself and her daughter out of harm's way.

After that revelation, I didn't bother Tara with anymore questions. Instead, I hung on for dear life. It seemed like forever until we stopped. Tara hopped down from the back of the massive horse like it was nothing. I tried to swing one leg over and discovered my legs were jello. I gripped the saddle, rolled to my stomach, and managed to slide off the horse, but it was far from graceful.

My feet hit the earth with a thud. "I have never been so thankful to have my feet back on the ground in my entire life!" I said, moving well back from the horse.

"You did well," Tara said.

"I am not a horse person, that's for sure." I grimaced and walked around a bit, trying to get my feet and legs to cooperate. I felt motion sick and shook my head to clear it.

"For this last leg of the journey, we go on foot." Tara spoke to the horse and with a bobbing of its head, it trotted off back into the forest. "He knows the way home," she said, before I could ask.

"Where to now?" I asked.

"Follow me." Tara began to walk forward, and I noticed for the first time that the sky was lightening.

We walked maybe fifty yards before coming to an

outcropping of stones at the edge of a bluff. Rocks jutted out, and trees were twisted and growing up around and between hunks of stone. Between two huge slabs an unusual tree grew at an angle. It was bent down toward the ground and then it curved dramatically upward again, creating a sort of U shape.

I began to see, as we moved closer, that the lower trunk section of the tree had a large oblong wound. It had clearly been there for years and had rolled edges from the tree attempting to mend itself. The wound in the trunk was taller than I was.

"We are here," Tara said. "This is the gateway between the worlds." She ran her hand over the rolled edges of the mark in the tree, and a light spilled out.

I stood there in awe as the tree yawned open; I could see straight through and I recognized the landscape. *It was home!* "Do I just step through?" I asked her.

She reached behind a large rock, pulled out a satchel, and slung it over her shoulder. "*We* both step through together," Tara corrected me.

The sun was beginning to rise, and I looked out over the Fae landscape one final time. I blew out a breath and faced the portal. "I'm ready."

"It's a bit of a jolt, mind you," was all the warning I got before Tara linked her arm with mine and we stepped into the portal together.

The light was blinding, and we were surrounded by a loud rushing sound. My ears popped and I blinked rapidly as my eyes tried to adjust from the once bright light to the soft light of dawn.

A few moments later I could see that around me the woods were parading butterscotch and orange leaves. Wood smoke stung the air, and it was crisp and cool. *It's still autumn!* I thought. *Surely, I haven't been gone too long.* A mist hovered over the ground and I recognized the property. I was standing at the edge of the backyard of the cabin I had planned to purchase on Nightshade Court.

I glanced to the right and saw the little garden gnome that marked the path from the Channing's property to the Shaw family's. The birds were singing in the trees, and as I gazed across the back of the property, I smiled.

"I know where we are," I said to Tara. "This time you can follow me."

Tara hitched her satchel higher on her back and fell in step behind me. I started out at a brisk pace, but as I began to recognize the woods around the Shaw's property, I broke into a jog. By the time I had spotted the Shaw's A-frame home, the sun was above the horizon. I heard the howl of a Lycan and knew I'd been spotted.

"Daphne…" Tara's voice sounded unsure. "Are we safe?"

I grinned back at her from over my shoulder. "Yes! I'm an ally to the Lycans. Hurry we're almost there!"

I ran past the remains of the Shaw's garage, and saw that my daughters were standing on the porch in their pajamas. Phoebe Shaw was with them.

"Mama!" Kenzie waved furiously.

"Mom, you're back!" Kayla yelled and leapt off the porch.

We raced for each other and I scooped them both into my arms. Dropping to my knees in the leaves, I pressed kisses to their faces and held on tight. "I love you both, so much."

"Love you too, Mama," they said in unison.

***

The reunion with my family and the Shaws was loud and filled with happy tears. My parents held on tight and cried over me, exactly the same way I'd cried over my girls. Harper had given me an enthusiastic hug, and Grandpa Geoffrey told me he was pleased to see that I had recovered. Phoebe and Randall had also given me hugs, and the Shaw kids were excited to have me back. Winter crowbarred his way in between everyone to get to me, and I stopped and gave the husky some attention.

I introduced Tara, and she was warmly received. The first chance I had, I took a shower—I'd missed those while I'd been in Fae—and changed out of the gown I'd been wearing when I'd escaped. Comfortable in a pair of jeans and a sweatshirt, I rejoined my family, and I wasn't surprised when my grandfather took me aside to speak to me privately at the first opportunity.

While the girls ate breakfast with the Shaw children,

Grandpa and I, with Winter following, stepped out on the porch. Grandpa confided that he was relieved that I was back in plenty of time for what he felt would be the final showdown with the Witches of the hollow.

"How much time do we actually have, Grandpa?" I asked.

"Eight days," he said. "Halloween and the blue moon are a week from tomorrow."

"I've only been gone a little over two weeks in the mortal world?" My jaw dropped at the discovery. "Wow, it felt like much longer while I was in the Fae realm."

He nodded and shut the doors to the kitchen. Quietly, he brought me up to speed on what had happened since the battle. "A half dozen Lycans have been seriously wounded, and one has died from their injuries," he said.

"Damn." I shook my head over it.

His eyes narrowed. "We also have three confirmed losses to the Witches of *the cause*."

I shifted slightly so I could see my children through the French doors. "I imagine Icarus Hedge was one. I saw the Lycans drag him off."

"That's right." Grandpa nodded. "Ashton Lowell was another."

"Good," I said, with no vocal inflection at all.

"The third confirmed Witch fatality was Jasper Prentiss."

I tucked my hands in my pockets. "And how are the residents of the hollow reacting to the news of a battle between the Supes?"

"They aren't," he said. "It's like it never even happened. The word in town was that Jasper Prentiss and Icarus Hedge died in a fiery car accident out on the highway."

"A car accident?" I asked incredulously. "Who thought that up?"

"Me and the Sherriff thought that would be the best explanation. There wasn't a lot left once the Lycans were finished with them. What was left—we burned."

"And Judith Hedge?" I asked. "She was a part of the group that attacked the ridge. Where is Icarus' wife now?"

"She ran from the battle. Judith took her snot-nosed teenagers with her and they left town the day after the memorial," he said. "Her house went up on the market a couple of days ago."

"I see," I said. "Grandpa, I have to ask. Are you absolutely certain that Ashton is dead? Especially with the necromancy thing."

Next to me, Winter made a sympathetic type of grumble.

"I *am* sure," he said. "I personally added his body to the pyre and stood watch until it was completely destroyed."

I felt nothing other than relief hearing his words. There was no anger and no grief. I was simply over it. Winter leaned into me and I accepted the canine support. "Well, there's one less thing for me to worry about, anyway."

"That still leaves Artemis Bradbury and the Albright girl unaccounted for."

"Meaning what, exactly?"

"Neither have been seen since the night of the battle," he said.

"Jessamine?" I frowned, thinking of my former best friend. "Do you think she survived the battle?"

"Jessamine Albright, Artemis Bradbury, and Judith Hedge all retreated after you took out Lowell. I saw them run off into the woods."

"Has Jessamine's mother said anything about her absence?"

"I spoke to our mayor after the memorial services for Jasper Prentiss and Icarus Hedge. She told me that her daughter had left town." My grandpa shrugged. "And I think she has, because *Belladonna's* has been closed up since the night of the battle."

"*Belladonna's* is closed?" I tried to wrap my mind around that. "During the Haunted Pumpkin Walk? This is the busiest time of year for local businesses."

"Yeah, well..." My grandfather scratched his chin. "Never thought I'd be thankful for all the damn tourists. Usually they're a nuisance at Halloween. This year they've been a blessing in disguise."

"So the residents in town are using the busy holiday season as a cover for all the shady events that have been going on?" I guessed.

"Exactly," he said. "Your parents put out the word

that you had a nasty flu bug and would be away from the ice cream parlor for a few weeks, until you regained your strength."

"That was clever," I said, running my fingers over the dog's ears.

"It was Allen's idea. Gina, Meg and Glynis have been running things for you while you've been gone. And your father has had that old shyster of a realtor, Martin Boggs, keep the wheels moving on that property that you put an offer on."

"Okay," I said. "I will call Martin later today, after I check in at the ice cream parlor."

My grandfather stared at me for a long moment. "I thought I was gonna lose you a few weeks ago," he said and astonished me by pulling me close for a big old bear hug. "You look damn good, Daphne."

"You look good too." I hugged him back.

"Sweet talker." He laughed. "Did Finnlagh do you right?"

My jaw dropped at the unintended double entendre. "He took excellent care of me," I said, grateful my grandfather couldn't see my face. "Thanks to him I survived a direct blast from witch fire and I am very happy to be back with my family."

My grandpa patted me on the back before he let go. "Good. Cuz we have a hell of a lot of work to do."

"Yes, sir." I nodded in agreement.

"It has been quiet while you were gone, Daphne, but it's the kind of quiet that makes me twitchy," he admitted. "The Witches are going to use the power of the upcoming Halloween night blue moon to their advantage, and we only have eight days to prepare for whatever comes next."

"And we will. However, I have to get back to work. I have a business to run and children to support."

"Poppy tells me the ice cream parlor has had a lot of Witches in lately. They've been hanging out and asking about you since the battle."

"Hoping that I was dead, were they?" I said with a half-laugh.

"Yes," he said, completely serious.

"Hells bells." I whistled under my breath. "They hate me that much?"

He nodded. "I happened to overhear Judith Hedge tell Agatha Prentiss at the memorial service that she was sure you had died. Agatha responded that she was glad, considering that you were responsible for Ashton Lowell's demise."

I smiled. "I imagine the Witches of *the cause* will all be pretty shocked to see me tomorrow, looking uninjured and working again."

He grinned. "They will at that."

"My returning to the ice cream parlor will also bring out the nosey towns folk in droves." I crossed my arms as I thought it over. "It would be an excellent way to see what I can learn *and* to try and get a finger on whatever move the Witches are planning next."

"I like the way you think." He wiggled his beetled

brows at me. "Which reminds me. I have a few things for you."

"Oh yeah?"

"Yup. Consider them presents." He patted my shoulder. "And because you love me you will be sure and keep one of them with you at all times. Come with me."

I followed him to his jeep, and he popped open the door, reached in the back, and handed me my first gift.

I started to laugh. "I really love you grandpa," I said, as I looked it over.

He gave my hair a tug. "I love you too."

***

The next morning, I was going through my pre-opening routine at the ice cream parlor. It was a Saturday and officially one week until Halloween. It felt great to be back. I was wearing a pair of jeans and an orange, untucked *Haunted Pumpkin Walk* t-shirt. My sphalerite pendant was tucked under my shirt and against my chest, and I had also added a brand-new waist holster, and my Glock 43.

Grandpa Geoffrey had retrieved my Glock from the battle, cleaned it, and refilled the magazines. He also gifted me with the waist holster and had installed a custom holster in my car.

After my talk with my grandfather, my parents had brought me up to speed on business. I was very relieved to know that the holiday sales had been strong in my absence. My mother informed me that she had also smudged the hell out of the parlor, as well as worked a banishing spell on both the front and the back rooms while I'd been away. There was no lingering energy or magick from Ashton Lowell, she explained, and I believed her.

For extra security on my first day back, I had driven to my parents' house first and then followed them in my car to the pharmacy. We all parked around back, and I got a hell of a jolt when I saw that my father was armed as well.

Seems he'd been taking lessons from my grandfather. I could only applaud his decision. The three of us went inside together without incident, and I went through my pre-opening routine. My mother had checked on me no less than three times before my employees came in for work.

I said nothing about that. I'd already texted my girls twice in the hour since I'd left them. Fortunately, my cell phone had been left behind in the Shaws living room the night of the battle; all I had to do was recharge it.

I made a few minor changes to the pink and white pumpkins in the front window display, and was happy to discover that the décor for the Haunted Pumpkin Walk still looked every bit as good as the last time I'd seen it weeks ago. Today we would be open until nine pm. It was going to be a long shift, but I was relieved to see everything looking so well.

Stopping, I gazed out across the town square to Jessamine's shop *Belladonna's*. It was odd to look out my front window and see dark empty windows where there were normally displays. Sure enough, a large sign was across the windows and the shop door announcing that they were closed until further notice. With a sigh I turned away.

"How's it going, Daphne?" My mom poked her head through the opening that connected the pharmacy with the ice cream parlor.

"All good," I said, trying to act like I hadn't been staring over at Jess' shop.

"I'm so glad that Harper, Kayla and Kenzie are staying with the Shaws for now," my mother said, tugging down the cuff of her orange Halloween sweater. "I want them all away from town until this ugliness passes."

"The plan I had originally put in place to home school the girls until after Halloween has worked out well."

"Phoebe has been so wonderful. Welcoming the children into her home." My mother walked behind the counter and helped herself to the pot of coffee I had brewing.

Joining her at the counter, I began to make myself a hot chocolate. "Tara volunteered to stay behind on the ridge to help guard the property, and the children."

"That's good." My mother nodded. "It certainly

makes it much easier for us to run the pharmacy, knowing that Kayla, Kenzie and Harper are safe, and far away from the Witches of *the cause*."

I stirred the cocoa mix in the hot water. "Phoebe mentioned last night that the Lycan kids from the Wolfsbane Ridge pack are all staying out of public school until November, as well. They're using online learning."

"Well, it's not a perfect solution." My mother sipped from her coffee cup. "But I hope this situation will be resolved in the next few days. Until then Lucas will be making sure you have no issues when you close up at night."

Normally I would have argued over the idea of needing the sheriff to watch my back, but after everything that had happened, it would be foolish not to accept the extra security. "All right," I said.

My mother sighed. "I can't tell you how much I am looking forward to the day when things return to normal for us here in the hollow."

"*Normal* is merely an illusion," I said, adding a flourish of whipped cream to my cocoa. "A wise woman once told me that."

My mother gave me an arch look. "Oh, so, *now*, you remember what I tried to teach you?"

"You have no idea how grateful I am to be able to remember you and Dad again," I said. "Mom, while I was recovering in Fae, I—"

My mother laid her hand on my arm, cutting me off.

"I didn't mean to upset you, sweetheart."

"You didn't," I said. "But it's difficult for me to accept that for a while there, I sort of floated along, in a cotton candy colored world that wasn't mine. I lost myself for a time. It was very easy to forget my responsibilities and frighteningly easy to..." I paused, searching for the correct word, "indulge myself."

"In a romance?"

I narrowed my eyes. "I never said that."

She smiled. "You didn't have to. When your grandfather told me about Finnlagh, and how hard he fought to keep you alive, I figured it out for myself."

"I did something foolish, Mom. I started something...Something that I can't finish. I gave my word to someone, made a pledge really, and I probably won't be able to keep it."

"Would this involve Finnlagh O'Brien?"

"Yes."

My mother raised her eyebrows. "A pledge with a Fae? That's problematic."

I shook my head. "There's the understatement of the century."

"The girls talked about him quite a bit." She took another sip of her coffee. "I was surprised that he didn't come back with you."

"There are circumstances..." I paused, wondering how much would be safe to tell her. "Finnlagh holds a rank, you could say. And there was this big political thing going on when I left the Fae realm." I blew out a long breath. "A day later, and it doesn't even feel *real* that I was ever there; or that I played a part in any of it."

"Well, you're back now," she said. "After a Saturday of Haunted Pumpkin Walk craziness, you may very well wish yourself back in Fae and away from reality."

"Nope." I shook my head. "Here in Hemlock Hollow is where I belong."

Gina and Meg arrived a half hour later, and I assured them both that I was fully recovered from 'the flu.' Twenty minutes before opening, while Meg worked in the back, Gina and I sat together at one of the tables, and she filled me in on our sales numbers and any ice cream supply orders she'd made while I'd been away. I heard a tapping on the glass front door and discovered Beau Stone, standing outside.

I got up immediately to let him in. "Morning, Beau," I said as I opened the door.

"I'm so happy that you're back!" he cried, tossing his arms around me.

I patted his shoulder. "Mind the waist holster," I said softly, and he let go immediately.

"Sorry," Beau said and ducked inside. He stayed by my side while I relocked the door. "I came to tell you that Glynis has gone home to—" He cleared his throat nervously. "Help her family."

Gina stood up from the table. "What happened? Was there a family emergency?"

Beau slid his eyes over to mine, in a silent plea for

help.

"They are at war, then?" I asked in a low voice, so that only he could hear.

"Yes." He breathed the word.

"What's going on?" Gina asked, looking from him to me.

"Gina and Meg might as well know," I said to him.

"Know what?" Gina asked. "Is something wrong with the wedding plans, Beau?"

"No, Gina," Beau said. "Glynis was called home to duty."

"Duty?" Gina tilted her head. "You make it sound like she is in the military."

"Daphne?" My mother was hovering in the doorway to the pharmacy. "Is everything okay?"

"Yes, Mom," I said, "but maybe you should stay for a moment."

"All right." My mother nodded and walked into the parlor.

"One of you tell me what the hell is happening," Gina said, planting her hands on her hips. "My family might be all mortals, but even *we* know that something is horribly wrong here in Hemlock Hollow."

"You are right, Gina," I said. "Something *is* wrong in the hollow. And it is affecting all of us. Mortal and Supe alike."

Beau tucked his hands in his jacket pockets. "Glynis was called home because the Fae are at war," he said, and for the next few moments you could have heard a pin drop.

My mother blew out a quiet breath. "I was afraid of that."

Gina's eyes were huge in her face. "War?"

"Yes," Beau said. "As Glynis holds both a rank and a title in the Fae realm, she had to return to her people."

"Well, duh, *of course* she does." This comment was from Meg as she came out from the back room carrying a stack of waffle cones. "I figure Glynis has to be like, Fae special forces."

"That she is," Beau said.

"I knew it!" Meg smiled. "When I first met her, I had the weirdest dream about her being a soldier but wearing a crown all at the same time."

I smiled at my teenage employee. "That's dead on the money, Meg, but still, you and your mom deserve to know what's at stake and decide whether or not you wish to remain here as my employees."

Meg slid a sleeve of cones into their holder. "I figured that shit was about to hit the fan, with that full moon on Halloween."

"Megan Lovari!" Gina scowled. "Watch your language."

"Sheesh, Mom." Meg brushed off her hands. "We all talked about the Witches of *the cause.* It's hardly a secret that the other Supes are on high alert. The Lycan and the Fae kids have pretty much vanished from school. We've got witch-bitches dressed all in black prowling the halls at Hemlock High. They pick on anyone who doesn't follow along with their dark magick club."

I considered the teen. "What else have you heard at school, Meg?"

Meg raised her eyebrows. "Do you truly want to know?"

I nodded. "Yes, I do."

"The word at school is that the story about the principal and Mr. Hedge supposedly dying in a car crash—is total *bullshit*," she said, walking out from around the counter. "Everyone has their own theory about why there was a cover up. Personally, I have a hunch those guys tried to take on the Lycans, and became wolf chow instead."

My mother pursed her lips. "That's a very interesting hunch."

Gina narrowed her eyes. "Daphne, where have you *really* been all this time?"

I turned to her. "I was in the Fae realm, recovering."

"Recovering?" Gina asked.

"Yes." I nodded. "From the wounds I sustained when the Witches of the hollow attacked my family and the Lycans on Wolfsbane Ridge a few weeks ago."

"Holy shit!" Gina pressed her hands to her lips.

"So I was totally right about the 'wolf chow' thing after all," Meg said. "And that also explains why Jade Prentiss has been running her mouth, happily telling anyone who will listen that you and Ashton Lowell were both dead."

"Well, as you can see…" I held out my arms to my sides. "I'm not dead."

"Is Ashton back as well?" Gina wanted to know.

"No, Gina," I said quietly. "He's gone."

Gina looked confused. "You mean he's gone, as in he left town?"

"No," my mother piped in. "Ashton Lowell is gone —as in he's deceased."

Gina frowned. "The Witches killed Ashton?"

"No," I said, very calmly. "I did."

Gina gasped.

"Because he tried to kill you first." That statement had been from Meg.

"He tried," I said, meeting her eyes. "He did not succeed."

"I had the weirdest dream a few weeks ago," the teen said, "that you faced off with someone and fired that gun you always wear. You got them first, but you were still hit with this glowing green fire." Meg rubbed at her left shoulder. In the same spot where I'd been hit. "In my dream you were dying, Daphne, but someone picked you up and carried you away."

Stunned, I stared at the teen. "That's exactly right. I was stuck right where you are rubbing your shoulder."

"No kidding?" Meg shivered.

"Do you often have precognitive dreams, Meg?" my mother asked.

Meg shrugged. "Sometimes the stuff I dream about hasn't happened yet, and sometimes it already has. It's confusing and weird because there's no way I could have known about it—not the details and stuff. But when I end up being right, it does kinda gives me a déjà vu feeling."

"You are describing precognition and retrocognition," my mother said.

Meg wrinkled up her nose. "Huh?"

"Retrocognition means that you have psychic visions of the *past*," my mother said, "while precognition is knowledge or visions of future events."

Meg frowned. "It's all really confusing. I wish I understood what the dreams meant."

"If it's okay with your mother, Meg, I will work with you on that after Halloween." My mother made the offer and smiled over at Gina.

"Of course," Gina nodded. "Poppy, I'd feel better knowing that you'll be the one helping Meg with this."

"That'd be awesome." Meg grinned. "Thanks, Poppy."

"Daphne?" Gina rested her hand on my arm to draw my attention back to her. "Are you all right now?"

"I've got some dandy scars. But, yes, Gina. For the most part I'm recovered."

"Ha!" Meg flipped her blonde ponytail over her shoulder. "Jade Prentiss is gonna freak out when she hears you are back. Plus, she's gonna look so stupid for saying all that nasty stuff about you."

I smiled. "I'd love for you to tell me exactly what Jade Prentiss has been saying, Meg."

"Are you sure?" Meg asked uncertainly. "I wouldn't want to hurt your feelings."

"You won't," I assured her.

Meg blew upwards at a strand of hair that was in her eyes. "Well, she said that Ashton Lowell had been cheating on you with a bunch of women."

I folded my arms over my chest. "Anything else?"

"She said that you tried to leave him when you found out." Meg grimaced. "Everyone in town has been talking about it."

I rolled my eyes. "Terrific."

"Well, he ended up being a creep, so I'm glad he's gone," Meg said and then bounced to another topic. "Hey, can I show you the *Wicked Witch* sundae I created for Halloween week here at the parlor?"

Gina balked. "I think, all things considered, perhaps we should come up with a different name for that special."

"I disagree." My mother smiled. "I think it's clever, and besides we need some light-hearted fun to counter-act all the negativity from *the cause*."

"Wait 'til you see!" Meg said with a bounce. "I made these cute witch hats out of chocolate covered cookies and ice cream cones."

I smiled at the teenager. "I bet the tourists would love it."

"Exactly!" my mother said. "Why don't you build one for us Meg and we can all sample it together?"

"Okay!" Meg said and went to begin working on her

sundae.

My mother spoke, keeping her voice low. "What Meg said about all the Witch students wearing black applies to not only the teenagers in the hollow, but for the adult members of *the cause* as well."

Gina ran a hand through her short blonde curls. "It's true. Daphne, for the past two weeks all of the Witches in town have been skulking around looking sinister in capes, cloaks and all black outfits."

My mother nodded in agreement. "We've actually sold out of black eyeliner and black nail polish in our cosmetics section."

"Seriously?" I asked.

"I have *never* seen the Witch community behave in such a way," my mother confided. "Flouting the rules of discretion in this way."

"Before this, the Supes were always discreet, for the most part," Beau said. "But this is brazen. Most of the mortals in the hollow have noticed the shift in their attitude."

How much damage did Ashton's necromancy cause? I wondered. "Could it be an energetic change maybe?" I said to the group.

"I'm not sure." Beau shrugged. "But the majority of local Witches are riled up and very confrontational."

"Even old Agatha Prentiss has been wearing all black clothing," Gina said. "I saw her at the bank when I made the deposit yesterday. She wore tons of occult jewelry and very dark makeup. Even her manicure was black."

My mind reeled at the mental image. "But Agatha Prentiss has got to be eighty years old!"

"The 'all black clothing' seems to be a statement, in a way," my mother said. "The Witches of *the cause* want everyone to know who they are."

"Mom?" I asked. "Are the teen Witches still wearing those horrible black and red bracelets? The same kind that cursed my girls?"

Gina sucked in a horrified breath. "*What?*"

My mother patted Gina's arm while she addressed me. "Yes, many of them still are."

"The bracelets you're speaking of..." Gina asked. "Would they be a braided friendship type of bracelet with silver charms dangling from them?"

"Yes," I said. "Have you seen many of the teenage Witches wearing them?"

"Dozens." Gina swallowed hard. "But not only on the teens."

"Daphne," Beau said, calling my attention back to him, "I should go, but if you need me to pitch in and help cover any of Glynis' shifts while she is away, call me."

I thanked him and let him out the front. When I relocked the door, I found Gina and my mother speaking in low voices.

I turned to Gina. "Are you sure that you are still comfortable working here, considering everything?"

"I am not gonna let a bunch of asshole Witches scare

me out of a job I love, or ruin my town," Gina said. "The Lovari family doesn't run from conflict."

"Lovari?" my mother repeated. "Gina, is your husband's family from Hungary or Poland, perhaps?"

"I think they're from Romania, but it might be Hungary. I'll have to ask him." Gina checked the clock. "We open in five. I need to restock a few flavors of ice cream," she said and hustled off to the back room.

"What are you thinking, Mom?" I asked as she studied Meg, while the teenager worked behind the front counter.

"I wonder if Meg's Romani roots are coming through." My mother tucked her auburn hair behind her ear. "It might explain the psychic ability that the girl is displaying."

"Mom." I shook my head. "We have enough to worry about at the moment besides Meg's psychic talents."

"Oh I know." My mother patted my cheek. "I was simply wondering what I'll find when I start working with Meg after Samhain."

Mom ducked back to the pharmacy, and I made every effort to pull my head back to the business of the day, which was opening and getting back to work. I had a life to reclaim.

CHAPTER EIGHT

The *Wicked Witch* sundae the Meg made was so cute that I took photos of it and posted it to the parlor's social media page. She had taken round chocolate wafer cookies and attached them with melted chocolate to dark chocolate ice cream cones, creating pointy witches' hats. The bottom scoop of the sundae was chocolate ice cream and the top scoop making up the Witch's head was a green mint chip. Using white candy eyes and pieces of candy corn, she added a nose and mouth. Finally, she placed the cookie/cone hat at an angle on the top of it all.

Meg was beaming with pride at her creation being featured, and when I opened the doors the tourists and locals began to trickle in. The three of us settled back into our routine of working together, and I found a huge sense of relief at being back at the ice cream parlor.

The day was busy. Being a Saturday and with only a week left before Halloween, our sales were strong. I caught more than a few wide-eyed stares when the locals saw me behind the counter again. I also overheard a few tourists ask about the recent troubles, the blogger who'd died, and the couple whose bodies had been located on a local hiking trail. One gentleman had even asked to interview me for his online paranormal site, since I had been the one to find the blogger's body behind the ice cream parlor back in August. I simply smiled and said, "No, thank you."

The locals who came in avoided the amateur press asking about the murders, but happily talked up the legend of the town's founding for the tourists looking for a good ghost story. Lucas Archer, the sheriff, popped in after lunch and ordered a coffee to go. He smiled, told me he was happy to see me back, and asked how I was feeling.

"Fine," I said, holding out his to-go cup. "I'm good as new."

He nodded and took a careful sip. "I'll be here right after nine to make sure there are no problems when you walk out to your car tonight."

"Thank you, Lucas."

"See you later," he said and moved his way through the crowd of tourists gathering at the counter.

There was always a lull before night fell during the Haunted Pumpkin Walk. We took advantage of it by taking turns with supper breaks, cleaning, and running the glassware through the dishwasher. I ate some cheese and crackers for supper and sipped some ginger ale. My appetite was off. I figured it was due to the stress of coming home from Fae. By sundown we'd be slammed again, and it would keep up until right before closing.

Before six, my cell phone buzzed in my back pocket, signaling a text. I checked and discovered a message from my grandfather. My heart pounding, I tapped the screen to read it.

Do me a favor, it read. *Go down to Bittersweet Books and pick up a title being held for me before you come back to the ridge tonight.*

I exhaled and told myself to calm down. Not every text had to be a crisis, but still, it was a weird request from my grandfather. He'd never done that before. Since my parents had closed the pharmacy for the night and had already gone home, I supposed I'd been the next logical choice to run his errand.

Okay, I texted back. *I'll walk down at my supper break.*

Thanks. Let me know when you pick it up.

I stared at his last text for a moment. That was odd. Why would my gun-magazine loving grandfather be so concerned about a book? With a shrug, I pocketed the phone and since we had a lull in the customers, I told Gina I had to run an errand. Grabbing my wallet from my purse, I shrugged on my jacket and stepped out onto the sidewalk.

The sun was setting, and the tourists were walking around the square taking photos of the hundreds of jack-o'-lanterns as they were lit. I dodged quite a few people on the sidewalk and headed down Hemlock

Lane to our new and used bookstore.

Bittersweet Books sat four buildings down from the pharmacy and my ice cream parlor. I passed up the hardware store, an Ozark crafts gift shop, and a building that had recently been converted into a two-unit condo. Finally, I came to the two-story bookstore. It was old, built of red brick with decorative white trim. To the left side of the building was a roofed second story deck. That deck neatly created a covered set of stairs that allowed access to the private apartment on the second floor.

A trio of tall, skinny windows on the second floor were illuminated with strands of orange lights. On the street level there was a charming wooden front door and a big display window. I rarely had time to come down to the bookstore myself, but the window display for the Haunted Pumpkin Walk was cheerful and clever. I moved closer to admire several lit foam jack-o'-lanterns in the front window. They rested on top of stacks of books. Silk fall foliage added some flair, and a long, dried vine of bittersweet was cleverly wound over and around stacks of books and pumpkins.

Reaching for the handle of the carved wooden door, I let myself in. The tinkling of an old bell announced my arrival. The calm and quiet of the bookstore was such a contrast to the bustle outside that I felt my shoulders drop in relief. Perky Celtic music was playing over the speakers and a few shoppers were browsing in the stacks. Intrigued, I walked deeper within the bookstore.

In the center of the room, a large round table was draped with a black, sparkly cloth. There were books stacked and displayed on stands all around the table. Here, smaller foam pumpkins were placed strategically, and large LED pillar candles flickered away. At the center of that display table was a large cast-iron cauldron. The cauldron was filled with books and a gothic black and white sign that announced, "Spooky Books."

Walking closer to the display, I saw that there were books on Ozark ghosts, mysteries, paranormal romances, classic horror novels, and children's Halloween picture books. The cauldron held pride of place at the center of the display, and it was an effective point of purchase arrangement. But while the jack-'o'-lanterns and candles flickering away were clever and cheerful decorative items, the cauldron itself was an antique and more than likely once owned by a local Witch.

To my left, a woman stepped out of the stacks. "Hello," she said. "May I help you?"

She was a serious looking redhead. I estimated her to be in her late twenties. "Hi." I smiled. "I'm here to pick up a book for my grandfather."

"Certainly." She nodded and gestured for me to follow her.

I summed her up as she walked to the wooden front counter. Her dress was deep purple, long sleeved, and fell past her knees. She wore practical flat shoes, and when she faced me from across the counter, I figured that her long straight hair was her natural color, as it perfectly matched her eyebrows and complimented her pale skin.

"Name?" she asked and began to tap on an iPad attached to a stand on the counter.

"Geoffrey Sullivan."

Her eyes flashed quickly up to mine. They were green and seemed to shimmer in the light as she held my gaze.

"Hello Daphne," she said formally. "It's nice to meet you. I'm Ruby."

"Hey, Ruby." I did my best to appear nonchalant even as my pendant vibrated a warning against my chest. It wasn't unexpected that she knew my name—the curse of small towns and all—but still, I went on guard.

Magick, I thought. *That vibration was definitely a warning that I was near magick.* I considered the red-head and tried not to react when a large, black cat leapt to the checkout counter. The feline sat, wrapped its tail around itself, and glared at me.

"Is your cat friendly?" I asked as the cat and I eyeballed each other.

"He is." Ruby reached under the counter and pulled out an old leather-back book. Gently, she slipped it inside of a brown craft bag. "His name is Pythagoras. He's the boss around here."

On cue Pythagoras let out a loud *meow.*

"The boss, eh?" I said, playing along. "I bet he's a popular store mascot at this time of year."

"He is." She patted the cat on the head, and he purred. "He also has a bigger social media following than I do." Ruby's voice was dry and made me chuckle.

She passed the bag over to me by the handles, and when I reached for it, Pythagoras leaned forward and head-butted my arm.

I glanced at the cat, considered those golden eyes, and the tension in my shoulders decreased significantly. As the cat's purr increased in volume, I tried to get a read on Ruby. I'd been around Witches all my life, and could typically spot one, but she didn't add up for me. She didn't have the attitude—or the wardrobe—of the Witches of *the cause.* Ruby was too polite, and she wore no occult jewelry…But I'd bet the last of my pumpkin-spice ice cream that Pythagoras was her familiar.

"What do I owe you?" I said, keeping my tone casual.

"The book has already been paid for."

"Oh, okay. Thanks," I said and stepped back.

"You are welcome here any time," she said, passing me a business card. "I am always more than happy to help you find whatever you might need."

"Thanks." I smiled and inclined my head politely. "Well, I better get back to the ice cream parlor."

"Of course." She inclined her head. "How late are

you open tonight?"

"Until nine."

"Oh good, I close here at eight. I'll stop in and try your new Halloween week special sundae. Pythagoras and I saw it posted on your social media today," she said. "It's cute."

A friendly Witch with a sense of humor? I thought. *Interesting,*

"See you around, Ruby." I waved. "Bye, Pythagoras." The cat yawned in response and I let myself back outside.

I had walked about half-way back to the parlor when a glimmer of gold caught my eye. I stared down at the business card that was still in my hand and jolted. As I watched, handwriting shimmered to life across the back of the card.

I blinked at the message that had suddenly appeared. It read: *Daphne, be aware that I am currently working with your grandfather as an operative inside the cause.*

As quickly as the metallic words had flashed into life, they began to fade. I blinked again, and they were gone.

I spun on my heel and reconsidered that pretty brick bookstore. *Ruby is a magickal spy?* It wasn't the weirdest thing that had happened in the past few months...However, my grandfather asking me to go get his book made a hell of a lot more sense now.

Hopefully, with a woman on the inside of the cause Grandpa would be able to find out what their next move would be. I flipped over to the front of the bookstore's business card and got another surprise as the owner's first and last name was shown there as well.

The name of the owner of *Bittersweet Books* was listed as: Ruby Prentiss.

The surname was not a common one in the hollow. In fact, it only belonged to one family as far as I knew. A Witching family led by their matriarch, Agatha. Next in line had been the recently deceased Jasper, which left his horrible teenage daughter Jade. I had thrown Jade and her mean girl pals out of the ice cream parlor a few weeks ago for bullying Harper, and for doing malicious magick against her and Glynis.

I saw Ruby move into view at her front window. Our eyes met and she acknowledged me with the barest of nods. Tucking the card in the front pocket of my jeans, I gave it a pat and headed back to the parlor. I didn't have much time to worry or wonder over this latest revelation as I suddenly realized that we had a line of customers forming. They were lined up all the way to the sidewalk and so I hurried to get back inside to help.

About quarter after eight, the crowd began to thin out. Meg ran out to the floor with a dish tub and cleared, Gina helped her load everything into the dishwasher, and I began to wipe the front counters down.

It suddenly dawned on me that I'd forgotten to let Grandpa know I'd picked up his book. Taking out my phone, I fired off a quick text and slipped the phone back into my pocket. As I finished, the shop door swung open and Ruby Prentiss strolled into my ice cream parlor. She'd obviously come straight from closing the bookstore, as she was still wearing the same purple dress and flat shoes.

"Hello," I said casually.

"Hey, there." Ruby slid onto a stool at the front counter directly across from me.

"What'll ya have?" I asked.

"I'd like to try the *Wicked Witch* special sundae," Ruby said.

"Coming right up." I nodded and went to work.

Gina came out from the back, wiping her hands on a clean towel, and rang Ruby up. They chatted casually with each other, and as I finished building the sundae I heard Gina ask about a popular mystery writer's newest release.

"The release date is in mid-November," Ruby said, dropping her change in the big tip jar we had on the counter.

"Can you reserve me a copy when it comes in?" Gina asked.

"Sure," Ruby said. "I'd be happy to."

I tucked a long-handled spoon in the dish and placed the sundae in front of her. "Here you are," I said. "Enjoy."

Martin Boggs, my realtor, came in next and he had a stack of papers for me to sign. Thanking him for waiting to come by until after we were slowed down, I moved to the end of the counter and signed everything.

We spoke briefly and he confirmed the closing date. He agreed that I should be able to move me and the girls into the cabin before Thanksgiving. We shook hands, he tucked everything away in his briefcase, and then ordered a pumpkin spice cone to go. He left with a wave, telling me he'd be in touch within the week to get the inspections going on the cabin on Nightshade Court.

Martin leaned his back against the door, holding it open for Mrs. Hickston who came in with a couple of her grandkids. They all placed their orders—Meg's *Wicked Witch* sundae was proving to be very popular— and Shirley switched things up and instead of her usual double scoop of strawberry and vanilla, requested the Haunted Pumpkin Walk special.

Gina rang her up and Meg and I went to work on the sundaes. I had just drizzled the butterscotch sauce over her pumpkin-spice ice cream when Shirley reached over the counter and tapped me on the shoulder.

"Daphne," she said, "I am so happy to see you back and fully recovered. Poppy said you had been very sick with a nasty bug."

"I feel fine, now, Shirley," I said, getting a scoop full of the gingersnap crumbs to sprinkle on her sundae.

"I'm sorry to hear that things with Ashton Lowell didn't work out," she said next.

I did my best not to react, and instead made a sort of neutral sound. I'd been expecting that sort of comment from one of the regulars, especially after Meg had told me that my 'breakup' had been quite the topic of conversation in town. Fighting to maintain a neutral expression, I added Shirley's completed sundae to the tray.

"Well, you're healthy and back on your feet now," Shirley said, shooing her grandkids over to a four-top. "That's all that matters."

"Daphne's tough," Meg added, placing the final sundae on the tray.

"She certainly is," Shirley agreed, closing her large purse with a snap. "It's a good thing that idiot man left town too…Why I'd smack him with my purse if he dared to show his face 'round here again!"

"He'd never stand a chance against you," I said. "You're my hero, Shirley."

Shirley preened at the compliment. "I'm glad he's gone." She nodded briskly. "Good riddance to bad rubbish."

I cast my eyes over toward Ruby, wondering what her reaction would be to the conversation. She sat quietly, eating her sundae.

I carried the tray with the orders over to the table for Shirley and no sooner had I placed the desserts in front of everyone, when two Witch teens walked in. I felt the buzz from the sphalerite gem lying against my skin, and I knew all too well what it meant.

One of the girls had brown highlighted hair. She wore dark blue jeans with a Halloween t-shirt, and small silver pentagram around her neck. Her companion had dyed black hair, was dressed all in black, and wore heavy, dark eye-makeup. The belligerent attitude that the goth kid exuded was so strong that it made my stomach clench.

I recognized the teen with the highlights; she was a local high school student and I'd seen her in the parlor before. But the other girl, with her severe makeup and dye job, made it difficult for me to tell who she was.

My gut response was to toss the two of them out of the shop immediately. The last thing I needed was magickal trouble. But I did not. My ice cream parlor had always been neutral ground. As long as they did not break The Accords, there was no legitimate reason for me to make them leave.

Silently lecturing myself not to overreact to their presence, I stood and chatted with Shirley Hickston and her grandkids for a few minutes, which gave me the opportunity to observe how the younger Witches were conducting themselves. Also, if needs be, I could intercept them very quickly in my current location if either of them tried anything hinky.

Gina took their order for a float and a cone, and Meg started working on them. I noticed Meg had made sure not to come into physical contact with the girl who had ordered the ice cream cone. Instead of simply handing it to her, Meg placed the finished cone in our acrylic stand on the counter and slid the cone stand closer.

The gothic teen Witch rolled her eyes. "Afraid of me, mortal?" she sneered at Meg.

Meg scoffed. "I'm not afraid of you, Blair."

"Can I help you with anything, girls?" I asked, stepping forward.

"Nah." The Witch in the Halloween t-shirt took her friend by the elbow and gave her a tug away from the counter.

I spotted the red and black woven bracelet the gothic girl was wearing. "Would you like a table, ladies, or are you taking your treats to go?" I asked them pleasantly.

"I think we'll sit for a while." The friendlier of the pair smiled. "I love the decorations in the front window. Your black, white and pink pumpkins? They're so cool."

I nodded. "Thank you."

With an impatient huff, the goth girl stomped over to a two-top in the far front corner.

Meg set the cream soda float down on the counter. "Here you go, Zara."

Zara picked up her ice cream soda float and thanked Meg. She took a sip, made a happy sound when she tasted it, and then looked back at me. "You know," she began, "I saw your help wanted sign in the window in August, but before I could apply, someone else had gotten the job."

I raised my brows. "Oh?"

"Anyway, I know the busy season is almost over, but if you ever need some more help..." Zara said, "I'd be interested."

"Good to know," I said. "Thank you, Zara."

She took a step back. "I do have sales experience. I worked part-time at the lodge in the state park over the summer." With a smile and a wave, she walked over to the table to join her friend.

I went back around the counter to Meg. "What can you tell me about your friend, Zara?" I asked.

"Her last name is Hawthorn," Meg whispered." She plays the flute and is in the marching band with me. Her family moved here at the beginning of the summer, and she seems okay." Meg flipped her ponytail over her shoulder. "I'm surprised to see her with Blair, though. Zara doesn't wear their bracelets or dress in all black like the other Witches at school."

"The girl with the bad dye job?" I asked. "Blair, you called her? I don't recognize her."

"Blair Radcliff. She's a Freshman." Meg shrugged. "I *don't* like her. She hangs around with the older girls in the shady Witchy clique."

A quartet of customers were leaving, and Meg grabbed the dish tub to go and bus their table. She bounced out front, with all the unbridled energy of a teenager.

After Meg left, Ruby cleared her throat delicately. "Not all of the Witches of Hemlock Hollow are involved in the movement, you know."

I pretended to wipe up my already clean counter as I stood across from her. Glancing up, I made sure no one was close enough to overhear us. Ruby was sitting alone at the front counter and between the Halloween theme music playing over the stereo system and the voices of the other customers, I doubted anyone would be able to listen in. However, I still needed to be cautious.

"I do know," I said.

"Are you aware that Witches have been trying to recruit new followers to their crusade?" Ruby asked, keeping her voice low. "It is a difficult time to be a Witch here in the hollow. You either believe as the members of *the cause* do, or you are shunned. Sometimes even hexed and cursed."

"Mob mentality," I agreed under my breath. "I saw what they did to Harper Wilson, when she spoke out against the Hedge's attack on my home."

Ruby turned slightly, making sure no one was close enough to hear. "Anything less than completely embracing their radical ideology is unacceptable, and the consequences are dire. However, there is a growing group of Witches who have walked away from this insanity. They smile, nod, and placate in order to protect their families, homes and their livelihoods."

"So they're playing along as to not become targets for a magickal attack themselves?"

"Yes," she said, picking up the cone hat from her sundae. "Believe me, Daphne, I'm not the only one working silently behind the scenes trying to negate some of the evil this fanatical movement has wrought."

"Which is how my grandfather found you."

Ruby inclined her head ever so slightly in

acknowledgment of my words. "I would imagine Blair is attempting to get Zara to join the ranks, even now," Ruby said. "I know they've already been pressuring her mother, Liz."

I slid my eyes over from where Ruby sat there nibbling on the cookie/cone witch hat of her ice cream sundae, to where the two teenage girls huddled together talking. Across the sales floor, Blair stopped speaking and sent me a hard glare.

"Is the Radcliff girl glaring at me or you?" Ruby asked, without bothering to turn around and look.

"Me," I said. "At least I think so. She's got so much black eyeliner on it's kind of hard to tell."

Ruby's eyes danced at my snarky comment, but she kept a sober expression. "I'm fairly certain that Blair's actual purpose here tonight is to confirm that the rumors of your healthy return to Hemlock Hollow are true," she said softly.

I smiled. "How fun for her."

"It may interest you to know that Blair was recently assigned to keep an eye on me at my store as well," Ruby said *sotto voce*.

"Why?" I asked just as quietly.

"Because I'm new to the movement," Ruby whispered and finished the last of her sundae. "That was great," she said in a conversational tone.

"Thank you," I said calmly. "It was Meg's creation and has been a strong seller."

Meg came back from the floor with the dish tub.

"Glad you liked it!" She smiled at Ruby, scooped up her spoon and empty sundae bowl, and took the dish tub to the back.

Ruby dabbed her lips with a paper napkin. "Be sure and let me know if your grandfather enjoys his book."

I nodded as she stood. "I'll do that."

"Goodnight." Ruby gave me a tiny smile and turned to go.

I watched her walk to the door, and she hesitated before opening it. She inclined her head, acknowledging the teenage Witches at the table. Their reaction was very interesting. Zara smiled and waved back, while Blair scowled. Deliberately, Ruby flipped her hair back with one finger and at the same time, the top scoop of ice cream fell off Blair's cone and dropped into her lap.

All on its own.

Blair swore, and her friend grabbed napkins to help her wipe up her shirt. I bit my lip hard, as not to laugh.

The last hour rolled on and finally nine o'clock was upon us. Blair and Zara had hung out until the last moment when I announced that we were closing. Zara gave me a friendly wave goodbye and Blair followed along behind her, looking sulky.

I locked the door and flipped the sign over to *Closed*. Through the glass front door, I watched as the girls meandered over to the town square to look at the pumpkins. I thought about everything I had learned today. The Lycan and Fae kids had all left the school, and the teenage Witches were bullying the other remaining kids, as well as recruiting for *the cause*.

I'd met a previously unknown member of the Prentiss family; and not only had she been friendly, but she was apparently working with my grandfather to spy on the nefarious local coven of Witches.

The mortals in town had indeed bought the story that Ashton had left town and I'd been out with 'the flu' for the past few weeks. Meanwhile—according to Meg—the Witches had been spreading tales that Ashton had been cheating on me, which he had; and that I was dead, which I wasn't. Finally, according to Ruby, Blair Radcliff had been sent to spy on not only me—but her and her business as well.

I frowned, wondering about the Radcliff girl. I supposed she was a relative of Hazel's. *That poor kid is doomed,* I thought. Hazel was a spiteful old busybody.

Catching Meg's reflection in the window glass, my thoughts shifted, and I smiled. Meg was energetic, cheerful and a hell of a hard worker. She was singing along with the old classic "Monster Mash" song on the radio and was busy first wiping tables and then seat tops. Once she finished the padded seats, she would pick up the chairs and flip them seat-side down on top of the tables.

I went in the back and got the mop bucket, while Gina began the closing reports and counting down the register. I filled the bucket with steaming water. Rolling it out front, I started by the front door, and mopped behind Meg while she worked.

"I can do that for you, Daphne," she offered.

"I've got it," I said, swinging the mop across the floor. "It feels good to use my arm in a new way."

"Okay, boss." Meg moved to the padded aqua barstools at the counter. She spritzed them with cleaner and wiped them down.

"Hey, Meg?" I said a few moments later. "Do you suppose that Blair Radcliff's eye makeup was an attempt at a smoky eye?"

Meg snorted out a laugh. "Well, the attempt was *tragic*, in my opinion."

"Maybe you can recommend some of those makeup tutorials you like to watch online the next time you see her at school," Gina said. "Perhaps that would help the girl."

"Hmm...I don't know," I said, "maybe she was going for a 'hung-over panda' look."

"A hung-over panda doing the walk of shame the next morning, maybe," Meg tossed back.

***

Gina and Meg went out the front, and Lucas dropped by as promised and walked me to my car out back. I think he had half-expected some sort of confrontation from the Witches now that I was back at work in the hollow, but there was none. Perhaps, as my grandfather had said, the surge in tourism was a blessing in disguise this year. There were so many people attending the festival that it was fairly safe for me—so long as I stayed in a crowd and remained alert.

On the downside, however, it took twice as long as usual to navigate my way through town due to the traffic. While I sat at our one stop light, I called the Shaw's landline to tell them I was headed back to the ridge.

The light turned green, and three out of the eight cars ahead of me were able to turn onto the highway. But it was a short turn light and all too soon it was red, and traffic stopped again. I pulled the ponytail holder from my hair and scrubbed the soreness from my scalp. Tiredly, I leaned my head against the headrest.

Alone, I could confess that I missed my friends from the Fae realm. I was worried about Torian and Imogen, and I hoped that Darren, Hamish, Moira and even Bagley were safe considering that war had come to the realm.

Finnlagh was probably up to his neck in court politics; I hoped he wasn't on the front lines. His sister Glynis was a capable warrior, and although Finnlagh had admitted that he had known war, I had no inkling as to whether or not he was an experienced soldier.

While he'd been gallant with me, romantic and kind, I had simply assumed that as a prince he was trained in combat. What would war with the Dark Realm mean for the royal family? What would happen to Princess Oona's children now that the uprising had begun? I'd tried not to think about it all day, but now, worry engulfed me for *all* of them. My lover, his family, my friends, and even the Leprechaun tribe and the army that I'd seen moving through the woods.

I shut my eyes for a moment and offered up a prayer. "Please, let Finnlagh, his family, and my friends be safe," I whispered and reopened my eyes.

A few more cars were now pulling onto the highway. Telling myself to be patient, I eased my SUV into the turn lane with the rest of the traffic. I'd never seen such heavy traffic before, not even during the Haunted Pumpkin Walk in years past.

In the intersection before me, someone tried to push through the red light anyway. Cars screeched to a halt trying to avoid clipping each other, and horns blared. "Jeez! Talk about reckless!" I swore at the impatient driver. "Everyone wants to go home. The point is to get there in one piece."

"Mortals are often reckless." Finnlagh's voice had come from nowhere.

I jolted and reached automatically for the Glock 43 that was in the custom holster of my car.

"*Mo ghrá*, put away your weapon," he said, materializing in the passenger seat beside me.

"Damn it!" I left the gun in place. "I really hate it when you literally *appear* out of nowhere."

"I cannot stay for long," Finnlagh said. "I only wanted to be sure that you were indeed reunited with your girls."

I shifted in my seat to make eye contact. "Did Imogen get my message to you?"

"She did."

"Are you and your family safe?" I asked.

"We are," he said. "Considering how you snuck off at the first opportunity, I am surprised that you asked."

I huffed out a breath at the condescension in his voice. "It's not like that."

"Then how is it? Explain yourself to me."

"You're gonna want to check that royal tone, Finnlagh."

Beside me he let out a little growl of frustration. "If you would be so kind as to explain to me the circumstances of your leaving, my lady," he said, so politely that it bordered on being rude.

"It's simple," I said. "My memories came back, and I wanted to be reunited with my children. When Princess Oona offered to get me out of the castle, I took her up on it."

"Wait." One of his eyebrows rose. "*Oona* offered to get you out?"

Shit, I thought. *He didn't know about Princess Oona being a part of the opposition.*

"Why would she do that, for you?" he asked suspiciously.

I decided to stick as close to the truth as possible. "I suppose, as she was forced into marriage herself, that she felt sorry for me."

"I have *never* forced you in any way," he argued.

"No, but you still manipulated the situation *and* tricked me into accepting," I argued back. "Before I could blink or even try to talk some sense into you, Finnlagh, you were rushing me straight to the altar."

Behind me a car horn honked, and I gave my attention to the road, rolling forward with the traffic. I made it to the front of the line, but the light went to yellow again before I was able to turn onto the highway. I braked and looked over at him once more. "I don't want to fight with you, Finnlagh."

"You left me," he said. "Practically at the altar."

"Don't you dare play the jilted bridegroom with me, pal." I gripped the steering wheel hard and struggled to keep my voice down. "I was stuck in that stupid room with a bunch of ladies in waiting, having a god-damn panic attack. Do you have any idea how mortifying it was having them insinuate that the real reason you were in such a rush to marry me is because I was pregnant or something?"

His eyes grew wide. "Are you?"

I opened my mouth to speak, found that I couldn't and tried again. "I don't know," I said finally.

"But, it is possible?"

"I suppose. I mean we went after each other for weeks."

"That is not a very romantic way of putting it,." He frowned.

I tossed up my hands. "Okay, fine. We had a lot of sex, and it was fun. But I swear to whatever god that is listening…If all this time you've been trying to get me pregnant simply to fulfil your duty to provide an heir —"

He made a strangled sound.

"I will kick your balls straight up to your throat," I continued pleasantly. "And *that* is only for starters.

"Daphne, I had not been making love with you only in the hopes that we would conceive," Finnlagh said, completely serious.

I gave him a doleful stare.

"You do not believe me," Finnlagh said, and he actually sounded hurt.

"Finnlagh, when you called in your debt you said, and I quote, 'be my wife and mother to my children.'"

"I do not deny that," he said.

I narrowed my eyes at him. "Glynis once told me there was tremendous pressure on you to wed and to produce an heir right away. It makes me wonder if all the times we were having sex was for our mutual enjoyment, *or* because you had an agenda in mind."

"Agenda?" He frowned. "What exactly do you mean by that?"

"A baby agenda," I said. "I will *not* be used as a brood mare."

"Nor do I want you to be one," he said firmly. "Daphne, I am sorry you felt so overwhelmed before the ceremony." He sighed. "I should have never left you alone."

I shook my head. "You're totally missing the point."

"What is the point?"

I grit my teeth. "The point is that all that anxiety brought my memories to the surface. They all came crashing back. The force of those emotions pulled me under hard. It literally took me to my knees."

He rested a hand lightly on my thigh. "I should have been there with you."

"I think it took something big and overwhelming to make my memories return," I said. "However, once they did, I realized that I simply couldn't stay and play faerie-tale wedding with you."

Beside me, he flinched. He lifted his hand and was no longer touching me.

Realizing that my words had hurt him, I tried again. "Finnlagh, you know better than most what is at stake here in the hollow."

"Yes." He nodded in agreement. "Yes, I do."

"I had to return home and help with this crisis with the Witches." I reached for his hand and gave it a squeeze. "You're not the only one who has a *duty* to their family, to their allies, and their land."

He twined his fingers with mine. "You are truly the warrior bride that was foretold."

"Cut that shit out," I said. "It sounds like a—"

"Faerie tale?" he said, lifting my hand to his lips.

"Finnlagh…Hey, I'm driving here. Don't distract me." I tried to sound firm, but it came out as more of a moan as he pressed kisses over my wrist.

"I love you," he said, and it made my heart slam into

my throat.

"Behave yourself," I said, and my request sounded weak, even to my own ears.

"Very well," he said, giving my hand a pat. "We will both attend to our duties; and when the battles are over, *mo ghrá,* I will come for you."

"Come for me?" I frowned. "What the hell does that mean?"

"Be safe, my love." Finnlagh smiled, and with a shimmer of light he disappeared.

CHAPTER NINE

Sunday was a shorter working day at the parlor, and Tara announced that she'd like to accompany me and see the town. The girls wanted to come along too but I refused, worried about their safety. On the ridge they were much safer since they were about as far away from the Witches as they could get.

My announcement was not met well, and there was whining and squabbling. Phoebe tried to intervene, but the girls were wound up and spoiling for an argument.

"It's not fair!" Kayla said crossly. "I wanna go and see all the pumpkins!"

"Yeah, me too!" Kenzie piped up. "Everybody else gets to go."

"Girls," Phoebe began, "your mother will be working and it isn't a good idea for you to be in town right now. Alison, Annabelle, and Adrian aren't allowed to go to the Haunted Pumpkin Walk this year either."

"It totally sucks," Adrian said, grabbing an apple from a bowl on the kitchen table.

"Yeah, it *sucks*!" Kayla said.

Seeing that she wasn't going to win, Kenzie switched tactics. "Don't leave us again, Mama!"

"It's only for six hours," I told Kenzie, who had thrown herself at me.

"Don't go!" she cried dramatically and held on to my waist for dear life. She started to cry. Real tears this time.

Realizing they were both afraid, I bent over and picked her up. "Why don't the three of us go outside and talk for a bit, hmm?" I glanced over at Kayla and tipped my head toward the porch. "Kayla, let's have a family meeting."

Once the three of us went outside I set Kenzie on her feet, and we strolled over to the pond on the Shaw's property. The bench was still in place and so we all sat down with me in the center and the girls on either side.

I explained to my girls again that I was only going to the ice cream parlor, and that I would be home by 6:30. But clearly, they were very anxious about me leaving them.

"What if you go away to the Fae realm again?" Kenzie asked.

"I won't," I said. "I promise."

Kayla leaned in closer. "You did before, and you didn't even say goodbye."

"I didn't go there on purpose," I tried to explain. "Grandpa Geoffrey sent me there with Finnlagh so I could get better."

"Finnlagh took you to his house?" Kenzie asked.

"Yes." I ran my hand over her hair.

"Did he do magick on you the way he did when we were sick from the bracelets?" Kayla wanted to know.

"Yes." I nodded. "I stayed at his house and his mother helped take care of me too."

"What is his mom like?" Kayla asked. "What's her name?"

"Finnlagh's mother is the queen of Fae," I said. "Queen Aine."

"Queen Awn-ye." Kayla sounded it out.

"She's a *queen*?" Kenzie asked. "Will we ever get to meet her?"

"Maybe," I said. "Someday. The queen was very kind to me."

Kenzie smiled up at me. "I'm glad she helped you get better."

I dropped a kiss on the top of her head. "Me too, baby."

"I want to see where you were hurt," Kayla said, tugging on my sleeve. "Show me."

"All right." With a nod, I slid my left arm out of my sweatshirt sleeve. Pulling the sweatshirt aside, I pushed my bra strap down so they could see my shoulder and collar bone area.

The girls stood up. Together they moved in front of me while I sat, and they stared at the pink puckered scar with very large eyes.

Kayla leaned in and touched a fingertip to the scars.

"Does it still hurt?" she wanted to know.

"No. It doesn't," I assured her.

"Mama, that's bad," Kenzie said, her breath hitching in her chest.

I slid my arm back in the sleeve and tugged the sweatshirt down. "I'm sorry that seeing it scared you, baby." I pulled her on my lap.

I tucked an arm around Kayla and drew her to sit beside me. The three of us sat together silently for a while.

"Mom?" Kayla finally asked. "Who did that to you?"

"I was hit by witch fire during the battle," I said.

"I know that," Kayla said, tipping her face up to mine. "I'm not a baby anymore, Mom. I meant which of the Witches did that to you? *Who* hurt you?"

"Ashton did," I said honestly.

Kenzie burrowed tighter into my arms.

Kayla kept eye contact with me. "I'm glad he's dead."

"Me too," Kenzie whispered. "Stupid Witches."

"Do you still love me even though I might be a Witch?" Kayla asked.

"Of course I do!" I pulled her in tighter. "Kayla, you are smart and so brave! You were the first one to know the Witches had gathered and were attacking that day. You fired off your arrows into those magickal clouds and defended not only your family, but the Shaw's as well. I was so proud of you baby!"

"I wondered..." Kayla's voice was timid. "Well, since Ashton, Aunt Jessamine, and some other Witches turned out to be bad...That maybe you thought that I would be bad too."

"Now you listen to me, young lady," I said firmly. "Your Grandma Poppy is one of the most talented Witches I've ever known. She is good and kind and loves us with everything she has. Her great-grandmother was named Brigit O'Reilly and *she* was one of the original Witches that worked to heal the hollow after old Goderich Stein tried to destroy it with his evil."

"I remember that story," Kenzie piped up.

"It isn't merely a story," I said. "It's a part of our heritage, the three of us are descendants of very powerful women. Good Witches who work their magick to help, heal, and to protect others in their community, and don't you *ever* forget that."

"Okay," the girls said in unison.

"I love the both of you so much," I said. "I'd do anything to keep you safe. Even if that means you have to stay on the ridge with the Shaw family while I go to town to work. It's not perfect, but we will get through this together."

"Do you think I'll be a Witch too, Mama?" Kenzie asked.

I shrugged. "You know, I'm not sure baby. We'll have to see what gifts you develop as you get older."

"Grandpa Geoffrey says I'm a Fae seer," Kenzie said

jumping to her feet. "But I think I'd rather be like Glynis and be a warrior!" She grabbed a fallen stick from the ground and began to fight an imaginary foe. "I'll destroy any bad guys who try and get us!"

I grinned. "There you go."

Kayla leaned her head against my shoulder. "You took after great-grandpa Geoffrey, didn't you, Mom?"

I glanced down at my eldest. Those blue-green eyes missed very little. "That's the way it looks," I said.

"Grandpa Geoffrey is the Hunter, isn't he?" Kayla asked me quietly while Kenzie danced along the edges of the water of the pond, jabbing the air with her stick.

"Yes," I said. "He is."

"So he's like the sheriff for the Supes, right?"

"Exactly." I nodded.

"And he's super good at fighting and weapons and stuff?" Kayla asked next. "Like you are?"

"Correct," I said. "Well, except for archery. You'll always be better than me with a bow, Kayla."

Kayla grinned at that. "I'm glad you're home, Mom."

I pressed a kiss to her hair. "Me too baby. Me too."

***

I had been working at the parlor for maybe an hour when Lucas Archer walked in. Besides the fact that he was wearing his uniform, I took one look at the set of his handsome face and knew: Something had happened.

Again.

Despite my heart rapping hard against my ribs, I managed a smile and a cheerful hello. "Hi, Sheriff Archer," I said. "What'll ya have?"

"Hi, Sheriff." Meg smiled at him and went back to busing a table.

He approached the counter and the light bounced off his mirrored glasses. "Your girls and parents are fine," he said in an undertone. "I'd like a coffee to go, please," he added, loud enough for anyone else to hear.

"Coming right up." I poured the coffee in a to-go cup and congratulated myself on doing so without spilling anything. I snapped the lid on the coffee and handed it over with a smile. "On the house," I said.

He slipped his shades on top of his head. "Daphne, do you have a moment?"

"Of course," I said.

"Can we go in the back?"

"Yup." I nodded and asked Gina to cover the counter.

"You know I will." Gina gave my hand a squeeze.

I opened the door to the back room and held it for Lucas. He smoothly walked around behind the counter and entered the room. Gently, I shut the door behind us.

He set the coffee cup down on the old table I kept in back and faced me. "I am here in my official capacity as sheriff, to make notification that your ex-husband's body has been found."

I flinched. "Where?" I asked.

"His body was discovered at the edge of the Lycan territory and the national forest a few hours ago. Geoffrey was called in to consult."

I blew out a long breath. "Meaning you believe the cause of death was supernatural."

"Technically, I'd say ritualistic." Lucas tucked his hands in his pockets. "Owing to the condition of the body and the paraphernalia recovered at the scene."

"Are you telling me this, because you believe I'm a suspect?"

"No." He shook his head. "You only returned from Fae two days ago. Our best estimate, due to the condition of the remains, is that he was killed at least a week ago."

"I understand." I nodded. "Thank you for telling me."

He nodded and picked up his coffee. "I have to get back to work, but I want you to be careful out there, Daphne," he said.

I patted my waist holster in response.

He started to go but hesitated in the doorway. "If you or the girls need anything, please don't hesitate to give me a call."

"I will," I said. "Thank you, Sheriff."

After he left, I stood there in the back and wondered what the hell to do now.

Gina had managed to wait maybe fifteen seconds after he'd left before she rushed to the back. "What happened?" she whispered.

"Zane's body was found," I said quietly.

Gina rested her hand on my arm. "Hadn't he been missing for a few weeks now?"

"Yeah." I blew out a long breath.

"Are they suspecting foul play?"

"Yes." I answered her as honestly as possible.

"When they first began looking for him…It appeared as if there'd been a struggle at his apartment," she said. "I remember hearing Mrs. Hickston talk about that."

"I have to figure out what to tell the girls," I heard myself say.

Gina wrapped me in her arms and gave me a hug. "I'm so sorry, Daphne."

I hugged her back. "Kayla and Kenzie don't have much of an emotional tie to Zane." My voice sounded hollow to my own ears. "They rarely, if ever, saw him. Once we were divorced Zane gave up all pretense in being interested in the girls."

Gina patted my back. "I've never even heard the girls speak of him."

"That's because they don't. He's basically a stranger to them."

But still, how am I to explain his death to them? I wondered. Especially after this morning when the girls were so on edge and worried about me leaving them again.

I'd find the right way and time to tell them about Zane, but it wouldn't be today. Who I did have to notify next was Phoebe Shaw and my parents, so that we were all on the same page. They would be able to help protect the girls from any gossip.

My girls have been through enough, I thought. Surviving the fire and losing their home, the magickal attack on them, and then Ashton's betrayal...Our fleeing to the Shaws, and the night of the battle on the ridge.

Was it any wonder they were afraid of me even going to work? I rarely sought comfort, but now I tucked my head on Gina's shoulder and held on tight.

"How can I help?" Gina asked.

"If you wouldn't mind holding down the front counter for a while," I said. "I need to check in with my parents and my grandfather."

"Whatever you need," Gina said. "I got you."

I let go and stood straight again. "Thank you, Gina."

"Hey, Mom!" Meg poked her head in through the door. "We're getting a line out here."

"Coming," Gina said.

"Everything okay?" Meg wanted to know.

"It will be," I said.

Gina hustled out to the front and shut the door, allowing me some privacy. I pulled my cell phone from my pocket and called Phoebe, and next my parents. Once that was finished, I checked to make sure things were under control out front; and finally, I called my grandfather.

"Been expecting to get a call from you," he said by way of hello.

"Lucas said the cause of death was ritualistic," I said, getting down to business.

"Do you honestly want to know the details?" he asked.

"I'm going to have to, if we're going to be able to successfully combat this evil."

"Before we get into the particulars, I wanted to say that I sure am sorry, honey," my grandfather said. "You know, I always hated that sonofabitch, but still, he was the girls' father."

"He stopped being anything other than their biological father years ago, Grandpa," I said. "But I'm also sorry that he was killed."

"Yeah, well." Briskly, my grandfather cleared his throat. "Did you ever watch any of those old documentaries about how all the ancient Druids were supposedly into human sacrifice?"

"Yeah…" I said, wondering where he was going with that. "Every time one of those documentaries came on television Mom would go ballistic about the inaccurate portrayal of the old religion."

He laughed. "I'll bet she did."

"So what does this have to do with the crime scene?"

"Well, we have a sort of reenactment of that style of sacrifice here."

"The victim was killed three different ways?" I asked.

"Yup," he said. "Head bashed, strangled, and the throat slit."

"God," I whispered.

"The killer even bound the victim's hands behind their back."

I opened my mouth, but nothing came out. I was trying to stay impartial, and I was failing. I kept thinking that if I didn't use my ex's name— instead saying, *he* or the *victim,* that it would be easier to discuss this somehow.

It wasn't.

My knees were wobbling and so I sat down. "Was the murder weapon recovered?" I managed to ask. "Lucas said they had 'recovered paraphernalia.'"

"Yes. It was left very prominently displayed."

"I'm guessing the murder weapon was an athame?"

"No," he said. "It was a big-ass boline."

"Wait," I said, rubbing my temple. "A boline is traditionally used only to harvest herbs."

"Well this bad boy was more along the lines of a sickle. Big enough to do the job and then some."

The mental image made me cringe. "*Shit.*"

"The weapon is a real beauty too. Probably an antique. The handle is decorated and carved with occult symbols, and I'm pretty sure the blade is—"

"Silver?" I interjected. "Is the blade silver and precious stones are inlaid in the handle?"

"Yes. How did you know?"

"I saw one once at Ashton's house," I said. "It was in a large case with other occult weapons and gear."

"Sonofabitch!" he hissed. "I wonder if one of

Lowell's cronies went and helped themselves to whatever was left in that house."

"Maybe," I said, thinking that over. "It's a good theory."

"Would you be able to tell me if the weapon had belonged to Lowell, if you saw it again?"

"Yes," I said. "I'm not likely to forget it."

"I'll see about getting a photo of it to you..." He paused. "If you think you can handle that."

"So long as it's a photo of the boline *only*."

"Of course," he said and blew out a long audible sigh. "Hells bells. This is an unholy mess."

"Speaking of unholy," I began, "there's no polite way for me to ask. Will he—" I stopped myself from saying my ex's name and instead cleared my throat. "Will the victim, reanimate?"

"In an abundance of caution, I made sure that this corpse won't be able to go walking again."

My stomach lurched, and I shut my eyes. What my grandfather was telling me as gently as possible was that he had decapitated the corpse. I tried not to think about the details of that, and instead focused on *not* getting physically sick.

Eventually I tuned back into my grandfather, who was still speaking.

"—have a friend of mine go by and check out whatever is left at Lowell's house."

"Ah, okay," I managed.

"You been keeping that gun on you?" my

grandfather asked.

"Yes sir, I have," I said.

"That's good," he said. "Because I'm sure that we have another goddamn necromancer working in the hollow."

***

By Monday morning, word had spread through the hollow the Zane's body had been found. The details were mercifully vague, and of course there were plenty of students and football players at the high school upset over Coach Hart's untimely passing.

Today it was Gina and myself manning the parlor, and Tara had come along to help out. By noon we were slammed, and I was happy to have an extra set of hands —even inexperienced ones—to bus tables and deliver orders to the customers waiting at the tables.

"Tara's having a great time," Gina said, elbow nudging me once we had things back under control.

I squinted over at Tara and saw that it was true. She had a mile-wide smile on her face and was chatting up the customers as she worked. Tara was wearing brand new jeans and a work apron over her orange Haunted Pumpkin Walk t-shirt.

She'd been busy while seeing the sights in town yesterday, buying herself clothes and a leather jacket at the second-hand store. Tara had gotten herself a hair cut as well. Now her blonde hair swung to her chin in a sleek and sassy bob.

"I got more tips!" Tara said and paused to stuff a roll of singles and a pocketful of change into the big communal tip jar on the front counter.

"Wow!" Gina's eyes were huge. "That's a lot of tips for a Monday."

Tara shrugged and took the dish tub in the back. "Just lucky, I guess."

A part-Fae part-Leprechaun who was 'just lucky'? I doubted that. Wiping my hands on a towel, I followed my new helper to the back.

"Hey, Tara," I said.

"Yes?" She turned from where she was loading up the dishwasher. Tara was currently fascinated with the industrial grade appliance. She loved loading and unloading it.

"Do you know about The Accords?"

"Yes." She nodded. "Your grandfather told me about them. Mortals are not allowed to persecute or kill the Supernaturals and the Supes aren't allowed to bewitch, devour, faerie-lead, or trick the mortals."

"There is also a no-glamoury decree."

"And?" Her eyes narrowed in confusion.

"That means you can't use Fae glamour on the customers in the ice cream parlor."

"I'm not." She waved that away. "Don't be worrying yourself about that."

I crossed my arms over my chest. "Tara, in all the years I've been open for business I have *never* seen that much cash hit the tip jar on a Monday afternoon."

"It's the Leprechaun side of me," Tara said, wringing her hands. "I can't turn that off, Daphne. I tried."

"Meaning what, exactly?"

"It means that even though I look like a mortal female now…" she paused and ran a hand over her new hairdo, "I still have the powers of my father's people."

"As in good luck?" I guessed.

She folded her hands at her waist. "It is *not* a Fae glamour, but I can't seem to help the coins and the good fortune. It's drawn to me, whether I will it or no."

I frowned. "So you're like a good-luck magnet?"

Tara nodded. "Yesterday, I won a free haircut, and a gift certificate for something called a mani-pedi. *And* the used clothing store happened to have a brand-new pair of the blue breeches in my size, in stock."

"We call them blue jeans," I gently reminded her.

"Ah, yes." She nodded. "Now, I certainly don't want to be causin' any mischief here at your place of business. I promise to work on trying to turn down the Leprechaun powers…But you should know that it's as much a part of me, as me green eyes."

I tried not to smile. "You slip into an Irish brogue from time to time," I said. "Did you know?"

"Will it make me stand out or identify me as a Fae?" Tara asked. "I want to blend in. Truly. I thought with my new hair style you wouldn't be able to tell…No one can see my ears. Not anymore."

"You look great Tara," I said. "What I *meant* was,

that the accent may draw a bit more attention from the males. Most folks around here aren't used to hearing the brogue. It's charming."

"I can handle the compliments on me accent. I don't appear short in the mortal world, either," Tara said proudly.

"No, you're average height as compared to a mortal female."

"You are still taller than me," Tara said.

"Not by very much," I admitted.

"I saw a female wearing these boots, yesterday," Tara said, continuing to load up the dishwasher. "They were very long, and went up her leg. The heels were tall. If I had a pair of those to wear, I would appear even taller."

I couldn't help but grin. All females, no matter their species were suckers for a sexy pair of shoes it seemed. "I tell you what," I said. "We get through the next week and past all of the unrest in the hollow and I'll take you shopping for some high-heeled boots."

Tara held out her hand. "I'll hold you to that oath." I shook her hand and proceeded to help her with the rest of the dishes.

A few hours later I was working at my desk in the back. I needed more toppings for the sundaes, and at the rate we were going, I'd be out before Halloween.

"Daphne?" Gina's voice drifted back to me a bit later. "You have a visitor."

I stepped back out to the floor and discovered

Catherine Albright, the mayor, standing by the front counter. Immediately, I knew that her visit was not a social call.

Catherine, as always, was impeccably dressed. Today she wore dark slacks and a white top under a Halloween cardigan with a vintage black cat pattern. The outfit was both seasonal and professional, which befitted her political role. However, Catherine was much more than merely the mayor, she was also the leader of the Witch community—and had, until recently, been dear friends with my mother. Just as her daughter, Jessamine, had once been *my* BFF.

That is until Jessamine had slept with Ashton Lowell and joined the other Witches of *the cause* in their attack on Wolfsbane Ridge. My stomach gave one hard jerk of surprise and then settled. I scanned the room, checking to see if she had any other members of *the cause* with her. I saw none that I knew of; it appeared as though she'd come alone. I was however very suspicious of her visit, and of her intentions.

"Hello, Catherine," I said coolly.

She slipped her cat eye shaped sunglasses from her eyes. "Hello, Daphne. I came by—"

"To gloat?" I guessed.

"To offer my condolences," the mayor said.

I gave her the barest of smiles. "How kind."

"How are your girls doing?" she asked next.

Instead of answering her, I asked a question of my own. "How's Jess? I see that *Belladonna's* is closed.

That's not like Jessamine to miss the biggest tourism influx of the year." I waited a beat. "I was concerned, considering the last time I saw her was under...Shall we say...Less than cordial circumstances?"

Catherine flinched. It was a tiny movement, almost completely controlled, but I saw her reaction, nonetheless.

"Jessamine has decided to take some time for herself and is traveling with her father," Catherine said.

"How exciting." Gina handed the mayor a coffee in a to-go cup and ranged herself beside me.

"Yes, isn't it?" Catherine smiled at Gina. "I believe they are in Europe at the moment."

Even as I processed the news that Jess had not only left town, she'd left the entire damn country, I managed a polite nod. "She wanted to get away from *everything,* is that it?" I asked.

Catherine tucked her sunglasses in the front of her shirt. "Sometimes a little distance is required, in order to see a situation for what it truly is."

Tara came bursting through the door behind me and bumped solidly into me with the dish tub. "Ah, feck it! I'm always trippin' over me own two feet."

Now Tara was many things: skilled horsewoman, accomplished rider, a spy for the Dark Fae. But she was not, by any stretch of the imagination, clumsy.

"Hello, dear, you must be new. I don't think I've seen you in town before." Catherine smiled and extended a hand. "I'm Mayor Albright."

"Ah, tis herself, is it?" Tara said to the mayor with an exaggerated accent. She kept ahold of the dish tub and did not offer her hand.

"Tara is a new employee," I decided on the spot. "She's been helping us while Glynis is out of town."

"I'm Daphne's friend, as well," Tara said. "I'll be making Hemlock Hollow my home for the foreseeable future."

"It is exciting to look forward isn't it?" Catherine took a sip of her coffee. "Then again, sometimes, in order to solve a current dilemma, we must look to our past for the answers we need."

"Sure," I said, wondering where she was going.

"The legend of how the town got its name, for example," Catherine said, picking up one of the tourism flyers displayed on the counter. "Have you told her about that yet, Daphne?"

When I didn't respond, Catherine smiled. "Ask her to tell you all about it, Tara. There is much to be learned from taking a careful look at our local history."

"No doubt." I inclined my head and wondered what she was trying to tell me.

"Well, I should return to city hall." Catherine dropped the tri-folded flyer to the countertop and stepped back. "It was nice to meet you, Tara. Welcome to Hemlock Hollow. Oh, I'm sorry, I don't believe that I ever caught your last name."

"Green," Tara said easily.

"Again, my condolences, Daphne." Catherine

nodded. The mayor walked casually out the door, and the three of us stood at the counter watching as she moved off and down the street.

Gina was the first to speak. "Take a careful look at the town's history? What was she insinuating?"

"Who knows?" I shrugged it off.

A couple approached the ice cream case and began to choose flavors for their cones and Gina went to wait on them. Picking up the flyer from the counter, I saw that it was open to the section of the tale of the evil lumber baron, Goderich Stein.

Immediately, Catherine's words replayed in my mind: *There is much to learn by taking a look at our local history*...I stared at the black and white photo of the old sawmill that was once owned by Stein.

Look to the past for answers, eh?

All the locals knew the tale of how the hollow had gotten its name...Over one hundred and sixty years ago, on a full moon night on Halloween, one brave man had fought against an evil sorcerer—a necromancer—and he'd won. After Stein had been defeated, the elders of the settlement decided it was best to destroy the body so he would not rise again. The local Witches had gathered together to cast a banishing spell, removing all traces of evil from the land that Stein had once despoiled.

Grandpa had once told me that the man who had taken the necromancer on directly had been an ancestor of Ashton's. It had been an ancestor of mine, Brigit

O'Reilly, who had been one of the original Witches to work the healing spell on the land that Halloween night. Her magick had played a part in the hemlock flowers that had sprung up. The protective plant covered the ground, keeping men and animals away so that nature could slowly rebalance the scales, giving the earth time to turn the energy away from the dark, and back to the light.

I stared at that photo. I was pretty sure that the old sawmill was still standing. It had been condemned years ago, back when I was in school. But...*If* someone was trying to model themselves after Stein by practicing necromancy, then that sawmill would be an incredible source of power for a dark practitioner to tap into.

I needed to go and see for myself if that was the case. It was time to do some recon—and the sooner the better. I'd be damned if I was going to sit around and wait until the Halloween blue moon...Because that's when the necromancer and any other Witches of *the cause* would be at their most powerful.

I reached for my cell phone. "Excuse me," I said to both Gina and Tara. "I need to make a phone call."

I slipped into the back room again, shut the door behind me, and called my grandfather. "Grandpa?" I began. "Catherine Albright was here. I think she was trying to tell me where to look for answers to the problems in the hollow."

"Oh, yeah?" he said. "I'm surprised that she risked

her cover to come and speak to you."

"Her cover?"

"Of course," he said. "Daphne, I had more than one spy in place within the ranks of the cause."

"Wow." I tried to let that fact sink in. *Catherine was one of the good Witches, after all.* "Anyway…" I said, trying to steer the conversation back on track. "I now have reason to believe that we need to go investigate the old sawmill."

"Goderich Stein's mill? That place was condemned years ago."

"And if someone is trying to remodel themselves after Stein?" I asked. "You know, claim the powerbase of the original necromancer?"

"Shit," Grandpa swore. "That's a damn good point."

"We should go today," I began. "There's no point in waiting until the full moon to give them more pow—"

"Hang on." My grandfather cut me off. "I have another call."

Shocked at being put on hold, I pulled the phone from my ear and stared at it. "What the hell?"

"Daphne." He was back a minute later. "Ruby Prentiss has informed me that her sister Jade, and several other young Witches from the hollow are missing."

"*What*?"

"The magickal community is in a panic," he said. "Have your mother check on Harper. Right now. I'm worried they may come after her too."

"I will," I said. Yanking the door open, I worked my way through the ice cream customers and walked over to the much quieter pharmacy side. "Mom?" I motioned her over to me.

"Yes?" She asked walking to my side.

Call Harper. I mouthed the words. "Make sure she's where she's supposed to be."

My mother nodded and pulled her phone from her pocket. Quickly, she called the teen. "Honey?" she asked a moment later. "Is everything okay?"

"She's fine," she said to me.

I nodded and spoke in my phone. "Grandpa, she is fine."

"Good," he said. "That's one less Witch kid to worry about. You tell that girl *I* said to stay indoors with the Shaws. Make sure Kayla and Kenzie do as well. Now hand your phone to your mother, I want a word with Poppy."

I held the phone out. "Grandpa wants to speak to you, and now I need to speak to *her.*" I deliberately did not speak Harper's name out loud.

With a nod, my mother passed me her phone and walked around to the far aisle for more privacy.

I put my back against the wall, smiled and waved at a few regulars, and acted like nothing was amiss. "Hey, kiddo," I said casually into my mother's phone.

"Daphne?"

"Geoffrey says for you to stay indoors with your hosts. There seems to be something nasty going around out there. Do you understand?"

"Sure, I guess."

"He also wants you to keep my girls indoors as well. That's a direct order, my friend."

"Oh, damn. Okay, I get it." Harper blew out a breath. "Poppy told me about your grandpa's *status* when we left town a few weeks ago. But if he's giving me a direct order, shit must be hitting the fan."

"Yes, it is," I said pleasantly and lowered my voice. "Do me a favor and tell Mama Wolf to expect a call from me or my mom in a few minutes, with more information."

"Of course, I'll tell Phoebe right away. And I promise to help keep the girls safe," Harper said. "I won't let you down, Daphne."

"You keep yourself safe as well, girlfriend," I said. "Gotta go."

"Bye," Harper said and disconnected the call.

My mother told me that Grandpa was wanting to speak to me again, and we swapped phones.

"Go down to Bittersweet Books." My grandfather's voice was brusque. "Meet up with Ruby. She's closed the bookstore and is waiting for you. Share with her what you told me and follow up on that. Do the recon at the sawmill, let me know what you find."

"Of course I will," I said to him as Tara walked over to me. "I'll leave immediately."

"Do you need my help?" Tara asked softly.

"Daphne?" my grandfather said. "At this point we're

not sure if the kids went willingly or not. But bottom line? Do *not* go to that mill alone."

"I won't go alone," I agreed, meeting Tara's eyes. "I'll take back up."

Silently, Tara nodded in acknowledgement and went immediately to the back.

"Text me when you are on your way to the sawmill. I'm going to reach out to the sheriff. If you discover anything, let me know."

"Yup," I said. "You do the same."

I disconnected the call and saw that while I had been on the phone, Meg had come in for her afternoon shift.

Slapping a smile on my face, I slipped the phone in my pocket and walked over to the front counter. "Gina," I called, "Tara and I have to run out and pick up a few supplies in Rolla."

"No problem," Gina said. "Meg and I can handle it."

"Beau did offer to help out," I reminded her, reaching for my purse under the counter. "So if you need an extra set of hands, give him a call."

Tara and I let ourselves out the back. I shrugged on a denim jacket, locked the door behind us, and reset the alarm codes.

"What has happened?" Tara asked, slipping her oxblood vintage leather jacket over her bright orange shirt.

"Come on," I said. "We'll use the alley behind the stores. I don't want to draw extra attention to us by walking in the front entrance of her bookstore."

Together, we walked quickly toward Bittersweet Books, and I filled Tara in on the way.

CHAPTER TEN

I knocked on the delivery door of Bittersweet Books. A moment later I heard the click of the lock and the metal door was slowly pulled open. Only it wasn't Ruby waiting for us. Instead we discovered Pythagoras, Ruby's black cat, sitting inside, staring up at the both of us with unblinking golden eyes.

There'd have been a time when having a cat unlock and open a door would have shocked me; now I didn't even blink. "Hey, Pythagoras," I said and stepped inside.

Tara followed me and barely made it over the threshold before Pythagoras hissed a warning.

"This is Tara,' I said to the familiar. "She's an ally. I can vouch for her."

Pythagoras looked her up and down and seemed to nod in approval. He let out a long meow and took off for the front of the store.

I rushed to follow the familiar through the aisles of books and was concerned at how dark and quiet the bookstore was. On my previous visit there was warm lighting and Celtic music being piped through the shop. Now it was silent, except for the distinct sound of weeping.

"Ruby?" I called out.

Tara and I stepped out from the stacks and discovered that the red-haired Witch was sitting behind her carved wooden counter with her head in her hands and she was sobbing.

Tara made a sympathetic sound. "I'm going to make sure we're alone and the building is secure," she said.

I nodded in agreement and walked directly to the counter. Ruby did not hear me call her name for a second time. Gently, I rested my hand on her sweater covered shoulder. "Ruby?"

She flinched and then her green eyes focused on me. "Daphne? You got here quickly."

Pythagoras leapt to the counter, reached out a paw, and patted Ruby's face. The red-haired Witch leaned into her familiar, and Pythagoras rested his head against hers.

"The store is empty, but for us," Tara announced. "Front door is secure."

"You're not a mortal," Ruby said, studying Tara.

"No." Tara folded her arms. "I'm not."

"Your energy reads as Fae, but yet…" Ruby paused, wiping her eyes. "You're more."

"Hey." I crouched down next to her chair. "I'm sorry to hear about your sister."

"She's not the only teen missing," Ruby said, wiping her eyes.

"Who else is unaccounted for?" I asked.

"Jade's friends, Robyn and Tabatha. Also Blair Radcliff, her younger brother, Brayden, *and* Zara Hawthorn. And those are the ones we know about for sure." Ruby reached for a tissue on the counter, blew her nose, and tried to compose herself. "I can't help but feel responsible."

"How?" I asked.

"I should have insisted Jade live with me, after our father died. Instead I was relieved when she wanted to live with my father's mother, Agatha."

Tara moved closer to the counter. "Are you and your sister not close?"

"No, we're not. Anyone who has ever met Jade knows she's spoiled, selfish and mean." Ruby tucked her tissue in the pocket of her jeans. "After our mother left, my father doted on Jade. She was the apple of his eye, and he spoiled her rotten."

I could personally attest to Jade's bad behavior. I'd witnessed it more than once in my ice cream parlor. But I did not say so. Instead, I said, "my grandfather is reaching out to the sheriff, right now. But in the meantime, I have a lead we need to follow up on. As there is safety in numbers I'd like you to come with us."

"Aye," Tara said. "A Witch would be a handy thing to have along."

"What sort of lead?" Ruby wanted to know.

"Did the members of *the cause* ever speak about a power source?" I asked her.

"They did." She nodded. "But I was never able to find out what they were hinting around about."

"It's not a what," I said. "I think the power source is a place. The old sawmill owned by Goderich Stein."

"By the goddess." Ruby rose to her feet. "That makes a horrible kind of sense." Ruby reached under the counter and pulled out a black backpack. "I put together an emergency magickal supply bag a couple of weeks ago. We can take it with us."

"Smart," I said approvingly. "I'll go get my car and come pick you and Tara up and we'll leave immediately"

"No." Ruby slung the bag over her shoulder. "We can take my truck."

***

Once upon a time the land owned by Goderich Stein was stripped of most of its timber and wildlife. But after one hundred and sixty years, nature had reclaimed the land. We turned off the highway and down a rutted gravel road that had seen much better days. Slowly we traveled, trying to keep any noise or dust down that might alert someone to our approach.

Tara leaned forward and pointed. "There. Park the truck over in that clearing. We should go on foot from here."

Ruby nodded and eased the pickup off the gravel road. We exited the truck, Ruby grabbed her pack from the truck bed, and I rechecked my holster, gun, and spare magazines.

Ruby checked her phone. "I still have coverage out here. Do you?"

I checked. "I have two bars. We should switch our phones over to silent though."

"I have something for the both of you," Tara said.

I swung my gaze to Tara and saw she was holding out bracelets. They appeared to be made of some sort of clear resin and held within the cuff was a four-leaf clover.

"These will bring you luck," she announced, and in a flash the bracelets had gone from her hand onto mine and Ruby's left wrists.

"*Go raibh maith agat,* Tara," I said.

"It's beautiful, and much appreciated," Ruby added.

Tara grinned, and in the blink of an eye she stood holding one of the long, obsidian-bladed spears of the Fae. "The sawmill is this way." Tara inclined her head. "I will take point."

I didn't bother asking how she knew. But Tara was correct. I made an 'after you' gesture to Ruby, and we fell in step behind Tara in the autumn woods. The later afternoon light slanted beautifully through the trees. We walked as quietly as we could through the leaves, while more drifted down.

Tara began to follow a rocky old creek bed. At one

time I imagined the creek had more likely been a stream that had helped power the mill. Now however, the creek was down to a slow trickle of water.

"Lucky for us both that we wore sneakers and jeans today," Ruby whispered as we traveled further upstream.

"I don't think it was random luck," I said softly. "I'm betting it was Tara's influence."

Ruby glanced meaningfully ahead at Tara and then down at her bracelet. "Oh...I see," she said slowly.

"Do you?" I asked.

Ruby nodded and pulled a hair tie from her pocket. "Daphne, do you shoot right-handed? I wanted to ask, so I knew what side of yours to stay on."

"Yes, I do," I said. "So if it all goes to shit out there, stay on my left,"

She nodded and secured her hair back from her face. "Personally, I can cast with *either* hand."

I grinned. "I will remember that and do my best to stay out of your line of fire as well."

Tara climbed up the hill from where we'd been walking along the creek and stopped. "We are here." She knelt, and Ruby and I followed suit.

About fifty yards ahead of us Goderich Stein's sawmill stood. At one time the sawmill would have been at least two stories tall. Now, a section of the roof had caved in and only about half of the faded gray building was still covered.

The side of the building we faced had the ruins of a

water wheel. One lone window remained high on the second floor but there was no roof above it. That direction would probably be the safest to approach. Once I got there I could ease around the side of the building and see what, if anything, was inside.

I judged the position of the sun in the sky. We had an hour, maybe a tad longer before sunset, but I wasn't going to stay in the cover of the thicker woods and wait until darkness fell. I wanted to check out the mill right now.

I pulled my gun from its holster. "Ready, ladies?"

"Wait," Ruby said, and cast her hands out. A misty fog coalesced and began to blanket the area between the woods and the mill.

"Nice," I said. I'd seen a mist like this once before, but this time it was to our benefit and for our cover. I could only be grateful.

"This is wonderful, Ruby." Tara dropped her hand on Ruby's shoulder. "Let me help." No sooner had Tara's words been spoken when the mist morphed into a thicker fog.

While Tara and Ruby's magick swirled around the mill, a hush fell over the woods.

A few moments later they were finished, and Ruby brushed off her hands. "Do not try and open any windows or doors," she said. "If anyone is inside, they will have the building warded. If anything crosses the threshold, window sashes, or door, they will know."

"Okay," I said, and moved out.

Staying as low as possible, I approached the old mill. Tara and Ruby were right behind me. No sooner had I eased alongside of the building, and the sphalerite pendant began to vibrate against my skin. It heated up, warning me that I was close to a powerful source of magick.

I judged the right side of the building to be easier and quieter to navigate and indicated which way I would be going with a tilt of my head.

Carefully, I picked my way along the side of the old mill. My sneakers were noiseless, and Ruby stayed behind me and to my left. I eased up to one of the broken windows and slowly leaned over far enough to see inside.

The missing teens lay on the floor, and none of them were moving. Illuminated by candlelight, they were bound and gagged and arranged in a circle, with the feet of one teen touching the head of the next. I counted eight of them. Six girls and two boys. I spotted Jade Prentiss' pale blonde hair, and to my surprise I also saw Cassandra Hedge. Her wild red curls were hard to miss.

So much for the Hedge kids leaving town, I thought. Easing away from the window, I glanced back at Ruby. Using my left hand, I held up three fingers, and then five.

Ruby's eyebrows rose almost to her hairline.

Tara slipped forward to see. Being sure not to touch the building itself, she scanned the room, and I watched her eyes slide over the dimly lit interior. With a nod, she eased back. Ruby looked inside as well, and beside a hitch in her breathing when she spotted her sister, she remained silent.

She moved away and I steeled myself, checking again to see whether or not the teens were still breathing. This time I took in the elaborate ritual circle that had been drawn on the floor. The candles weren't only for light, they'd been strategically placed as well. The kids seemed to be alone. Nothing else was moving around inside of the building as far as I could tell.

But I didn't like it. It was too easy. It had to be a trap.

Focusing on the closest teen, I was relieved to see her ribs rise and fall and let out my own breath that I had been holding.

I wanted to go rushing in and grab those kids. But there were only three of us. It would take a couple of trips each to get everyone out. Besides, this wasn't an action movie. It was hard to say what sort of magick or foe we would encounter when we went inside. And the sawmill was so still and quiet that it made my neck prickle.

I eased away and went back the way I came. Despite the cover of the swirling fog, I remained close to the side of the building and kept my head down. Tara and Ruby were right behind me, and we all hurried back into the cover of the woods once again.

I pointed down to the creek bed and none of us spoke until we were farther away from the sawmill and down along side the creek. Here in the ravine, the air was clear, and I could see my companions clearly.

Ruby spoke first. "They seemed to all be breathing."

"I didn't see anyone else inside of the mill," I said. "Did either of you *sense* anything or anyone?"

"No," Tara said. "I did not see anyone other than the children, but my instincts tell me someone else *is* there."

"Agreed," Ruby said. "Also, that mill was warded out the ass. As it stands now, trying to cross the threshold would be suicide."

"My gut is warning me that this is a trap. The way the kids were arranged, it's almost like a dare to come and get them. No way is it going to be as simple as slipping in and getting everyone out." I pulled my phone out, saw I had service and sent off a text to my grandfather and to Lucas.

At sawmill, I texted. *No longer recon. This is a rescue. Eight teens are inside bound and gagged.*

It seemed like forever until the 'delivered' message popped up on my cell.

Ruby shrugged her pack from her shoulders. "Tell him the building is heavily warded."

I sent that text next and saw three dots on my phone almost immediately. Grandpa was messaging back.

"He's on the way," I said, reading his responding text to Tara and Ruby. "Fifteen minutes out. He's bringing back up."

Ruby sat on the ground in the fallen leaves beside

the edges of the creek. "Good, that gives me time to get to work. Tell him I will lower the wards before he gets here."

Dutifully, I texted that information to him. I got a thumbs up emoji in reply and I tucked my phone away. Grandpa would know where we were. A perk of being a Hunter was that he'd be able to track me, a Fae, and a Witch quite easily.

Tara knelt down beside Ruby. "May I help you with the spell?"

"Yes, I'd appreciate that, Tara." Ruby pulled a small cauldron from her pack. "Daphne, if you joined us too, we'd have a better chance at succeeding. The magick of three and all that."

With a nod, I sat beside her. "I can try. Tell me what you want me to do."

Ruby added some of the water from the creek to her tiny cauldron. A water smoothed pebble was next, along with a small red feather. With a snap of her fingers a tiny ball of fire danced above the cauldron.

"Elements four now hear my call; bring balance and power to one and all," Ruby chanted.

I settled in cross-legged and tried to clear my mind. Energy was energy, and the very least I could do was lend some of that to her spell.

Ruby had us repeat a spell verse with her three times. I carefully spoke along with her and Tara. Sitting in a loose triangle, I held hands with them and was surprised when sweat began to roll down my back. A tingle began at my tailbone, and then, a rush slammed up my spine.

For the first time, I felt power rise up from within me.

Red energy flowed from Ruby, green shimmered from Tara, and a white light pulsed irregularly from me. Together they combined into one, and as twilight fell, that iridescent energy spun in a circle between us. Slowly it rose higher, until it shot through the misty air and off in the direction of the sawmill.

I felt it in my chest the moment the wards were broken. Although there was no sound, I felt it like a deep bass concussion from a firework.

Ruby nodded and released our hands. "That'll do."

"Well, fuck me!" I whispered. "Ruby, did I just do magick?"

"You did." Ruby grinned at me, and with a snap of her fingers, the tiny fire was extinguished. "The wards are down."

"But," I said, "that's not possible."

"There are more things in heaven and earth, Horatio," Ruby quoted.

"But…" I sputtered, "I'm not a Witch."

"I think your magick runs along the lines of battle magick," Tara agreed, squeezing my hand. "With your grandsire being the Hunter and your mother a Witch, your magick only shows itself in times of serious conflict, or life and death situations."

My thoughts immediately went to the night of the

ridge. My shot at Judith Hedge had been deflected, but when I'd fired on Ashton it hadn't.

So what had been the difference? I wondered. I shut my eyes and allowed myself to remember those last few moments. While Judith had thrown her magick in my general direction, Ashton *had* intended to kill me. He'd thrown his witch fire directly at me, and I had fully expected to die. Could that had been the impetus required to force my magick out? I had acted in self defense and my shot had miraculously gotten through his shield.

"I have a question," I said to Ruby. "Would this battle magick be sporadic at first?"

"Absolutely," Ruby agreed.

I sat on the ground and my mind spun with the possibilities...I thought about everything that had happened over the past few months. Beginning with the zombie break in that I managed to thwart. Granted, I'd been about to go for the head shot when someone else had beaten me to it. But I had successfully defended myself and my home.

I'd knocked Cassandra Hedge's hand down when she'd been about to throw magick in the ice cream parlor, and yes, I'd received a burn, but in the grand scheme of things I had avoided a debilitating injury. Later that very night the Hedges attacked, and my house on Hemlock Lane had gone up in flames. I had run through that green witch fire to try and find my girls and had escaped with nothing other than a few blisters on my back, and some singed and smoky clothes.

I considered the charm I'd spontaneously spoken when Finnlagh had broken the curse that had been cast on the girls, the way I'd discovered Ashton's dark ritual room...Maybe the door hadn't swung open on its own after all. Slowly my magick had been getting stronger. Which would explain how I'd been able to disarm Seamus, even while I was injured, when I'd been recovering in the Fae realm.

I shook my head and came back to the present.

Efficiently, Ruby had tucked all of her magickal supplies away. "Put it all together, did you?"

I rose shakily to my feet. "You say that like you've known all along."

She stood as well. "Your grandfather suspected as much after the battle on Wolfsbane Ridge. He told me so himself."

"Would have been nice if he'd have told me," I groused.

Ruby shook her head. "That's not how magick works, Daphne. You can not simply tell someone, 'by the way, you have battle magick.'"

I opened my mouth to argue, reconsidered, and shut it. "Well, you've got me there."

Tara patted my shoulder. "Some things must be discovered at their own time and in their own way."

I nodded, took one step, felt suddenly lightheaded, and staggered.

Tara grabbed my arm before I could fall. "All magick has a price, my friend."

"Do you know how to ground and center?" Ruby bit back a smile.

"Yeah." I half-laughed. "I do. My mother taught me when I was a kid."

"Then do so," Ruby suggested briskly.

Taking advantage of two of the natural elements I stood with one foot at the edge of the creek water and the other on the rocky bed. I took in a few deep breaths and blew them out slowly. A few minutes later I felt like myself again.

"You did well," Tara said. Her head whipped around. "The Hunter approaches," she whispered.

In the gathering darkness three figures emerged. Two of them I recognized immediately. The first was my grandfather, toting his crossbow and a large pack on his back. Lucas Archer, the sheriff, was the second, and the third was a tall, broad bull of a man.

His hair was fair, cut military short, and he was beyond ripped. He wore fatigues, a tactical vest, and his arms were left bare. He moved soundlessly along side my grandfather and Lucas, and as he grew closer there was something about him that was vaguely familiar...

Ruby stepped forward. "The barrier is down."

My grandfather nodded. "Good."

"Who's your friend, Grandpa?" I asked.

Grandpa tilted his head toward the man. "This here's Val, and I trust him. Now let's get down to business."

"Okay." I said. "There are eight teens inside the sawmill. First floor. They appear to be breathing but are bound and gagged with what looks like fabric strips. The kids are arranged head to foot inside of a ritual circle that is drawn on the floor."

"Was there magick working when you saw them?"

Ruby spoke up. "Yes. There are candles arranged at the cardinal points. They were lit at least when we saw them."

Lucas joined in the conversation. "Maybe the kids were drugged."

Tara spoke up. "I can phase in and out of the building and take out the children one by one."

"Good." My grandfather nodded. "You get the kids to Ruby, Daphne, and Lucas. They can wait at the edge of the woods. Ruby you work any magickal first aid that's required. Daphne and Lucas? I want you guarding our flank and protecting the kids."

I didn't bother to argue. There was too much at stake and too many captives inside the mill.

The sharp crack of a stick punctuated the night. From farther down the creek bed the sound of voices came. Being down in the creek ravine, we were far too exposed and not in a good defensible position at all.

"Everyone join hands!" Ruby hissed. "I can cloak us!"

I jumped to do her bidding. Grabbing Tara's hand in my left and Grandpa's in my right, I watched as Ruby took my grandfather's other hand. Quickly, Tara took

Lucas' hand, Lucas clasped Val's, and Ruby and Val finally closed up the circle by joining hands.

Ruby jolted hard when Val's large hand engulfed hers. I watched her head fall back, and an instant later a bubble appeared to surround us. Everything was now muffled. Almost as if we were underwater.

I watched, amazed, as a group of hooded figures walked past on the rise above us. I couldn't see their faces, but they moved quickly along the ground and through the leaves on their way to the mill.

"God damn it," my grandfather grumbled. "That's ten more Witches to contend with."

As they traveled by us, completely oblivious, I risked a glance over at Ruby.

Her back was arched, and her head thrown back. Whatever magick she had conjured had her stretched back almost defying gravity. Val, standing directly across the circle from me, was watching her too. Once the group of Witches had safely passed us, Val yanked his hand free from Ruby's.

His action broke the spell. Ruby's eyes rolled back in her head and she collapsed. Grandpa tried to catch her, but Val was there. He caught her and lay Ruby gently on the ground.

The rest of us dropped hands and moved forward to help Ruby.

Val knelt down beside Ruby. It was then that I noticed a massive sword in a sheath across his back. "If you will allow me?" he said.

I looked to my grandfather. He nodded. "Val knows what he's doing. Watch."

Val ignored the accolade from my grandfather. Muttering something under his breath, he taped with one thick finger on Ruby's breastbone.

With a harshly sucked in breath, Ruby sat straight up. "Damn it!" she hissed, and took a swipe at Val.

"You are welcome." He nodded to Ruby. When Ruby scrambled away from him, the newcomer slowly stood.

It was a long way to travel. I estimated the man to be at least six foot five.

"I go now," Val said.

"Move into position. I'll be right behind you," my grandfather said. The tall fair man nodded once and took off at a fast clip up the creek bank. He disappeared into the darkness a second later.

My grandfather met my eyes. "If any of those cloaked Witches shows hostile intent, take them out."

I nodded. "I understand."

Beside me, Lucas shifted.

"They won't give it a moment's thought, Sheriff," my grandfather said. "They *will* kill you if given a chance. You've already seen what they are capable of."

"I know," Lucas said. "I've seen enough magickal carnage to last a lifetime."

Together the five of us walked to the edge of the woods. Ruby's magickal fog was still holding. Tara snapped a salute to my grandfather, which made him grin, and she disappeared a second later.

"Give me five seconds, then drop the fog," my grandfather said to Ruby.

"I will." Ruby nodded.

Grandpa pulled a cigar out of his shirt pocket, clamped it between his teeth, and gave me a wink. "Time to go to work." He took off at a run toward the mill.

Beside me, Ruby counted under her breath, and suddenly the fog was gone as if it had never been.

A heartbeat later and chaos broke out. There was an explosion of light and screams, and gunfire sounded from inside the mill. Tara shimmered into view holding a young boy in her arms. I reached out immediately to take him from her and moved back a few yards into the cover of the trees. Ruby was right behind me, with a teen slung over her shoulder in a fireman's carry.

Lucas stood with his gun out, watched over us, and protected the area.

I rushed back to the edge of the woods and Tara was there again. I recognized Zara Hawthorn as I took her under the arms and drug her away from the clearing. I laid the teen down beside the first boy and ran back for the next.

Ruby went past me dragging her sister, much as I had done the last teen. Jade's feet bounced along the ground. The girl was still unconscious.

For the next few minutes Ruby and I raced back and forth, taking the kids from Tara as quickly as we could.

Ruby went to grab an unconscious Sage Hedge, but he was too tall for her and she staggered. So, Lucas reached out and slung the boy over his shoulder.

Out of my peripheral I saw movement. Two cloaked figures were flying right at us. They were screaming curses as they approached. The faces of the Witches were hideous, both white and misshapen. There wasn't time. I drew my gun and fired on the closest one.

The Witch went down, and the second abruptly shifted her direction and was now moving toward where the children all lay. I spun, trying to track the movement, while Lucas let the teenage boy roll off his shoulder. The sheriff aimed and fired on our attacker in one smooth motion.

The second Witch was down. Ruby grabbed Sage's feet and tried to drag him to safety. Lucas grabbed Sage's wrist with his free hand to help.

Tara reappeared. "This is the last one!" She carried the teenager over to the others and set her down. Ruby grabbed a fallen branch and began to draw a large circle around Tara and all of the children. "Quick!" She gestured to us. "Get inside the circle!" I ran through the opening and Lucas was right behind me.

Ruby completed the circle and stamped her foot on the ground. At once, bright white light beamed up through the leaves and surrounded us all.

While Lucas stood guard, Tara produced a long obsidian blade and began to cut through the gags and binds from the children's hands. Ruby followed along behind her, working magick on each rescued teen. Slowly, one by one, they began to awaken.

I went to stand guard with Lucas. There was no more gunfire—that had been brief—but there was a fire. A natural fire. Its orange and red flames were glowing brighter. I wondered about that for a moment, but then my grandfather came around to the front of the mill and I saw that he was using a flame thrower.

He was making sure the sawmill would be completely destroyed. From out of the flames, Val appeared. He had a sword in one hand and a severed head in the other. He held the head by the hair, which was long and red.

I gasped. "Is that?"

"Artemis Bradbury," Lucas said.

Behind me one of the teens squealed. I turned to find Zara with her eyes far too large in her face.

"Go help Ruby with the kids," Lucas said to me. "It's over now. Geoffrey's got it."

I stayed long enough to watch as Val tossed the head back into the burning building, and my grandfather moved in spraying the area with more cleansing flames.

"God, I love my work!" My grandfather's voice carried gleefully over to us.

"There's a few more bodies over here," Lucas called over to Val.

The big man nodded and moved to gather up the bodies of the attacking Witches. He grabbed one body by the arm, drug it halfway across the clearing, and flung it onto the fire.

My stomach lurched hard. I didn't wait to see how he handled the second body. Turning away, I holstered my gun and went to go and kneel beside Zara, who had begun to sob. "Hey, kiddo." I slipped my arm around her shoulders. "I've got you."

"That crazy bitch was going to kill us!" Zara said, turning her face into my shoulder.

The teens were all sitting upright now. Sage and Cassandra Hedge were huddled together, and Blair and her younger brother Brayden held each other tightly. Ruby was holding onto Jade's hand, and Jade's pals Robyn and Tabatha leaned together. Both girls were also crying loudly.

"I'm sorry," Jade said to her friends. She reached over to touch the foot of Cassandra Hedge. "I swear to you, I didn't know who she really was, or what Artemis was planning. I *swear* I didn't!"

"Tell me about those plans," I said.

"Artemis told me that she was the descendant of old Goderich Stein," Jade explained.

Blair piped up. "Ms. Bradbury kept going on and on about how she was meant to fulfill his work."

Cassandra Hedge shuddered. "I never realized she was talking about *necromancy*."

I shifted my focus back to Jade. "Are you saying that Artemis claimed that her ancestor was Goderich Stein?"

Sage rose to his feet. "She did. She's been telling us since the beginning of the school year that she was building a new coven of young Witches, and that we would be more powerful, even stronger than our parents…"

"Cassandra and Sage?" I addressed the siblings. "I thought you moved to a new town after your father died?"

"We decided to come back." Cassandra stood with her brother. "Our friends are here. Hemlock Hollow is our home. We'd been staying with Ms. Bradbury, at her place."

"At first, I thought we'd be okay," Sage said. "But things started to get sort of weird."

"How do you mean?" Ruby asked.

"She'd been calling us out of class to her office. We'd all go in for these special group counseling sessions." Blair volunteered the information.

Ruby frowned at the information. "At your school?"

Zara leaned against me. "I only went to one, and I turned her down. Still, she came after me."

"I'm sorry, Zara," Blair said. "I am sorry for getting you involved in this."

Zara glared at the goth girl. "You stay the hell away from me! From now on."

Blair ducked her head. "Okay."

Ruby glared at her sister. "Jade, how could you be so foolish! Why would you ever buy into that? You know what happens to those who work with dark magick."

Jade cringed. "Ms. Bradbury made it all sound so good," she said. "She showed us some of Stein's grimoires. And Dad…Well, *he* said that with the full moon falling on Samhain this year it was the perfect time for us all to ascend to a new level of power."

"Our *father* was in on these counselling sessions?" Ruby sounded horrified.

"Yes," the kids said together.

Lucas had been listening, even as he stood watch. Now he spoke. "Jesus, to use the children that way. The principal and the school counselor indoctrinating them into radical magickal beliefs while they were at school…"

"Daphne," Jade drew my attention back to her. "Artemis especially hated you and Ashton Lowell. She told us she was planning on removing him from *the cause*. She was planning on killing him too."

"Yeah," Blair added. "Something about him trying to usurp her rightful place as leader of the glorious revolution?"

"What's usurp mean?" Brayden wanted to know.

"It means, 'take over'," Jade said. "But yeah, she kept going on and on about how Ashton Lowell came into her town and tried to take over the dark coven that *her* family had built over generations…" The girl focused on me again. "But you beat her to it. Did you shoot him even after he struck you with witch fire?"

"In the end, Daphne's bullet was faster than his spell." This came from my grandfather. As one, all the teenagers gasped when they saw him.

The group reaction made my grandfather grin like a

lunatic, even with his cigar still clamped between his teeth.

"Oh. My. Gods," one of the kids squealed. "He's totally, like, the Hunter."

"I wish I had my cell phone," someone said, and there was a murmur of agreement.

I tried not to roll my eyes, but Geoffrey Sullivan did cut a larger than life figure. Between the cross bow, the flame thrower, and the military grade camo...He was impressive. In the end, my grandfather did not confirm or deny his identity. Instead he merely suggested that we get the kids home to their families.

Lucas, Ruby, Tara, and I all helped the kids back to Ruby's truck. It took a while. There's nothing like herding eight frightened and traumatized teens through the dark woods at night.

I fell into step with Lucas and brought up the rear. "Okay," I said quietly. "Who the hell is the *Terminator* guy with my grandfather?"

Lucas smiled. "Val does kinda have a *Terminator* vibe. Doesn't he?"

"Grandpa said he was a friend."

"When I was introduced to him, Val merely said he had come to help to fulfil a family debt." Lucas shrugged. "You may have noticed the guy is not big on conversation."

Ahead of me one of the kids stumbled, and I rushed to help them.

Eventually, we made it back to the truck. Tara sat

with Ruby in the cab, and Lucas and I piled in the truck bed with all eight kids. No, it wasn't legal, but it got the job done.

Zara stuck to me like glue. Not that I blamed her. She was still new to the hollow, and she didn't know many of the other kids. After this she wasn't likely to try and make friends with the other…survivors. I made a mental note to introduce her to Harper, Meg, and the Shaw girls.

"It sure is lucky, that your sister drives a pickup," Robyn said to Jade.

"We were all pretty freaking lucky to be alive, if you ask me," Jade replied.

I glanced over at Tara where she sat in the cab. As if she knew I was looking at her, she smiled at me through the back window and tipped me a wink.

I called my parents and the Shaws to let them know that everyone was safe, and that we were all headed back to town. While I did that, Lucas used his cell phone and called dispatch. Carmella promised to notify all the families of the missing children.

"There's no point in calling our mom," Cassandra said. "She abandoned us and left us to fend for ourselves."

"What?" Lucas said.

"After we moved away from the hollow, she rented a cheap apartment in Rolla, told us we were old enough to take care of ourselves, and took off."

"Do you know where she went?" I asked.

"Dunno." Sage shrugged. "But she took her passport."

"We'll find you someplace safe to stay while we sort this out," Lucas said to the Hedge siblings. "The rest of you?" Lucas pitched his voice to be heard. "Your families will meet you at the sheriff's station."

His announcement was met with varying degrees of enthusiasm.

"Tell you what," I said to the teens. "After you are reunited with your families, if you'd like, come over to the ice cream parlor. Free cones all around."

That offer was met with *much* more excitement.

CHAPTER ELEVEN

By the time we returned to town the teens' families had gathered, and the relief of the kids being safe was overwhelming for so many of the families. I reopened the shop since Gina and Meg had already closed up and gone home for the night, and Tara was excited to help.

Ruby and Jade also surprised me by pitching in. Ruby manned the cash register and Jade actually tossed on an apron, grabbed a dish tub, and began to bus tables.

"You don't have to," I began.

"It's cool." Jade tossed her blonde hair. "The ice cream parlor is rocking, and besides, it's the least I can do."

"Did you do a spell on your sister to get her compliance?" I asked Ruby.

"No." Ruby snorted out a laugh. "That's a big old dose of guilt you see there. Jade has learned a valuable lesson. Now it'll be up to me to make sure it sticks."

I gave her an elbow nudge. "Will she come live with

you now?"

"Yeah," Ruby nodded. "I think that would be for the best. I may need some parenting advice."

"Boundaries and rules," I said. "Set 'em and stick to them."

Lucas brought the Hedge kids over to the parlor himself, and he was accompanied by Catherine Albright. He informed me that Cassandra and Sage would be staying with her until he could locate their next of kin.

I saw Catherine watching me, and I inclined my head. The two of us would have to talk about what had happened, her working with my grandfather, and of course what had gone wrong with Jessamine. But that conversation was for later. The Hedge kids were quiet and sat at a table with the mayor. I could see her speaking with them. Despite their horrible parents, I hoped the kids would turn their lives around.

My parents showed up with Harper, Kenzie, and Kayla, and the girls were in heaven sitting at the counter in the midst of all the action. Harper took her cone and went over to speak to Zara and her family. Zara was still a tad wide-eyed even as she sat with her dad's arm around her shoulders. But she did chat with Harper, and whatever my favorite blue-haired Witch had said to the girl made her smile.

My parents were both speaking with the mayor, and I hoped my mother would be able to patch up her friendship with Catherine.

Jade stopped at the counter with a dish tub full. "Daphne, I'll load these up, if you can show me how to run that big dishwasher in the back."

"I can teach you!" Tara happily volunteered.

"Okay." Jade didn't smile but held eye contact with me. "I appreciate you letting me help. I needed to do... something."

I nodded. "Volunteering and helping others is a good start."

"Yeah," Jade said, and then was distracted when Harper took her seat at the front counter. "Harper?" she said as soon as the girl sat down next to Kayla.

"Jade." Harper inclined her head. She wasn't frowning, but she wasn't smiling either.

"I wanted to say I'm sorry. The things that have happened...Well, it has made me think about stuff." Jade paused. "Anyway, I wanted to apologize for how I acted and how I've treated you."

"Sounds like you've had a rough couple of days," Harper said.

"Yeah," Jade agreed. "It's making me reevaluate a few things."

Harper tucked a strand of her blue hair behind her ear. "That's good."

With a nod, Jade carried the dish tub around to where Tara was waiting.

Ruby shook her head once her sister went in the back. "Wow, she just *apologized* on her own."

Harper leaned forward. "Nothing like being rescued

from the clutches of evil practitioners and a whacked-out necromancer to change your perspective."

I smirked. "Truer words were never spoken."

"So tell me." Harper's eyes danced. "Was Geoffrey *really* using a flame thrower out there tonight?"

"He was," I said.

"That is so hard core," Harper decided.

And so, Hemlock Hollow returned to whatever passed for normal.

The cause was no more. Now that the dust had settled, I found out from Catherine that many local Witching families had tried to stay out of the insanity of the radical movement. It seemed, however, that no one save Artemis, Jasper Prentiss the principal, and the teens we'd rescued from the sawmill had been aware of Artemis' true plans: to wipe out the old covens and create a new one with her hand picked acolytes.

At sunrise on October thirty-first, my mother, Ruby, Harper, Catherine Albright, and a handful of other good Witches discreetly gathered at the ruins of the old mill. The building had been reduced to ash and keeping with the tradition began by the original Witches of the hollow, they worked a cleansing spell together to heal the land from the evil that Artemis had tried to reanimate there.

According to my sources, the field is now covered in not only wild blooming hemlock, but also bright red poppies. My mother added her own spin on the ritual and as the mayor put it: Poppy Sullivan-Grant's flair for good magick and herbalism had finally been given the credit it so richly deserved.

At sunset on Halloween night the town square was packed. The energy was festive and fun, and thousands of jack-o'-lanterns were lit. The annual trick-or-treating had begun, and my girls were out hitting all the shops and homes along the square with their grandparents.

Kayla had decided to go as a Glinda—thanks to a donation of an old dress from Alison. My mother had re-worked the pink homecoming dress for Kayla, and they'd added a sparkly crown and wand. Kenzie had decided to be a Fae soldier. Grandpa Geoffrey had managed to find some small army surplus items, and my mother had shortened and taken everything in. Kenzie had added wings and was defying convention by also toting a huge plastic sword.

I wore my favorite Halloween sweatshirt, jeans, and my waist holster. I figured it would be a long time before I felt comfortable enough to go unarmed. I was happy to stay in the parlor and oversee the passing out of sample cups of ice cream to the trick-or-treaters and their parents.

This year, in addition to Meg and Gina, we also had Tara working with us. And Tara was having a wonderful time celebrating her first Halloween in the mortal realm. She especially loved seeing all the kids in their costumes.

As always, we had a good crowd in the parlor. My regulars were lined up at the counter, and the mortal high school students had claimed the tables by the front window. This year Harper had joined them. She and Cal sat together and were holding hands. I slid a pumpkin spice milkshake down the counter to Mr. Watson, and even though he was eighty years old, he snagged it easily.

"Thanks, Daphne." He smiled.

The doorframe was suddenly filled. The man known to me as Val walked into the parlor and all the chattering voices fell silent for a few seconds. He spared a single glance at the patrons and immediately they all looked away and resumed talking.

I smiled as Val claimed the last open seat at the front counter. "Hi Val, what'll ya have?"

"Geoffrey tells me to try the Haunted Pumpkin Walk special sundae."

"Can't go wrong," I agreed and while I rang him up, Tara built the sundae. "Decided to stay in town to enjoy Halloween, eh?"

"Yes." He nodded. "I shall be staying indefinitely. There are a few more things I still must tend to."

"Oh?" I handed him his change and noticed for the first time that his eyes were a searing green. In fact, they were very much like Ashton's. My stomach clenched, and it was everything I had *not* to reach for my gun.

"Ah, so you have seen the resemblance," Val said.

"Who are you, really?" I asked, keeping my voice even.

"My name is Valentin Lowell. Ashton was my younger brother."

I took that in. "Why are you here in the hollow?"

"Your grandfather notified the family at my brother's passing. After he spoke to my parents, he asked me to come. My family and I felt, all things considered, the least we could do was to send me over to assist in cleaning up my brother's mess."

"Did you know that Ashton had turned?" I didn't add the words: *to evil*. There were too many people close by.

"My family suspected. The truth is he lost his way a long time ago, and then we lost him."

Tara passed me the sundae and I placed it in front of the man.

Before I could decide what to ask him next, my grandfather surprised me by waltzing into the ice cream parlor. "Happy Halloween!" he said loudly.

It took him a while to make his way to the counter. All the regulars wanted a chat with Geoffrey Sullivan. He came to town so rarely, and by the time he sat next to Val at the counter, the man had plowed his way through half the sundae.

"So." My grandfather slid on a newly vacant seat. "Did Val here tell you he's bought the old stone house on Hemlock Lane?"

"No," I said coolly. "He hadn't."

"Hello, Geoffrey," Tara said. "Can I get you anything?"

"I'll take a coffee, black."

I leaned on the counter. "And why would he purchase Ashton's house?"

"Well technically it was willed to his family," my grandpa said. "Val here—"

"Perhaps, Geoffrey," Val cut him off, "you will allow me to explain."

"Go ahead." Grandpa shrugged.

"I felt it best to take care of the property my brother had purchased," Val said. "To do whatever clean up or repairs are required. It will also allow me a place to live and to do my work."

"Besides," my grandfather said, "I asked Val to stay in the hollow for a while. I'm gonna need an extra set of hands until I can find and properly train my replacement."

I wasn't happy to hear there would be yet another Lowell in the hollow, but I tried to maintain a neutral expression.

"Despite what you may think," Val said to me, "the Lowell family does have honor. It is now my task to restore the family name and reputation."

"I see," was about the best thing I could think to say.

Mercifully, a line had formed at the register and I dove back in to help Tara fill our orders.

Eventually Grandpa and Val left, and I put my focus on enjoying the rest of my evening. It was time to put the Lowell family and the events of the past few months behind me and enjoy my life and my girls.

Kenzie and Kayla burst in. "Mom!" they shouted.

I went to them and made the appropriate oohing and aahing over all of their candy, as was expected.

"Ruby gave us books!" Kayla said.

"Did she?" I smiled. "That was nice."

"And everyone loved my warrior Fae costume!" Kenzie said proudly.

"Of course they did," I said.

"Do you think Glynis would like it?" Kenzie asked.

I ran a hand over Kenzie's hair. "I'm sure she'd be thrilled with it."

"When are her and Finnlagh coming back?" Kayla asked.

"I'm not sure," I said, surprised at how her question had made my heart ache. The truth was, I had been missing Finnlagh like crazy over the past few days. "There were some things they had to take care of at home."

"Was it important?" Kayla wanted to know. "Like royal stuff?"

"Yes," I said, keeping it simple. "But I'm sure they'll be here with us again as soon as they can."

***

November arrived and the weather became much colder. Tourism slowed down, which allowed me extra time for shopping for the girls and myself, as well as purchasing furnishings and housewares for our cabin on

Nightshade Court.

We moved into our new home the week before Thanksgiving, with plenty of help from my family, the Shaws, Tara, and even Ruby. I was glad for the help because I was exhausted. At first, I thought that all the inter realm travel and battles with evil Witches had finally caught up with me...Until I discovered that life had thrown me a hell of a curve ball.

Once I got over the shock of it, I told myself to cowboy up and to deal. I would figure out something. I always did. We celebrated our first Thanksgiving in the cabin with my family, and Ruby and Jade joined us as well.

It was Ruby who had noticed the change in me first, but by the grace of the gods my parents did not. The first chance we had to be alone, I told Ruby what was up, and she was supportive. She was turning out to be a true friend, and I was going to need all the friends I could get.

On Mondays in the off season, I closed the ice cream parlor. So, the first Monday in December found me sitting on my new couch, wearing a big slouchy sweater, thick socks, comfortable leggings, and enjoying a fire in the woodstove. I had set up our artificial tree earlier and plugged in the lights. Our totes of decorations that had been stored in the detached garage from our old house had been moved to the basement of the cabin. I had hauled all of them upstairs, so the girls could go crazy decorating the tree when they got home.

With the upcoming Yule season in mind, my laptop was out, and I was starting my online shopping for the holidays. I had beef stew in the crockpot. Winter, the husky was sprawled over my feet and the holidays were fast approaching. Contentedly, I glanced up to admire the bright multi-colored lights on the tree and caught the movement outside.

It was snowing. "Ha!" I set the laptop aside and went to the glass sliding door to the deck. "Look at that, Winter."

The dog whined to go out, so I opened the door for him. He was off like a shot, prancing through the snowflakes and snapping at them as they fell from the sky. I leaned against the open door and laughed at his antics. I doubted we'd get more than an inch at most, but it sure was pretty. The girls would go crazy when they got home in a little while.

I had only begun allowing them to walk from the security gate and down the driveway by themselves. The girls felt very grown-up, but the truth of the matter was, I had Lycans patrolling the woods and watching out for the girls as they walked home 'alone' down the driveway. As an ally to the pack, I was within my rights to request it, and so I did. In exchange, I allowed them to run my property on the full moons. Of course that drove Winter crazy. He was always wanting to go out and run with the Lycans...

My thoughts skidded to a halt. Across the yard I

thought I saw a person standing at the edge of my woods. Winter suddenly began barking.

"Winter, heel!" I commanded, and the dog returned to my side.

Instead of letting out a warning growl, the dog began to whine. He sat, gave an excited half bark, and his butt started to wriggle. It was snowing hard enough that I could tell the person was a female, but that was all. I moved back inside and slapped the wall. High up and next to the sliding door, my grandfather had installed a new hidey hole for my Glock 43. The panel dropped open, and I grabbed the pistol and racked the slide.

"That's close enough," I called out. "Identify yourself."

"Hello, dearest," came a familiar voice.

I immediately lowered the weapon.

It couldn't be.

But it was. Walking through the snow and stopping at the edge of my deck—dressed in jeans, a sweater and a pale blue winter coat—stood Aine, Queen of the Fae.

"Buh," I managed. *Oh Gods,* I thought. *Has something happened to Finnlagh?* "Is Finnlagh all right?"

She smiled. "Please do not worry. Finnlagh and Glynis are both fine. The rebellion is over, and we are hard at work to restore peace with the Dark Fae."

I pressed a hand to my chest in relief.

"May I come in?" she asked.

"Ah, sure," I said. "I mean of course. Come in, Your

Majesty."

Queen Aine hesitated at the door, brushed the snow from her hair and coat, and stepped inside. "You have a lovely home," she said.

I managed to close the slider behind her and to replace the gun. But I wasn't sure what to do next. The last thing I'd ever expected was for the queen of the Fae to drop by.

"Er…" I cleared my throat. *What the hell is the correct thing to do?* I wondered frantically, as the queen moved to the woodstove. "Can I offer you some tea, ma'am?" I said out of desperation.

She smiled. "That would be lovely, and please here in the mortal realm, call me Aine."

Winter still sat by my side and he was quivering. "Go ahead," I said to the dog. "Show your manners." The husky went bounding across the room and skidded to a stop in front of the queen.

"What a beautiful dog," the queen said, removing her coat. She folded it and laid it on a chair.

Winter offered his paw, and when the queen cooed over him Winter fell into a puddle of adoration at her feet.

I scrambled to make some tea for my guest. I dropped a tea bag in a thick mug and hit the hot water for the coffee maker. While I bustled around the kitchen, the queen made herself at home on the end of the couch closest to the woodstove.

Winter promptly dropped his head in her lap.

I joined her a few minutes later and wondered what to say. The queen sipped her tea and smoothly began the conversation before I could.

"Now that things have begun to settle down in the realms," the queen said, "I wanted to come by and see how you were doing, and to visit my future granddaughters."

I did a double take.

"True," she went on speaking, "you and Finnlagh were unable to be handfast that last night at the palace, but as you are my son's betrothed, I wanted to check on you myself and make sure you were well."

"I...I haven't heard from Finnlagh in quite some time. I wasn't sure if he was all right, or even if that whole betrothal thing still held."

"Of course it does," she said gently. "My son loves you very much, surely you know that."

"Your Majesty," I began.

"Aine," she corrected.

"Okay, Aine," I said. "Things are a bit more complicated than that. My life, my family, and my business are here in the mortal realm."

The queen's brow puckered. "I fail to see what the complication is. Your property sits at the borders of the Fae realm. It will be quite simple for us to visit each other."

Winter lifted his head from her lap and barked. He got up and scrambled for the front door. A second later, and my quiet little angels came bursting into the house.

"Mom! It's snowing!" they shouted.

The backpacks hit the floor with a thud. As usual they were both talking over and on top of each other, and at the same time. Kayla hung up her coat and scarf neatly, and Kenzie chucked hers in the general direction of the wall hooks.

I stood and when our guest did as well, the girls fell to silence. "Girls." I made the introductions. "This in Finnlagh's mother. Queen Aine."

"Awn-ye?" Kayla tried to pronounce it.

"That is correct." The queen's eyes sparkled. "Hello, Kayla."

Kayla narrowed her eyes. "How do you know my name?

The queen smiled. "Glynis and Finnlagh have told me all about the two of you."

"Hi!" Kenzie bopped over. "You're Glynis' mom?"

"I am."

"Are you a real queen?" Kayla stared up solemnly at her.

"Yes," Aine nodded.

"Neat." Kenzie decided.

"What's it like to be a queen?" Kayla wanted to know.

"Hey, Mom?" Kenzie looked to me. "Can we have hot chocolate? You always make that for us the first time it snows."

While the girls visited with the queen, I dutifully went to the kitchen to make hot cocoa. By the time I loaded up their mugs with mini-marshmallows, I discovered that the girls were snuggled up on either side of Aine and were talking on the couch. As if they'd known her forever...

"Our Mom escaped the castle *before* she and Finnlagh got married?" Kenzie asked.

I bobbled the tray, managed to save it, and quickly set it down on the coffee table.

Kayla grabbed her mug. "Mom, you didn't tell us that Finnlagh asked you to marry him."

"No," I said, tugging the oversized sweater further down over my hips. "No I didn't share that with you girls, because..." I trailed off, trying to come up with a suitable answer.

While the queen smiled innocently at my answer, Kayla and Kenzie were both glaring at me.

"Where's your ring?" Kenzie asked. "The girl always gets a ring."

Aine sat back on the couch and grinned mischievously. She was clearly enjoying the hell out of my predicament.

Troublemaker, I thought at Queen Aine. Hard enough that I hoped she would pick up on it.

She merely inclined her head in acknowledgement.

"Look, nothing is settled yet," I told my girls. "My priority was getting home to you two. Everything else will work itself out in time."

The queen tactfully changed the subject, and Kayla and Kenzie kept her entertained for a good hour.

"I should go," Queen Aine said, drawing loud whining protest from the girls.

"Can't you stay?" Kenzie begged.

"I must return to my home. Otherwise my husband, the king, will fret."

"What's the king like?" Kayla asked.

"He is kind and wise," the queen answered. "But if I am gone for much longer he will send out the troops to bring me back."

The girls thought that statement was hilarious, but I understood it to be the sterling truth.

"Do you have to go home and make him supper?" Kenzie wanted to know.

The queen laughed until she cried. "Something like that."

The girls and I stood on the front porch and waved as Queen Aine strolled across the dusting of snow and over to the far edge of our property that bordered the Fae lands. One second she was there, and the next, she was gone.

"She was nice," Kenzie said, leaning against my side.

"Will she be our new grandma if you and Finnlagh do get married?" Kayla asked.

I shut my eyes, took a deep breath, and changed the subject. "Who wants to decorate that tree?"

"I do! I do!" the girls shouted in unison and raced back inside.

I shut the cabin door, locked it, and wondered when

I'd see Finnlagh again.

***

The girls were finally asleep. Between the excitement of the first snow, our surprise visitor, and decorating for the holidays, they had crashed hard. I banked the fire, closed the woodstove doors, and shut off all the lights. After checking on the girls, I made my way upstairs to my bedroom.

I wasn't used to having a bathroom of my own, and I took a long shower and slipped into an oversized red plaid flannel nightgown. I grabbed a thick robe from the door and stepped into the bedroom.

I pulled the quilt back and was preparing to climb into bed, when I realized that I was no longer alone. Reaching for the gun in my bedside holster, I turned and aimed in one motion.

Only to discover Finnlagh standing by the large windows looking out over the property.

"Shit!" I swore, pointing the gun away from him. "You have *got* to stop doing that! One of these days I'm going to accidentally shoot you."

He grinned. "I have missed you too, my love."

I secured the gun and tried to calm down. "I'm glad you're here. We need to talk, Finnlagh," I managed to say before he swooped in and laid one on me.

There was something about him. Always had been. I'd once thought that he would ruin me for any other male, and he truly had. My brain clicked off and my heart fell. I wrapped my arms around him and kissed him back, every bit as thoroughly as he was kissing me.

Eventually he lifted his mouth from mine. "You *have* missed me."

"Don't gloat," I said and kissed him again.

He smiled and tried to pull me directly against him, but I eased back.

"Finnlagh," I began as he held onto my hands, "there's something you should know…"

"Enough talk," he said, pressing a tender kiss to my knuckles. "I am taking you to bed." With a firm tug he pulled me to him and scooped me up in his arms.

"Listen, I appreciate the attempt at a romantic reunion," I said as he stepped closer to the bed.

"This is not an *attempt*," he chuckled.

"Finnlagh!" I hissed. "Put me down. We really have to talk!"

"As my warrior bride commands." He bent over and dropped me on the mattress. I landed on the bed with a soft bounce.

I couldn't help but laugh. "Trust you to be so god-damn literal."

He leaned forward, planting his hands on either side of my hips. "You demanded to be put down," he said. "I have obliged."

I sighed. "Can you back up for a minute?"

He frowned. "Why won't you let me touch you?"

"It's not that," I said. "Finnlagh, you need to see

something."

"Oh?" With a grin, he sat down immediately on the bed. "You have my complete attention, my lady."

I stood up and stepped in front of him. My heart pounding, I untied the robe, and shrugged it off. I was slightly embarrassed standing before him in my extremely unsexy flannel night gown. The gown was oversized, red plaid, gathered at the neck, and it hid my shape. Taking a deep breath, I cupped my hands beneath my tummy and turned so he could see my profile.

His breath was harshly drawn in. "You are with child?"

"I am," I said shakily. "With your child." I dropped my hands and faced him again. "Been having a hell of a time hiding that fact."

"Why would you hide it?" he asked.

"Because when I first found out I was pregnant I was so far along that I was terrified that it might have been Ashton's." I took a deep breath and continued. "But the doctor gave me a due date of April. Which would mean that in the mortal realm I would have had to have conceived in *July*. And the timing of the conception made no sense."

"No sense..." He began to smile. "Unless you had been in the Fae realms."

"Right." I nodded. "The first time Ashton and I ever slept together was early September. Before that I hadn't been with anybody for *three years*...At first, I couldn't figure out how I was so far along in the pregnancy, and then I remembered that you told me how in the other Fae realms time ran even more dramatically differently for mortals. Hours would be days, and days would be like weeks."

"Are you and the babe well?" he asked.

"We're fine," I assured him. "Baby is growing by leaps and bounds and kicks up a storm." I felt a thump. "He or she is performing right now."

Hesitantly he reached for my belly. I took his hand and laid it against my bump. A second later and the baby kicked against his hand. Finnlagh's smile lit up the room.

"Do you know the gender?" he asked.

"No," I said. "I wanted to be surprised."

"We will be handfast immediately," he said.

"Let's not start all that again," I said, as the baby kicked against his hand.

"Ha!" he laughed. "Our child agrees with me."

I reached down and took Finnlagh's face in both my hands. "We shouldn't get married simply because of Fae oaths or even because there's a baby on the way. In my book we should only get married if we are both in love and plan to spend the rest of our lives together."

"I do love you," he said. "How many times must I tell you?"

"How would a marriage between us even work?" I asked. "The girls and I have to stay in the mortal realm. I've fought too hard and too long to make my home safe again. I'm not leaving. And you need to be with your people."

He covered my hands with his and held them. "Thanks to Diamant's three children, there's not much of a chance for me to ever become king." He smiled. "Besides, I also have news. I have been appointed as the official ambassador for the Fae here in the mortal realm."

"Ambassador?" I blinked. "You were?"

"Yes. Many Fae are living in the mortal world now. The position is perfect for me." He pressed a kiss to the palm of my hand. "I am very much looking forward to living in the mortal realm with you, the girls, and this baby."

"Are you sure?" I asked. "Because this is it for me. If we get married, you become a dad to two young girls overnight. My girls haven't ever had a man truly committed to being their father. And I won't see them hurt. Not ever again."

Gently he took my hands in his. "I understand you have fears. But in truth, after you agreed to be wed in front of the king and queen, there are those that would say we are *already* bound by handfast. Whether marriage vows were spoken or no."

"What?" I did a double take.

He drew me onto his lap. "You are my mine, and I am yours. Your children are my children. *Mo ghrá*, our lives are already bound together."

I sniffled. His words hit me right in the heart.

"Are you crying?" he asked.

"Pregnancy hormones," I told him, resting my head against his shoulder. "I'm more emotional than usual."

"I love you, Daphne," he said. "From the moment we met, you were the only one my heart beat for."

"Yeah well, I fell for you despite the fact that you're tricky, chivalrous, loyal, sneaky, and sometimes overly romantic," I said. "But I love you too." I cuddled closer. "I suppose now that the zombies and the evil Witches are gone from Hemlock Hollow...We could go ahead and get married."

"My lady." Finnlagh hitched me higher on his lap. "I am overwhelmed at your eloquent proposal. However, I may need a few days to compose myself sufficiently to give you an answer."

I snorted out a laugh. "Smart ass."

Finnlagh kissed me and it was sexy, dreamy, and well...It was everything. Before we could go any further, however, Kenzie and Kayla burst into the room.

"Yes!" they cried in unison.

"Please get married right away!" Kenzie shouted. "Before Yuletide!"

"Were you eavesdropping?" I asked the two of them and felt myself blush.

Kenzie launched herself at Finnlagh and he caught her easily. "I met your mom today," she told him. "She said she was going to be our new grandma."

"My mother was here?" For the first time Finnlagh looked uneasy.

"She was," I told him as Kayla sat on the bed next to me.

"Since everyone is awake, can we have a pajama party?" Kenzie wanted to know.

"A what?" Finnlagh was confused by the words.

"Yeah, let's stay up all night and have cookies and snacks!" Kayla agreed.

"I suppose it would give us a chance to talk about the wedding and our future," Finnlagh said. "As a family."

That was all the girls needed to hear. They went tearing down the stairs, and lights on the lower level began to come on. Finnlagh glanced longingly toward the bed.

"Welcome to real life, pal," I told him. "Privacy is now a precious commodity."

"We will have plenty of time after they fall asleep for a proper reunion."

"If you let them stuff themselves with sugar, they'll *never* go to sleep," I said, holding out my hand. "Parenting 101."

"I will think of something to distract them from sweets." He took my hand and we started down the stairs together.

"Hey!" Kayla's voice traveled clearly. "Where did this big plate of fruit and cheese come from?"

I slanted a look at him. "I suppose we need to have a talk about you doing too much magick around the girls?"

He pressed a kiss to the back of my hand. "Wait until the baby arrives. Fae children often have wild and unpredictable magick."

I blanched. "I did not know that."

"Never fear." He grinned. "I will help the baby learn to control it.

"Baby?" Kayla stood staring at the two of us. "Did you say, *baby*?"

Caught, I could only smile nervously at the girls. "Yes," I said. "Finnlagh and I are having a baby in the spring."

"You are?" Kayla's eyes were huge. "You're not kidding us?"

"No, I'm not kidding and yes, I'm having a baby."

Kayla crossed her arms. "Prove it."

I cupped my hands under my baby bump and turned to the side, much as I'd done for Finnlagh earlier.

"Whoa!" Kayla said.

"Whoopee!" Kenzie ran to me and pressed a kiss to my belly.

"What do you think, girls?" I asked.

"I think you better hurry up and get married," Kayla said soberly.

"You are my favorite red-haired-girl," Finnlagh said, giving Kayla a one-armed hug. "I've been telling your mother the same thing."

"She's stubborn," Kayla told him. "But don't worry. I got your back."

"Hi, baby!" Kenzie spoke to my belly. "I'm your

sister."

Overcome, I ran my hand over Kenzie's hair.

"The baby says its hungry, Mom," she announced. "We should have that snack."

Finnlagh smiled at me. "It would be wise to listen to the advice of the resident Fae Seer."

"You're right." I smiled. "I'd forgotten about that. What else does the baby say, Kenzie?" I asked her.

Kenzie pressed her ear to my belly as if listening. "Okay, sure," she said to my belly. "I can tell them." Kenzie straightened and started to laugh. "Hey, Momma?"

"Yes?"

"The baby wants you to know that he's a boy."

EPILOGUE

Nine months later…

We stood on the porch of the cabin and waved goodbye to Finnlagh's parents. "Bye!" I waved again and managed a smile, but in truth it was strained.

"Bye, Grandma and Grandpa O'Brien!" Kayla and Kenzie shouted in unison.

"Finnlagh," I said out of the side of my mouth, "you *have* to talk to your father!"

"You're overreacting," Finnlagh said mildly.

"He can *not* keep giving the girls such extravagant gifts!" I whispered back.

"It's a grandparent's right to spoil their grandchildren." Finnlagh smiled down at Kayla and Kenzie who sat on the front steps with their new 'present' in Kenzie's lap.

"He's so soft!" Kenzie pressed her cheek to the top of the kitten's head. The tabby kitten was brownish-gray and black, with a bushy ringed tail. It made me think of a raccoon, as there were rings of solid black along its tail and the end of it was a solid black.

The kitten let out a *meow*, and the girls began to coo over him. Winter pushed his way in between the girls and gave the newcomer a thorough sniff. The dog finished his greeting by bestowing a lick on the top of the kitten's head.

"The dog likes him," Finnlagh pointed out.

"Even I can take one look at that kitten and know it's not an ordinary cat." I crossed my arms. "It's a *cat sith*, isn't it?"

Finnlagh smiled and adjusted the sleeping bundle that was against his shoulder.

"That faerie-cat is going to be huge when it grows up," I warned. "Look at the size of its paws."

Finnlagh smiled down at the girls. "What do you think girls? Will he be a great *tíogair*?"

The girls pounced on the Gaelic word and promptly proclaimed the kitten's name would be Tigger. I tried to tell them that he hadn't meant to use the classic literary character's name, but because the Gaelic pronunciation of *tiger* sounded like Tigger, the name stuck.

I sighed while the girls rushed back inside, and went to set up the cat crate, food bowls and litter box that had magickally appeared, right after King Donal had handed the *cat sith* to the girls.

I shifted my gaze to my in-laws, who were walking hand in hand toward the back of the property. One moment they were there and the next they'd gone through the portal and back to Fae.

"Seriously, you need to talk to him," I said. "He told

Kayla he was going to give her a horse for her birthday!"

"I know." Finnlagh grinned. "Kayla will love that."

I slapped a hand to my forehead. "Where on earth would we put a horse?"

"The pole barn is huge," Finnlagh said. "I'm sure I could modify a section of it for a horse stable…"

"A horse is a huge responsibility," I began.

"I'd love to have a horse or two here," Finnlagh said. "I could teach the girls how to ride."

I shook my head and wondered why I even bothered. When your in-laws were the king and queen of the Fae, sometimes you just couldn't win. Against Finnlagh's shoulder, the baby began to wake. "Someone is going to be hungry," I said. "I want to feed Kamden before we go to the Shaw's for the harvest moon bonfire."

Finnlagh handed over our five-month-old son, and I took the baby inside to change him. The baby was impatient for his bottle and he let the whole house know it. When I finished up the diaper change, Finnlagh was waiting with a bottle. He took Kamden, sat on the couch, and got him settled.

While Finnlagh fed the baby, I went to pack a diaper bag and the picnic basket and told the girls to get their jackets and shoes together.

"Can we take Tigger and show him to the Shaws?" Kenzie wanted to know as soon as I walked back in the living room.

"Maybe not the best idea to take a *cat sith* into Lycan

territory without asking first," I told her.

"We need to get Tigger a collar," Kayla said. "Something fancy."

Instantly, a bejeweled collar materialized in Kayla's empty hand.

"Look Mom!" Kayla jumped up and down.

I shot a suspicious look at Finnlagh. "Did you do that?"

"Wasn't me," he said. "My hands are full."

A parchment note floated down from the vaulted ceiling a moment later, with no small amount of glitter.

Kayla snatched the note out of the air. "The collar is a gift from Grandma O'Brien."

"Really?" Kenzie popped up. "Lemme see!"

While Kayla and Kenzie oohed and aahed over the kitten collar, I went and got a broom to clean up the glitter and made a mental note to add 'speaking to Finnlagh's mother about not spoiling the girls' on my to-do list as well.

Finally, the five of us—and the dog—were ready for the walk over to the Shaw's. I carried the picnic basket, Kenzie held Winter's leash, and Kayla carried the diaper bag. Finnlagh had the baby in a sling across his chest which left his hands free.

Baby Kamden snoozed away, lulled by a full belly and the movement of his father's walking.

"I still think the kitten should have come along," Kenzie complained.

"Perhaps next time," Finnlagh said, reaching back

for my hand.

Kenzie looked to Finnlagh. "Do you think he will be okay in his crate?"

"Tigger was snoozing away on top of a fleece blanket, like a king when we left," I pointed out. "He was worn out from meeting you and Kayla. He'll need a few days to get used to his new home."

Kenzie accepted that and promptly challenged her sister to a race. While the girls and the dog ran ahead, Finnlagh and I stopped for a moment beside the pond on the Shaw's property.

The pond was pretty all year long, but was made even more so as the autumn season began to unfold. It was the first place Finnlagh and I had kissed, and we had been quietly handfast there on those banks at Imbolc. We had kept the ceremony simple and small, with only my family, Glynis and Beau, Finnlagh's parents, Ruby, and the Shaw and Wolfram families in attendance.

We walked together, with the September woods turning to burnished colors all around us. The girls were happy, the baby was healthy, and my business was doing well. Finnlagh had set up an office for himself in the basement of the cabin, and he was content to work from home as the ambassador to the Fae while taking care of our son.

It wasn't exactly a conventional life, but it worked for us. So, no, my life wasn't normal, but I was more than fine with how everything had turned out.

Finnlagh lifted my hand to his lips and pressed a kiss to the knuckles above my wedding ring. "I love you," he said.

I smiled. "Anybody ever tell you that you look dead sexy in a baby carrier?"

One of his eyebrows rose. "Why no, my lady," he said. "No one ever has."

"You are a wonderful father," I said, "and I fall more in love with you every day watching you with Kamden and the girls."

"I am very happy with my life here with you, Kamden, and our girls."

I gave his hand a squeeze. "Although I'm the last person to have *ever* expected to have a faerie-tale life, I am happy to live my 'happy ever after' out with you, Finnlagh."

He smiled. "And I with you, my love."

"Mom. Dad. Come on!" Kayla shouted from up ahead.

Finnlagh paused. "Kayla just called me Dad."

I reached up and pressed a kiss to his mouth. "She did."

Kayla and Kenzie stood together with the dog, waiting on the trail, and both the girls were rolling their eyes as we joined them. "Can't you stop kissing for like, five seconds?" Kenzie wanted to know. "We're gonna be late."

"Sorry." I grinned at them.

Kayla reached back, grabbed Finnlagh's hand, and

tugged him along. "Do you think Grandpa O'Brien will give me a horse for my next birthday?"

Finnlagh slid his eyes to mine. "We'll have to see about that," he said to Kayla.

I snorted out a laugh and took Kenzie's hand. We continued down the path, all of us together, as a family.

The End

***

The Hemlock Hollow trilogy will continue with a new spin-off series:

Hemlock Hollow Anthology

Beginning with Ruby Prentiss' story!

Ruby Prentiss is a quiet bookseller. She likes order, peace, and a simple life. Her family's unfortunate links to the past incidents in the hollow are a shame to Ruby, and she is determined to restore some integrity to her family name. Which may be tougher than she bargained for considering she's now the guardian for her trouble-making younger sister.

When Valentin Lowell comes bursting into her life, he upsets all of her carefully laid plans. He's too big, too brash, and too…Well, too everything. They couldn't be more different, and yet the attraction is undeniable.

Unfortunately, he loves trouble and conflict, while Ruby is absolutely determined to avoid it.

However, things are *never* as they appear in the hollow, and Ruby and Valentin are on a collision course that will change both of their lives forever.

Bewitched in Hemlock Hollow, coming fall 2021

ABOUT THE AUTHOR

Ellen Dugan is the award-winning author of over thirty-five books. Ellen's non-fiction titles have been translated into over twelve foreign languages. She branched out successfully into fiction with her popular *Legacy Of Magick*, *The Gypsy Chronicles*, *Daughters Of Midnight*, and *Hemlock Hollow* series. Ellen has been featured in USA TODAY'S HEA column. She lives an enchanted life in Missouri tending to her extensive perennial gardens and writing. Please visit her websites:

www.ellendugan.com

www.facebook.com/ellen.dugan